# Pillars of Gold and Silver

Beatriz de la Garza

PIÑATA BOOKS

PIÑATA BOOKS
HOUSTON, TEXAS
1997

This volume is made possible through grants from the National Endowment for the Arts (a federal agency), Andrew W. Mellon Foundation, the Lila Wallace-Reader's Digest Fund and the City of Houston through The Cultural Arts Council of Houston, Harris County.

*Piñata Books are full of surprises!*

Piñata Books
A Division of Arte Público Press
University of Houston
Houston, Texas 77204-2090

Cover design by Gladys Ramirez

de la Garza, Beatriz Eugenia.
    Pillars of gold and silver / by Beatriz de la Garza.
      p.   cm.
    ISBN 1-55885-206-9
    I. Mexican Americans--Juvenile fiction. [1. Mexican Americans--Fiction. 2. Grandmothers--Fiction.] I. Title.
    PZ7.D36975Pi   1997
    [Fic]—dc21                      97-22161
                                          CIP
                                          AC

# Pillars of Gold and Silver

# Acknowledgements

The following persons helped me to gather and to remember the words of the rondas infantiles, both by collecting materials and by looking back into their own memories: María Eugenia Dubois, who sent me texts from Mérida, Venezuela, and my sister, Alicia M. de la Garza, who drew on her years as an elementary school teacher. To both I am grateful for their help. My thanks also to Jane Smith Garcés for putting me in contact with María Eugenia, to my cousin, Mercedes González de García, and her daughters, Evelina and Mirna, and my nephew, Fabio, all of whom contributed their own recollections of the rondas. To Leticia Garza-Falcón, my thanks for her always perceptive comments. And, as always, I remain grateful to my friend, Alice Lozano, who has been unfailing in her support and encouragement and in whose house were written parts of this book.

---

*Dedico este libro a mis compañeros de juegos
en aquellas noches de luna.*

# Chapter I

*Mambrú se fue a la guerra, qué dolor, qué dolor,*
*qué pena*

The first time that Blanca Estela saw the Río Grande she thought that it was an ugly, frightening thing. It was her first visit to Mexico, and she was alone in the back seat of an old black car, as big and heavy as an army tank. Her mother was in the front seat, talking to the driver as if they were old friends, although Blanca Estela had never seen him before. But then everything was new to Blanca Estela since she and her mother had packed their suitcases and got on a bus a few days ago.

Now they were on a narrow asphalt road, patched in some places and with open holes in others, flanked on both sides by dusty, thorny brush that pressed against the barbed wire fences that ran parallel to the road. And then suddenly Blanca Estela could see the river. It coiled inside its banks like a snake, slithering over flat rocks, churning in brown pools that threatened to suck you in if you fell in the water.

"The Río Grande," the driver said, turning his head and smiling at Blanca Estela. He was a broad-shouldered man with a brown face, gray hair, and large calloused hands, which rested lightly on the steering wheel. Blanca Estela nodded politely at his announcement, not wanting to let him see her dismay. To her the river seemed as ugly and desolate as the countryside they were passing. Then she saw the bridge ahead of them, and she was afraid. The bridge which they were getting ready to cross seemed to hang from wires suspended in the air and swayed from side to side in the wind.

"That's Revilla, just across the bridge," Blanca Estela's mother said, speaking in Spanish and smiling at her. It was the first time that she had smiled during the trip. Blanca Estela took heart from her smile and said nothing about her fear of the swaying bridge and the sullen river below them.

Blanca Estela remembered exactly when her mother had stopped smiling. It was two weeks ago, when a man and a woman had come to their house to talk to her mother. Her mother's beautiful green eyes had opened very wide when she saw the strangers standing on the porch. Her voice shook when she asked them to come into the parlor and then turned to tell Blanca Estela to go next door and play with June and Linda, her best friends.

Blanca Estela had gone next door and had stayed, playing with June and Linda in their backyard until some time after the strangers had left. For some reason she had felt reluctant to go back to her own house and to her mother. When she finally returned home she found her mother in the bedroom, lying in bed with the blinds closed so that the room was almost dark. Blanca Estela had stood timidly at the door, watching her mother as she lay on the pretty quilted bedspread, her eyes closed, clutching a handkerchief in one hand while in the other she cradled the photograph of Blanca Estela's father in his soldier's uniform. Sometimes a deep sigh, like a sob, would escape from her, but she never opened her eyes. After a few minutes, Blanca Estela tiptoed away without disturbing her. She went to the kitchen and quietly poured herself a glass of milk, which she drank slowly while she pondered whether she was still going to the picnic on Saturday with June and Linda.

She did not go to the picnic on Saturday because she was helping her mother to box up dishes after wrapping them in several layers of newspaper. Then they had packed their clothes—the woolens in boxes sprinkled with moth crystals, and the summer things in suitcases. Mrs. Akers, Linda and June's mother, had come by to visit them several times during those days, bringing food in casseroles and shopping bags full of black clothes for Blanca Estela's mother.

"Lili," Mrs. Akers had said, as she pulled out the black clothes from the sacks, "I really don't think you should wear mourning clothes. Nobody does it anymore."

"Thank you, Helen, for buying these things for me. I didn't feel like going out," Blanca Estela's mother had answered in her funny English. "I know that they don't wear black for mourning here, but people still do it back home, and that is where we are going. Blanca Estela and I are going to stay with my mother in Mexico until I decide what to do."

And Blanca Estela and her mother had taken their heavy suitcases, gotten on a bus and traveled for days until they had arrived at this lonely spot. They had left behind their pretty little house with the bright, green door and her mother's pink and red geraniums, which grew in pots set around the front porch. On the day that Blanca Estela and her mother left, Mrs. Akers, June and Linda were gone somewhere, so there was nobody to wave goodbye to them when they got in the taxicab, and there was no one to see them off at the bus station, either.

At the beginning of the trip, Blanca Estela had found it exciting to look out the window at the changing scenery—first green fields, then brown hills, and later blue mountains with white peaks, and even copper-colored cliffs—but after a while, the hours began to stretch out slowly and monotonously. Her dress clung to the back of her legs with sweat, and the upholstery on the seats scratched her face when she leaned against it and tried to go to sleep.

Sometimes they stopped in little towns, or even where there was only a gasoline station or cafe all alone in the middle of nothing. Then her mother would have her get out and go to the restroom or give her sandwiches to eat, even when she wasn't hungry. Other times when she *was* hungry, she had to wait a long time to eat until they reached their next stop. Once, when she was both hungry and sleepy, she began to fret and to complain about it to her mother, but then she stopped because her mother did not seem to be listening. She seemed to be far away in her thoughts and, instead of responding, she asked Blanca Estela, "You don't really remember him do you? You were still so little when he left. He only came back once for a visit after that. He was supposed to come back for good by the New Year. And now he is never coming back."

Blanca Estela was not sure that she understood what her mother was telling her. However, she hesitated to ask her questions because her mother had shut her eyes and turned her head away from her, as if she were closing the door to her room to keep everybody out, even Blanca Estela.

Now here they were, setting out across the river, suspended above the watery serpent below them, waiting for them to fall, so it could devour them. The wooden slats of the bridge rattled under the wheels of the heavy car, and Blanca Estela held her breath with a queasy feeling in her stomach. It reminded her of the sensation she had experienced on seeing the trapeze artists flying from one side of the circus tent to the other, high above her head. She looked at her mother, trying to divine from her manner if they were, indeed, in danger of falling, but her mother continued to talk to the driver and even to smile occasionally.

Blanca Estela had noticed that her mother had become more talkative after they got off the bus earlier that morning. They had stepped down from the bus slowly, their legs stiff from the long ride, and had gone into a small dark store. There, a very large woman waited, wedged between a wooden counter and rows of tall shelves crammed with cans of milk, boxes of rice, packages of buttons, spools of thread, and many other things that Blanca Estela did not recognize. The bus driver had set their suitcases down on the pavement outside, and a young man, who seemed to be strangely childish, had carried them into the store. The driver had come in, too, and bought a bottle of soda pop from the big woman. Then he took several packages from her, together with a canvas sack that said "U.S. Mail."

Blanca Estela had stood quietly just inside the screen door, waiting for her eyes to become accustomed to the dimness of the store after the glare of the sun outside. The heat that had met her when she got off the bus had made her slightly dizzy. It was like nothing she had felt before, except perhaps the heat that came out of the oven when her mother opened it to take out freshly baked cookies. Inside the store, however, it was not as hot, and she felt comforted by the unusual aromas of coffee and strange spices that permeated the room.

Finally, the bus driver returned to the bus and the bus pulled away. Then, after the bustle and noise had subsided, the storekeeper came out slowly from behind the counter and embraced Blanca Estela's mother. The two women began to talk, and Blanca Estela was forgotten for the moment. She looked around her at the walls painted a dull green and decorated with metal signs which advertised sliced white bread and orange soda pop.

Her mother and the storekeeper were speaking very quietly in Spanish, but Blanca Estela could not understand everything they said. Her mother had always spoken in Spanish to her, but back home everybody spoke English, and her mother also had to speak English in the shops and to the neighbors, even if she sometimes sounded funny and got embarrassed. Blanca Estela, though, talked to her friends only in English and sometimes translated for her mother when they went out. In this strange place, however, it was Blanca Estela who felt left out and understood only part of what people said.

The young man, who seemed to be the storekeeper's son, had come in then, very excited, to tell them that the car was outside. Blanca Estela looked quizzically at her mother, but she was busy saying goodbye to the large woman. The man, who was to be their driver, had come into the store at that moment and said "good morning" to the storekeeper. Then, when he saw Blanca Estela's mother, he broke out in a smile. He shook hands with her and patted her on the back, afterwards saying, "Lilia, welcome back. We have not seen you in so long—how many years? Since you got married and went away. Don't tell me this child is yours."

Blanca Estela had pressed herself against the wall, filled with a certain embarrassment, afraid that the storekeeper and the man would expect her to say something. She was relieved when they seemed to forget her and went on with their conversation. After a while the man said, "Well, if you're ready, let's go. *Doña* Anita will be impatient waiting for you. She knows you are coming."

He picked up their suitcases and carried them out, and Blanca Estela found herself being shepherded out until her mother stopped and said, "You had better go to the bathroom before we leave." Blanca Estela shook her head, but her mother insisted and took her to a small room behind the store. It was hot and dark in the cubicle, with only a little light and less air coming in through a small window at the top. There was a large tank with a chain hanging from it over the commode and a rusty washbasin under the window. Blanca Estela's mother stood just inside the door waiting for her to finish, so she could pull the chain which Blanca Estela could not reach. She handed her some toilet paper and afterwards had her wash her hands in the basin. "There are no towels, so dry your hands with the paper," she told her. Then they hurried out of the bathroom and got into the car, the two grown-ups in the front and Blanca Estela, all alone, in the backseat.

Blanca Estela guessed that they had been driving about half an hour before they got to the bridge. Crossing the bridge itself did not take very long, but she was relieved when they finally got off the tremulous wood surface and were again on solid ground. The road on the other side of the bridge was made of gravel, and at the end of it Blanca Estela could see a squat structure with a tin-roofed shed attached to it. As they approached these buildings, the car slowed down, and two men in khaki uniforms stepped out to meet them. They both wore dark eyeglasses to shield them from the brightness of the sun, and it worried Blanca Estela that she could not tell if they were looking at her.

"Good morning, Manuel," one of the men said to the driver. "What do you have with you today? Good morning, Miss."

"Good morning, Leopoldo, don't you recognize me?" Blanca Estela was surprised to hear her mother address the stranger, laughing.

"My goodness, is it you, Lilia? Lilia de los Santos? Who would have expected to see you here! I thought you were far away, on the other side, up north. You have been gone a long time. Have you come to see your mother? I know she will be very happy to see you. And who's that in the back? Have you taken to smuggling children, Manuel?"

The four adults laughed, but Blanca Estela found herself shrinking against the seat, trying to make herself invisible in the farthest corner of the car. She had a sudden fear that she would be told to step outside the car and be left behind, without her mother. Lilia shook her head, still laughing, and answered the man called Leopoldo, "This is my daughter, Blanca Estela."

"*Doña* Anita's granddaughter! How happy she's going to be to have her visiting here! Go on then. *Doña* Anita is probably waiting with dinner for you right now. You don't want it getting cold." The two men in the khaki uniforms waved them on, and the car started moving again down the long white dusty road.

Blanca Estela relaxed her clenched hands, and suddenly she felt hungry. After a few minutes she looked back, but the dust from the road, which trailed behind them like paper streamers, blurred everything behind them. The men and the buildings were no longer visible. Ahead of them, something white shimmered in the distance.

Manuel turned to her and said, "That's Revilla, over there. You can begin to see the houses from here. You have never been here before?"

Blanca Estela felt her mouth go dry. It tasted as if the dust from the road had caked on her throat. She could do no more than shake her head.

"Blanca Estela, you're supposed to answer when grown-ups ask you a question," Lilia scolded her, but then she turned to Manuel and explained, "I think she's very tired. We have been traveling for days. And then... what happened..." her voice broke, "... all this has been hard for her too."

Manuel reached out with his large calloused hand and patted Lilia on the shoulder. "We are all very sorry," he said. "Such a tragedy."

Lilia nodded, and they both fell silent.

The shimmering dots that shone like a mirage in the distance now resolved themselves into houses as they drove down the long, unpaved street. Blanca Estela was surprised to notice that the houses all abutted each other and were made of stone, their walls rising like cliffs, directly from the street. Many were whitewashed. She now realized that it was their reflection of the sunlight that had dazzled her eyes from far away. Other houses had exposed patches of sand-colored stone blocks where the plaster had flaked off. This gave them a mottled look, like an animal in the process of shedding its fur. They all had massive wooden doors that sometimes stood half-open and doorlength windows protected by iron bars. Nothing stirred in the noonday sun except a few stoic-faced dogs that huddled close to walls, looking for shade. She could hear no sound, save a chorus of cicadas and the cooing of turtle-doves in the distance.

They stopped before one of the mottled-looking houses, and Manuel sounded the horn of the car. A plump, gray-haired woman wearing a black and white print dress came running through the open doors, wiping her hands on a white apron. Lilia threw open the door of the car and ran to meet her. "Mamá," she cried out and threw her arms around the woman. The two stood embracing for a few minutes. Blanca Estela, looking out of her window in the back of the car, noticed with dismay that the two women had begun to weep. She leaned back against a corner of the back seat and shut her eyes. She wanted to shut her ears too. It frightened her to see grownups cry.

Suddenly the gray-haired woman opened the door next to Blanca Estela, and the next moment she was pulling her out of the car, kissing her and clasping her head against her bosom. Blanca Estela looked up at her mother, a question in her eyes.

"It's your grandmother, *tontita*. Don't you remember your Mamá Anita, you silly little thing? The letters she wrote to us? How about the clothes she sent you?" Lilia shook her head, half-laughing, tears still trembling on her long, black lashes like raindrops, as she said this.

"What did you expect, Lilia? I haven't seen the child since she was in diapers, but I would have known her anywhere, even without the photographs you sent me. She gets her eyes from Roberto, you know. She takes more after her father's family, but she is still my granddaughter. There is a little bit of your father in her, too."

"Let's hope it won't be the mustache," cried Lilia with a little desperate laugh. "It's what I remember most about Papá. And Roberto, too. I remember how his mustache used to scratch my face when he kissed me. Do you still miss Papá? Because I'm not sure how much I remember about Roberto. He had been gone so long before he... before he left."

"Come in the house," Mamá Anita said briskly. "Manuel, bring the suitcases and leave them just inside the door."

They stepped across the threshold of the heavy double doors and into a covered entryway that opened to a walled courtyard. Flowerpots with jasmines, ferns and geraniums lined the whitewashed walls of the entry and spilled down the steps to the patio. The floor and the steps were made of rough and uneven stones.

"Watch your step," said Mamá Anita as if she could read Blanca Estela's thoughts. "That's the *aljibe*," she continued, pointing to a square cistern in the middle of the patio. "We get our drinking water from there. We collect the rain water from the roof through those tin gutters that empty into the *aljibe*. You must never raise that screen lid on top of the *aljibe*. You could fall in; it's very deep. Besides, leaves and dirt can get in the water."

Blanca Estela nodded dumbly, already a little afraid of this efficient woman who seemed to anticipate questions.

"I have dinner on the stove. Come on, you must be hungry."

Mamá Anita took Blanca Estela's hand and led her through a door to her right into a long room with two floor-length windows where the wooden shutters were partially closed. Several portraits of stern-faced men and women hung from the walls in heavy, carved frames. A dozen or so straightbacked chairs stood like sentinels around the walls, and two rocking chairs flanked the second window.

They turned left at the end of the room and went through another door. They crossed two other rooms, one after the other, each with high, plump beds draped with frilly coverlets. Finally, they came to a large kitchen. All the rooms, from the parlor to the kitchen, had doors or windows that opened to the patio. From these there was a view of the *aljibe* in the middle, a spindly lemon tree that grew near the cistern and a small wooden building which stood against the courtyard wall farthest from the house.

In the kitchen there was a huge elevated fireplace built into the outer wall. The hearth came up to the height of Mamá Anita's waist. Blanca Estela noticed that underneath the hearth there was a recess where firewood was stacked. Coals were glowing under an iron trivet in the hearth, and on top of the trivet rested a clay pot.

"I still like to cook the beans over a wood fire. The rest of the cooking I do on that little kerosene stove," Mamá Anita explained, pointing first at the fireplace and then at the opposite wall where a two-burner stove stood on a table covered with bright green linoleum.

Blanca Estela was beginning to be convinced that it was not necessary to question Mamá Anita. She told you what you wanted to know before you had a chance to even utter a word.

In the middle of the kitchen was a round table surrounded by four chairs, and against the inside wall, the one adjoining the house next door, there stood a glass-fronted china cabinet. Mamá Anita opened a drawer at the base of the cabinet and took out a green-and-white checked tablecloth, which she gave to Blanca Estela.

"Go set it out on the table," she told Blanca Estela, while she took three large soup plates made of bright blue pottery from a shelf above.

Lilia then came in the kitchen, saying, "I hung up the clothes in the big wardrobe in the front bedroom. Was that right? It was empty."

"I emptied it so that you and Blanca Estela could put your clothes inside. I used to keep your father's suits and some of your brothers' clothes in it—clothes from when they were boys. I packed them up in a trunk. I guess I should really give them away to somebody who needs them. I aired out the wardrobe for several days, but I'm afraid it still smells of mothballs. Help me serve the beans, Lilia, and let's eat."

Three smaller pottery bowls came out of the cabinet, and Lilia ladled out pinto beans in their soup from the pot on the fire. They shredded strips of hot corn *tortillas* into the soup and ate them with blue-speckled tin spoons.

"Mamá," Lilia said, "I haven't eaten beans and *tortillas* like these in so long. I try making them sometimes, but they never come out like yours. What's the matter, Estelita?"

Blanca Estela, still filled with an overpowering shyness, got up from her chair and went to whisper in her mother's ear that she was thirsty. Lilia translated for Mamá Anita.

"Oh my goodness," exclaimed Mamá Anita, "I forgot that I have some lemonade cooling in a jug. Or would you prefer some orange soda? Here, let me give you some money, and you can run to Chabela's store. It's just on the corner. She has a refrigerator, and the sodas are cold. You know, Lilia, I hope this child can get used to the way things are here. I don't have all the modern conveniences that you're accustomed to having now."

"This is how I grew up, Mamá. I haven't forgotten how things are, and Estelita will soon get used to life here. Children adapt very easily. Estelita, do you want to go to the store and get yourself a cold soda?"

Blanca Estela shook her head. She would rather suffer the torture of thirst than go by herself to the store in this strange place which she did not yet completely understand. Mamá Anita then got up from the table and poured out three glasses of lemonade from a clay jug which was wrapped in wet burlap. It was cool and tart, and it quenched Blanca Estela's thirst better than the cold sodas ever could.

Next, Mamá Anita filled the large soup bowls from a pot on the stove with a broth which she called *caldo de res* and which gave off aromatic clouds of steam. It had large chunks of beef and wedges of tomatoes, onions, cabbage, squash and rounds of corn on the cob floating in the soup. Lilia showed Blanca Estela how to fish out the meat and scoop out the buttery marrow from the bones and spread it on the *tortillas*, which they then ate rolled up.

When Blanca Estela's bowl was empty, Mamá Anita asked her if she wanted another serving. She shook her head. The hot meal, the first she had eaten in several days, had made her sleepy.

Mamá Anita turned to Lilia and asked, "Does this child ever speak?"

"Of course she does, Mamá. It's just that she is tired. She is actually a little timid, too, and all this sudden change..."

"Does she speak Spanish?"

"She understands everything you say to her. I always speak Spanish to her, but where we lived, nobody else spoke it, so it was always English with her friends, the shops, the schools..."

"But when she talks to you, what does she speak?"

"Well, you know, it's Spanish mostly, but sometimes she doesn't know a word, and she mixes the two languages. I understand her."

Mamá Anita had become agitated, and Blanca Estela watched her with apprehension. "She's going to speak pure Spanish here," Mamá Anita said heatedly. "I don't understand any garbled up mixtures. But enough of this now," she added, calming down. "The poor child is falling asleep. Come on, Blanca Estela, I'm going to set up a cot for you, and you are going to take a nap."

Mamá Anita took her hand and led her in a reverse journey through the bedrooms and back to the long parlor. "This is the coolest room in the house at this time of day because it faces north and has cross ventilation from the street and from the patio," she said, stopping in front of the half-shuttered window. "Wait here while I get the cot."

She disappeared and came back in a few minutes with a folding canvas cot, which she set up in front of the window. The next thing she brought was a small pillow in a snowy case with a scalloped edge and embroidered daisies across the front.

"Now," said Mamá Anita, "before you lie down, let's remove your dress. Are you wearing a slip underneath? Good, you can use it as a nightgown. Let me help you." Mamá Anita unfastened the buttons in the back and pulled the dress over her head. "Now let's take off your shoes and socks."

It was heavenly to be rid of the wrinkled dress that had begun to chafe against her neck. She felt the breeze from the open window blowing over the perspiration on her back, which had soaked her thin slip. It was better than air conditioning. Blanca

Estela rested her head on the pillow and smelled on it the fragrance of lavender soap that her mother used sometimes. From her reclining position, she looked up at the heavy beams that supported the ceiling, the *vigas*, as she later learned they were called. There was something written on them, but she could not make out the words. Between the windows there was a marble-topped table that she had not noticed on her way in. On the table there was a stack of books and a sewing basket lined in red silk, overflowing with spools of thread and skeins of embroidery floss in every possible color. There was also a large photograph in a gilt frame. She turned her head to better see the photograph and was surprised that it was her mother in a wedding dress. Then she realized that the smiling man standing next to the bride must have been her father and drifted off to sleep.

When she woke up, she could hear the drone of soft voices close to her. She opened her eyes and saw her mother and her grandmother sitting in the rocking chairs, facing each other a little way from her. Mamá Anita seemed to be darning clothes with the sewing basket on the floor next to her. For some reason Blanca Estela was reluctant to move and let them know that she was awake. She willed herself to remain still, concentrating, instead, on seeing if she could read the writing on the ceiling beams. By narrowing her eyes and squinting she was able to make out the letters slowly. The words on the beam said, "Antonio de los Santos." She wondered who he was—perhaps one of those grim-faced men in long whiskers that looked out of the large portraits on the walls. There followed *Septiembre* (that meant

September), followed by the number "1876." This was June of 1952. She began to count back how many years ago that had been, but she gave up after a while and listened, instead, to her mother's conversation. There was always something secret about what grown-ups said when they thought you weren't listening.

Lilia was saying now, "I was surprised to see Leopoldo when we got to the customs office at the bridge, Mamá. I didn't know he worked there. He didn't recognize me at first. I must have changed a lot."

"You're thinner now," answered Mamá Anita. "Black clothes make you look pale and thin. And he hadn't seen you since before you got married."

"You know, when I was single and before I became engaged to Roberto, Leopoldo would always ask me to dance with him at all the parties. I think he wanted me to be his sweetheart, but Roberto started courting me. Do you remember—Roberto used to come every Sunday from across the river so he could see me at the promenade on the plaza? My brothers didn't like Roberto. They used to stand by the bandstand, glaring at us while we talked. Did you put them up to doing that?"

"Of course not. They just felt that it was their responsibility to look after you since your father was dead."

"Can you imagine what it felt like to have three older brothers watching every time you talked to a boy? It didn't bother Roberto, though. I think it made him more determined, and that's why he insisted that we get married so soon. That, and the fact that he knew that he was joining the Army. Oh,

Mamá, why did he have to go? Why did he have to go to war?"

"It was his duty. He was born in the United States, and that country was at war."

"But he volunteered for the most dangerous things," cried out Lilia.

"He was a brave man—whatever else he might have been. You knew what he was like when you married him. That's what your brothers were telling you."

"We had so very little time together, and he barely knew his daughter. I don't know if she remembers him."

"Have you asked her? Do you talk to her about him? How did she take the news about him?"

"I don't know," Lilia answered, hesitantly. "She's such a quiet child, always has been. Sometimes I can't tell what she's thinking or feeling."

"You did tell her, didn't you?" Mamá Anita insisted.

Blanca Estela could no longer ignore the heaviness in her bladder, and she knew that she had to get up and ask where the bathroom was. Her movement alerted the two women that she was awake. Lilia got up quickly from her rocking chair and came to her.

"Are you awake, my love?" she asked in a tremulous voice. "Are you thirsty? Would you like some lemonade?"

Blanca Estela shook her head frantically and sat up, swinging her legs over the side of the cot, saying that she needed to go to the bathroom.

"Oh, of course. It's been a long time." Lilia turned to Mamá Anita and asked her, "Shall I take her... in the back?"

"Yes," said Mamá Anita, continuing to sew. "You should go with her and show her where it is... and to be careful."

"Put on your shoes, Estelita," Lilia said when she noticed that Blanca Estela stood gingerly on the stone floor with its bumpy little cobblestones. "After a while you'll get used to going barefooted here, like I did when I was your age. I guess children still do that, don't they Mamá?"

"Oh yes, they go barefooted in the summer, even in the middle of the day when the sidewalks are as hot as the tortilla griddle. The sand in the streets, too, gets hot enough to burn your feet. But you had better hurry up and take the child to the outhouse; she looks desperate."

Lilia took Blanca Estela by the hand and led her out to the patio through the open door in the parlor. Blanca Estela looked down at the hard-packed dirt of the patio and was glad for the shoes on her feet, for there were red ants crisscrossing the ground. Lilia took her to the small wooden structure that Blanca Estela had noticed before at the far end of the patio, and Lilia unlatched the door. A hot, nauseous vapor was released, and Blanca Estela averted her face with revulsion.

"It's so hot in here," Lilia said. "Let's leave the door open. "Nobody can see you on account of the high walls that surround us. I'll stand here, in front of the door."

Blanca Estela looked at her mother in confusion. There was no familiar white commode in the little room. Instead, there was a wooden platform or box, with an opening at the top.

"Come on, Estelita, sit there before you wet your pants," Lilia encouraged her.

Blanca Estela did as she was told with the greatest reluctance.

"I forgot the roll of toilet paper," Lilia said. "Let me run in the house and get it. You had better not use that brown paper; it's rough."

"No!" Blanca Estela cried out in panic. "Don't leave me here. I will fall in."

"Of course you won't fall in," Lilia reassured her. "The opening is too small."

Mamá Anita appeared then and calmly handed Lilia a roll of tissue paper.

"I thought she might want this," she said. "And when you finish here, I will have a bath ready for her."

As soon as she was finished, Blanca Estela jumped off the seat and ran towards the house. Her grandmother beckoned from the kitchen door, and she followed her inside. A narrow door in the back wall of the kitchen stood open. She had assumed that it was a closet door, but it now revealed a small room in half-darkness whose only light came from the kitchen. A metal tub stood in the middle of the room. Mamá Anita began to fill a tin bucket under the faucet that protruded from the wall.

"I don't think we'll need to heat any water," Mamá Anita said, "but come test it, put your hand in the water. Can you stand it like that?"

She nodded. She felt shy at undressing and bathing in front of her grandmother, but the days of traveling without stopping to wash now made her long desperately for a bath.

Lilia walked in the room with a bar of perfumed soap. "Mamá, I'll do that," she said, taking the overflowing bucket from her. "Step in the tub Estelita."

Blanca Estela dropped her rumpled underclothes on the floor and stepped into the tub. Lilia unbraided Blanca Estela's hair and poured water over her head, soaking her first and then lathering her with fresh, lavender-scented soap. In spite of the tingling chill left by the water, Blanca Estela felt sleepy again, languid with the relief and the pleasure of feeling clean and sweet smelling.

When they were finished rinsing her, Mamá Anita wrapped her in a heavy cotton sheet while Lilia toweled her hair dry. After she was dry, they gave her a cotton nightgown printed with pink roses on a pale blue background, trimmed with eyelet ribbon around the neck. Mamá Anita had sewn it especially for Blanca Estela.

The sun had gone down, and the house, which faced north and east like an upside down 'L', was enveloped in gloom. Mamá Anita clicked on the switch above a lightbulb that hung from a cord in the ceiling, and the kitchen became illuminated by a yellowish light.

"We have electricity tonight since the river is running strong. That's how they run the generator of electricity, with water power," she explained for Blanca Estela's benefit. "I still prefer my oil lamps, though. They give a softer light. Let me light the one for the parlor."

Mamá Anita held a match to the wick of a lamp, which rested on the kitchen table. The lamp was made of crystal and had a base shaped like a goblet, which held an iridescent-green oil. The wick caught fire from the match, and Mamá Anita carefully arranged a glass chimney above it. The chimney top was a reverse shape from the base. It had two narrow ends with a bulbous middle. Mamá Anita took the lamp by its slender neck and walked away in the direction of the parlor, illuminating the way ahead of her.

When Mamá Anita returned to the kitchen, where Blanca Estela and her mother waited, she put out an enameled pitcher full of milk and some dark, flat bread sprinkled with pecans and brown sugar.

"Do you want me to scramble some eggs, or will bread and milk be enough? I never eat anything heavy at night."

"Bread and milk is enough for me Mamá," Lilia answered, "or coffee, if you make some. And I'll have some of that cheese that you have in the screened box."

Mamá Anita nodded and went to the window sill where she took a round white cheese from a frame made of a fine wire mesh, which kept out the insects but let in fresh air.

Blanca Estela sipped from her glass of milk and munched on a large slice of bread. It was different from any bread that she had ever tasted—not very sweet and with a faintly spicy flavor that she liked. She was used to cold milk though, and the lukewarm milk, with a buttery film floating on top, was not too pleasant to her.

"She doesn't like boiled milk," Mamá Anita remarked, noticing the small sips that Blanca Estela confined herself to taking. Tomorrow I will make chocolate with the milk, so you won't notice the taste," she added, addressing Blanca Estela.

Blanca Estela nodded sleepily. "Let's get you to bed," said Lilia, and the three of them trooped to the front bedroom, where another oil lamp on a corner table showed several pillows and coverlets stacked on the bed.

"We don't use the beds in the summer," Mamá Anita explained to Blanca Estela. "The mattresses are stuffed with wool, and they are too hot to sleep on at this time of the year. But they are wonderfully warm in winter. Your cot is already set out, but let me put this coverlet on it because it gets cool by dawn."

Blanca Estela looked at her mother with a wordless question, which Lilia understood. "Don't worry, Estelita. I'll put my cot right next to you, but you go to bed first."

Suddenly the sound of children's voices came in through the open windows, accompanied by shouts, laughter, and finally, a song. Lilia raised her head to listen and smiled. "Mamá," she exclaimed, "the children still play games and sing *rondas* in the evenings, just like they did when I was a child!'"

"Oh yes," Mamá Anita responded matter-of-factly. "I expect that Blanca Estela will join in with them as soon as she settles in."

"I don't know," Lilia said doubtfully. "It takes her time to make friends, and she doesn't know any of those games or songs. What's that one they're singing?" Lilia went very still, listening to the chant outside the window.

Blanca Estela edged quietly to the window and leaned out cautiously in the embrasure until her fingers were touching the cool iron bars that protected the window. The moon had just risen in the sky. It was almost full, and its silver light showed a circle of five or six children as dark silhouettes—shadows elongating and shrinking against the background of the shimmering sand under their feet.

They sang as they marched in a circle, swinging their interlocked hands. Blanca Estela heard her mother give a little sob behind her. "Do you hear that, Mamá?" asked Lilia. "Do you remember that song? *Mambrú se fue a la guerra, qué dolor, qué dolor, qué pena. Mambrú se fue a la guerra, no sé si volverá.* Roberto went away to war Mamá, just like Mambrú, and he never came back."

Out of the corner of her eye, Blanca Estela saw her mother throw her arms around Mamá Anita and sob against her bosom. Mamá Anita held her for a moment and then pushed her back gently saying, "Shh, stop crying, Lilia, you will frighten the child. It is time that we all go to bed. You must be exhausted."

Later on in bed, Blanca Estela lay quietly but awake. She could hear her mother's rhythmic breathing as she slept close by and Mamá Anita's soft snores from the cot farther away in front of the other window, and these sounds comforted her. She had never experienced such intense darkness before. There were no streetlights outside; there was only the diffuse glow from the stars and the moonlight coming in through the open doors and windows to lighten the blackness. Without street traffic, the silence magnified the occasional chirping of a cricket or the soft mewing of a cat. It was easy to feel alone and sad in the dark silence, but she would not allow herself to do so. If she gave in to the heaviness that weighed against her heart, then she, too, would cry and wake her mother and frighten her.

She thought about Mambrú. Who was he? Did he go away to war, as her own father had? She scarcely remembered her father. His memory was more a combination of sensations than a specific recollection—the scratch of his whiskers against her face when he kissed her, the feeling of being held secure atop a pair of broad shoulders. Mambrú had been a soldier, too, but she did not think that he would have looked like her father in the photographs she had seen of him.

Several months ago Mrs. Akers had taken her to the movies with June and Linda to see a picture about knights going off to wars which they called Crusades. King Richard had gone away to the Crusades and had been gone for a long time. His wife had thought that he was dead, but one day the king returned. He had just been imprisoned somewhere and had had a hard time finding his way home. Perhaps Mambrú would return home, too, and the singer of the song would cease to feel sad. Perhaps Roberto would come back to Lilia also, and she would no longer weep.

She wondered if the children would sing the song again tomorrow evening and whether she could learn it by memory. She wondered what would happen to her and to her mother if her father never returned. She wondered if they would live forever with her grandmother, who reminded her of a friendly little dragon.

As sleep closed in over her, the refrain of the song played on in her head: *Mambrú se fue a la guerra... que do-re-mi, que fa-sol-la...* Two tears rolled down her cheeks and fell onto the pillow.

# Chapter II

*Knock, Knock. ¿Quién es? La Vieja Inés.*
*¿Qué quiere? Un color.*

Sunlight poured into the kitchen through the
bow window and the open door when Blanca Estela
walked in the next morning to find Mamá Anita
rolling out flour *tortillas* at the table while Lilia
cooked them on a griddle on the stove. The *tortillas*
would puff up, releasing their freshly baked aroma,
and Lilia would press them down to make sure they
cooked thoroughly. Then she would flip them over
to cook on the other side.

"Good morning, my love," said Lilia.

"Did you sleep well?" asked Mamá Anita. Blanca
Estela nodded sleepily. She had, indeed, slept sound-
ly, dreamlessly, so much so that after waking up it
had taken her several minutes to recollect where she
was.

"Shall I cook you an egg for breakfast?" Mamá
Anita offered. "Scrambled with tomatoes and
onions, or soft and runny? The eggs are very fresh,
just gathered from the nest. Pedro, a little boy who
lives just up the street, brought them early this
morning. You will meet him later and perhaps
become friends with him. Would you like to eat a
banana first?"

Blanca Estela took a banana from a brightly
painted bowl in the center of the table, peeled it,

and ate it hungrily. A loud knocking at the front door startled her as she swallowed the last mouthful of fruit.

"Blanca Estela, go see who it is," said Mamá Anita. "I removed the bar from the entry door when I let Pedro in this morning, but I shut the doors again."

Blanca Estela looked down at herself and exclaimed, "But I'm still in my nightgown!"

Mamá Anita and Lilia both laughed. "It's quite all right," Mamá Anita assured her. "Your gown is quite modest. It can pass for a dress. Just go through the house; don't cut across the patio, because you're barefooted."

She ran back through the bedrooms and made a right turn when she came to the parlor, where at one end, the two cots were still unfolded and unmade, side by side. She slowed down when she reached the entryway, stopping to inhale the fragrance of the jasmines in the flower pots before she pulled on one of the heavy front doors. A boy somewhat smaller than herself stood nonchalantly on the sidewalk, a metal bucket dangling from one hand. She thought that this must be Pedro come to deliver more eggs. She stood aside to let him pass, but he did not move. Instead, he knocked again on the door although it was now open. Then he said, "Knock, knock," and waited. She made a gesture for him to pass. He shook his head and said, "You're supposed to ask who it is. Say, '¿Quién es?'"

"¿Quién es?" she repeated, puzzled.

"La Vieja Inés," he responded to her amazement. How could he say that he was an old woman named Inés'?

"Come on now," he encouraged her. "Ask me what I want: *¿Qué quiere?*"

"*¿Qué quiere?*" she repeated obediently, waiting to be enlightened.

"*Un color.*" She was completely at a loss now. How could anybody ask for a color? Something of a certain color, yes, but not a color by itself. "Name a color," he added, with a trace of impatience.

She looked down at her gown for inspiration and tried to remember the Spanish word for blue. "*Azul,*" she finally said.

"Well, yes," he responded, as if he were disappointed. "Of course I have blue," and she noticed then that he wore faded blue shorts and a shirt with a sailor collar of more or less the same shade.

"Why did you answer '*La Vieja Inés?*'" she could not refrain from asking.

The boy shrugged his shoulders. "I don't know. It rhymes with '*¿quién es?*'" He then stepped over the threshold adding, "My mother says, could she please have some water?" He continued, "You must be Blanca Estela."

She wished that he wouldn't call her that. Her friends, June and Linda, and their mother always called her Stella, which she preferred, and her mother called her Estelita, but to her grandmother she was Blanca Estela. It seemed as if everybody in this place was going to call her the same thing. She did not like double names, not unless it was something cute, like Mary Ann.

"I am Mario," the boy told her. "I live next door to you. *Doña* Anita told us you were coming." He skipped down the steps from the entryway to the patio and went to the *aljibe* while she followed him uncertainly. He raised the wire mesh lid and dropped the bucket that was attached to a long coil of rope, which in turn, was tied to a metal ring on the outside wall of the *aljibe*. She heard the metal hit the side of the cistern several times and the splashing of water before he hauled up the bucket and emptied it into his own pail.

"Thank you for the water, *Doña* Anita," he called through the bars of the kitchen window. "My mother sends her regards, and how are you this morning?"

"I am well, Mario," Mamá Anita answered from inside. "Tell your mother that I am enjoying the company of my daughter and my granddaughter."

Blanca Estela had forgotten that she was bare-footed until she felt a feathery brush against her foot, and then she remembered the red ants. She ran back up the steps to the entryway and waited there for Mario. He followed her, walking carefully as the overflowing pail splashed water on his feet, which were also bare and quite dirty.

"Do you want to come out and play with us tonight?" he asked her. "We played outside your window last night."

"Yes, I know," she answered. "I heard you."

"Why didn't you come out and join us, then? We would have let you play."

"I was tired. I fell asleep very soon." She was ashamed to remember that the night before, before going to sleep, she had cried very softly into her pillow. "I don't know your games. We didn't play them where... where I used to live."

"Oh yes, you're from the other side, aren't you? Evita said you probably didn't speak Spanish, that you probably spoke only English, or *Pocho*, you know, half and half, but you sound all right to me. Come out and play tonight. You can just watch at first if you like."

He left, closing the door behind him, and she went back to the kitchen to join her mother and Mamá Anita for breakfast. She was ravenously hungry.

That evening, after supper and after the sun had gone down, the children came out to play again. Blanca Estela, standing between the shutters and the metal bars in the embrasure of the window, could see them standing about, arguing over which game to play. Their mothers brought out rocking chairs and set them on the sidewalk to converse with their neighbors. Mamá Anita tried to convince Lilia to sit at least in front of the open door, but she refused, sitting, instead, in the parlor, in front of the open window, but away from the lamplight so nobody could see her.

"*Hija*," Mamá Anita said to her daughter, "you are carrying mourning too far. Those harsh customs of old that kept widows in hiding are past."

"I just don't feel like seeing anybody yet, Mamá. I don't want to talk to people now. It will only make me sad when the neighbors start remembering Roberto and the way things used to be. In a few days, yes, but not now. Estelita, why don't you go out, and you, too, Mamá, if you want to talk to your friends."

"They were your friends, too, at one time."

"That was before I went away. Things change so much."

"Blanca Estela, you go out and play if you want to, child," said Mamá Anita.

Blanca Estela did not want to go out, either. For her it was enough at this time to stand in the embrasure and listen to what the children were singing. They had formed a circle around a girl in a white dress while they sang something. At a certain point in the song, two of the bigger boys, who had not joined in the circle, attempted to break through the chain of interlocking hands as if they were trying to reach the girl in the middle. Twice they tried and twice they failed, and finally the two boys joined the circle too, and they all sang again.

This time she understood some of the words. It was something about "*Doña Blanca*" and about being surrounded by pillars of gold and silver. Blanca, like her own name. Were they making fun of her? Blanca meant white something also. Maybe it was the girl in white. The girl in white, although small, seemed to be important. Blanca Estela could not see any of the children's faces anymore as the twilight lengthened into night, but the girl in white seemed to be telling the others, even the bigger children, what to do. She recognized Mario's voice responding to her.

"No, Evita," he was saying. "You already got to choose a game; now it's somebody else's turn."

"*La Vieja Inés, los colores*," another boy said.

"You can't see colors in the dark," Evita's voice answered scornfully.

"Besides, we're not prepared. We should all bring an item of the color chosen. That way there is no cheating."

"Enough play for tonight," a woman's voice called out in the dark, and the children slowly marched away, still talking about what they would play the next night.

Blanca Estela rested her head against the cool iron bars of the window. In her mind new words buzzed around like frantic bees, which were not silenced until she fell asleep.

The following morning, after breakfast, Mamá Anita asked Blanca Estela to go to Chabela's grocery store on the next corner to buy half a kilo of tomatoes, since she needed them for cooking dinner. Blanca Estela stood very still, petrified at the thought of having to go out by herself and talk to a stranger who might not understand her. But how to refuse Mamá Anita?

"I don't have any money," she finally said.

Mamá Anita laughed.

"Don't worry, child. Just tell Chabela to charge it to me. She always does, and I pay her at the end of the month. Come, let's step out on the sidewalk, and I'll point to where you will go."

Mamá Anita opened the front door and turned to face the left. "See that yellow house at the end of the block? That's the store." The yellow house did indeed stand out in bright contrast to the white stucco and the dun colored stone of the rest of the houses.

At that moment a two-wheeled cart with rubber tires pulled by a dappled gray horse, stopped in front of them. "Oh, here's the meat," Mamá Anita explained to Blanca Estela. "It's so good of Pepe to bring it to me. He started delivering it last winter when my rheumatism got bad and I had trouble walking all the way to his shop. It was my knees, you know. Good morning, Pepe. What do you have that is especially good today?"

"Good morning, *Doña* Anita," answered the man, jumping down from his perch on the cart. "Ribs are good today, lots of meat on them. I don't know how much longer we'll get good meat. We haven't had any rain lately, so the pastures are dry and much of the cattle has been sold. We'll be left with only goat's meat if we don't get any water soon. Maybe we'll have rain before St. John's feast day at the end of June."

"We'll pray to St. John for rain, Pepe, to make sure the river doesn't dry up. Let me have the ribs. This is my granddaughter, Lilia and Roberto's girl. Blanca Estela, you go on to the store. Half a kilo of tomatoes, remember. Oh, and you might look and see if you want some mangoes or bananas, but make sure they're ripe."

Mamá Anita gave her a light push on the back and sent her in the direction of the yellow house. She walked slowly, keeping her eyes on the sidewalk, which on this block was made of the same little cobblestones as the floors of the house. She was reluctant to look in the open doorways or windows for fear that someone might call out to her, saying something to which she would not be able to respond. When she came to the yellow house, she hesitated at the open door and then, taking a deep breath, stepped inside the shop.

It was only a small room with a short wooden counter, behind which a small, thin woman frowned and peered intently at a scale. She was pouring rice out of a metal scoop into a pan with rounded edges, which rested at one end of the scale while a bar with metal weights on it danced up and down at the other end. Chabela very delicately adjusted the grains of rice until the bar was balanced exactly in the middle, the metal weights in equilibrium with the mound of rice.

"Here you are," she said to three children who stood on the outer side of the counter. "A quarter of a kilo of rice."

"Thank you," said the boy, "and half a kilo of beans, please."

Blanca Estela recognized Mario from the back. She had noticed the cowlick on the back of his head yesterday. He was leaning against the counter on one arm, talking to a girl on his right. Blanca Estela could see the girl's profile, and it reminded her of a porcelain doll's face that she had once seen in a glass case when her mother had taken her to a big department store back home. The girl was not quite Mario's height and built like a small bird, with dainty fragile limbs. She had dark, curly hair cut short and wore a pale green pinafore. Blanca Estela immediately longed to look like her.

Mario held some colored picture cards in his hand and was telling the girl, "I'll trade you Hedy Lamarr for Linda Darnell."

The girl shook her head and made her curls quiver like flowers in the wind. "I have my collection of movie star cards already complete." When the girl spoke, Blanca Estela recognized her voice as belonging to the girl in white from the night before.

"What about Erroll Flynn, Evita? Are you sure that you have him?

"Quite sure."

"One half kilo of beans and a quarter kilo of rice," said Chabela, interrupting the conversation.

"Mimi, you've got the money," Mario addressed the girl on his left without turning to look at her. The girl fished in the pocket of her dress and pulled out several bills, which she gave to Chabela. Chabela opened a drawer built into the counter and gave her some coins in change.

"What about you, Evita?" asked the storekeeper, talking to the girl in green, "What are you buying today?"

"My mother says please send her a kilo of avocados, half a kilo of tomatoes, and oh yes, some candy for me."

"Hrrmph," muttered Chabela, "we'll see about the candy, but I do have some very good avocados." She went to a wire basket where she had stacked a pyramid of shiny blue-black skinned avocados.

Mario turned to leave, followed by the girl who carried the small bundles of rice and beans. "Hello, Blanca Estela," he said. "This is my sister, Mimi."

Blanca Estela was surprised. They did not look like brother and sister. Mario was rosy cheeked, as if he had just scrubbed his face (although he did not look overly clean) and had bright dark eyes, while his sister seemed to have taken her color from the sandstones of the houses, or from the khaki of his shorts. Mimi had light brown eyes, tan skin and sandy-colored hair which was cut short, very straight, but it kept falling over her forehead. She was obviously the older of the two, although not much bigger than he and had a serious expression that seemed to say that she had worries of her own.

However, it was clear that she followed her brother's lead.

"Are you coming out to play with us tonight?" Mario asked Blanca Estela.

Evita, her arms laden with bags full of avocados and tomatoes, joined them before Blanca Estela could answer.

"Who is this?" she asked Mario.

"This is Blanca Estela. She's visiting her grandmother, *Doña* Anita."

"Oh yes, I remember now, the one from the other side. You come from across the river, don't you? My mother says that she knows your mother. Can you speak Spanish?"

"Of course she does." Mario came to her rescue, noticing, no doubt, that Blanca Estela's tongue seemed to be tied up in knots.

Evita shrugged her shoulders and immediately had to re-establish her grip on the avocados, which threatened to come cascading down from her arms.

Pouting a little, Evita said, "I have to go now; I must help my mother in the workshop. I am snipping off the loose threads from the bridesmaids' dresses that she's making. They're beautiful, but nobody is supposed to see them until they're ready."

"What do you want, child?" Chabela asked Blanca Estela, and she felt herself blushing.

"You go home with the groceries, Mimi," Mario told his sister, returning to his place at the counter. Blanca Estela suddenly realized that he meant to help her, if she needed it, and this knowledge gave her confidence.

"Half a kilo of tomatoes... please," she said, speaking slowly.

"This is Blanca Estela. She's visiting her grand-mother, *Doña* Anita," Mario introduced her to the storekeeper.

"Yes I know. And how is Lilia, your mother? I haven't seen her in a long time. Give her my regards... my condolences too. Here's the tomatoes. Tell your grandmother that I put them on her account."

Blanca Estela walked out of the store, clutching the bag of tomatoes tightly to her chest. Mario followed her. He seemed to be thinking of something. Finally he asked, "Why did Chabela say to give your mother condolences?"

She stopped and looked at her feet, tracing the contours of the buckles on her sandals with her eyes, not knowing how to answer. She came to a decision. "It's because my father is dead," she said, and looked at him to see how he took her announcement.

He said nothing for a few moments and then, as they began to walk again, he asked her, "What was he like, your father?"

"He was a soldier," she answered after some thought, and she noticed admiration in Mario's eyes.

"My father is a mechanic," he volunteered mat-ter-of-factly. "He runs the generator to produce electricity. The turbine is in the river; the water turns it. We... my brothers and sisters and I—we help him. We get to go swimming in the river when we help him. My father also knows how to repair radios, and my big brother runs the movie projec-tor—when we have movies. We don't always have electricity, either."

Blanca Estela was impressed by the multiple talents of Mario's family.

"Why don't you come out and play with us tonight?" he repeated the invitation of the day before.

"I don't know your games," she told him with less embarrassment than the first time.

"We'll play Colors... you know, *La Vieja Inés*. I already showed you how to play that one. Anyway, when you come out to play, bring something—a button or a ribbon or something like that for a color. I'll choose you for my team."

"All right, I will. After supper?"

"Yes, after the sun goes down. Bye."

She left him at the door of his house and went on to the next door to where Mamá Anita waited impatiently to make tomato sauce.

"What took you so long, child?"

"I was talking to Mario and Evita and Mimi," she answered, as if these were the names of her lifelong friends. "And," she added, "Chabela sends her regards to my mother."

Blanca Estela left out the part about the condolences.

That afternoon, when she got up from the afterdinner nap that Mamá Anita insisted that she take, Blanca Estela asked her grandmother if she could look through her sewing basket for a scrap of cloth. She explained about playing Colors.

"Oh yes," said Mamá Anita. "There are some ribbons in there, but don't take the whole length. Just snip off a short piece."

Spools of thread in a multitude of colors nestled against the red silk lining of the sewing basket, like precious jewels displayed in a jeweler's case. She did not think that Mamá Anita would approve of her taking a whole spool of thread for a game. There was also a profusion of white satin ribbon, but this choice did not strike her as sufficiently imaginative. There might be scraps of cloth or buttons elsewhere; however, she did not feel yet confident enough to ask Mamá Anita for them. She finally settled on a short piece of pale blue ribbon, apparently a remnant of that which adorned the nightgown that her grandmother had made for her.

That evening, after supper, she ventured out to join the other children who were just then negotiating which game to play. Evita had several suggestions, none of which was Colors, but Mario reminded her that the night before she, herself, had insisted on their bringing samples of color for the game. "We brought the samples, didn't we?" he asked the others. Several nodded, including Blanca Estela, who now clutched the piece of ribbon in her hand.

"All right," Mario continued, pressing his advantage. "I'll choose my team: Pedro, Blanca Estela, Mimi. Evita, you can be *La Vieja Inés*, if you like. "

Evita was somewhat mollified at getting the lead role in the game and picked for her team a boy and a girl who, until then, had kept themselves slightly apart from the group.

"They're visitors," Mario explained to her. "They come every year from the capital to visit with their uncle, the doctor, and his wife. They don't always play with us."

"I didn't know *La Vieja Inés* had a team," Blanca Estela commented, puzzled.

"She doesn't, really," Mario admitted. "They're just like her advisors, to help her guess the colors."

"What happens if they guess the right color?"

"In that case you go with them, to their side. The side that gets the most people wins."

Evita had already approached them and was miming knocking at the door while she said, "Knock knock." She and Mario then went through the opening routine, asking who it was and what she wanted, "*Un color,*" answered *La Vieja Inés.*

"Which color?" they all asked her.

"*Morado,*" Evita announced, after a dramatic pause.

"Purple?" Mario asked and looked around at his teammates, who shook their heads. "*No tenemos.* We don't have purple," Mario replied with satisfaction at turning her away.

*La Vieja Inés* went back to consult with her advisors and soon returned to repeat the performance. This time she asked for blue.

"*Azul?*" asked Mario and looked at his crew. Slowly, Blanca Estela opened her hand and revealed the pale blue ribbon in it.

Evita gave a little squeal, "She gave up, she gave up. She comes with me."

Blanca Estela looked at Mario and saw disappointment in his face. Like a lawyer, determined to fight for his case even after his client has let him down, Mario turned to argue with Evita.

"You asked for *azul.* That's not *azul.*"

"Well it is, sort of. Anyway, she gave up when she showed it to us," gloated Evita.

Blanca Estela felt confused and humiliated. Surely the ribbon in her hand was blue. She remembered asking Mario for *azul* yesterday after she had looked at the blue ribbon on her gown, and he had admitted that he had blue.

Crestfallen, she stepped away from them all and went to stand by herself on the sidewalk, gradually edging her way back to the open door of her grandmother's house.

Lilia and Mamá Anita were still in the kitchen, drying and putting away the supper dishes. They asked her if she had played outside with the other children. "Yes," she said, "but I am tired now and want to go to sleep."

"We'll set up the cots in just a little while," said Mamá Anita. "would you like to sleep outdoors tonight... in the patio? It's getting so hot now that we're not getting a breeze in the house all night long. It's perfectly safe to sleep in the courtyard. Nobody has ever climbed over the walls. Some people line the top of the walls with broken glass, but I never felt the need to do so. Most people are honest in this town."

As they were getting ready for bed, Blanca Estela felt that she had to find out what her mistake had been while playing Colors. She showed the ribbon to her mother and asked her, "What color is this?"

Lilia looked at it closely by the lamplight and said, "It's so pale that I can hardly tell. Oh, of course, it's *celeste*."

"I thought it was *azul*," cried Blanca Estela with frustration.

"Well, of course, it's *azul celeste*. That's the shade of blue, like the sky, *el cielo*."

"Which is *azul*, then?" she insisted.

"Well, it's darker," Lilia answered her.

Like Mario's shirt and shorts, Blanca Estela realized. She reflected that the game—and the
language—had many more subtle meanings than she
had guessed. Shades of meaning, just like shades of
color.

The following afternoon they had a visitor. It
was at the right time for short visits, after the siesta
but before supper. Long visits were made in the
evening, after supper. The visitor was a tall woman
with a longish face who embraced Lilia and gave
Blanca Estela a quick hug. Mamá Anita called her
María Eva. The woman carried something bulky
wrapped in a sheet. As she sat down in one of the
cane rocking chairs, she unwrapped the bundle and
revealed a long dress of pale green silk.

"Look at this," she said, in a confidential tone.
"Six bridesmaids' dresses just like this one, and each
is embroidered with crystal beads on the bodice. I'm
doing all the embroidery myself. That's why I
brought it with me, so I can work while we talk."

"Who's getting married?" Lilia asked, bending
closer to see the beadwork.

"Artemisa González. You probably don't know
her. She's only seventeen. She's José González's
daughter, an only child. Her parents used to stay
most of the time at the ranch, but now they live in
town. He's doing very well; he planted cotton
recently, rather than raising cattle, and made money.
They say the bride's dress is quite a creation. She's
having it made in Laredo. I'm only doing the bridesmaids' dresses."

"That's an unusual color for bridesmaids' dresses. In the past bridesmaids usually wore pink, and
there wasn't such an army of them, either," Mamá

Anita said, putting on her eyeglasses and starting to darn a pillowcase.

"Nile Green, it's called. It's very much in style." It's supposed to be the color of the waters from the River Nile," María Eva explained.

Blanca Estela looked at it closely. The cloth did have a watery-green look to it, but it was not like the water of the Río Grande. That had been brown. Somewhere else rivers must be green.

The woman turned to Blanca Estela and said, "Evita tells me that you were out playing with them last night. I am so glad that you're making friends already."

Blanca Estela was taken aback by two thoughts. This woman was Evita's mother, was her first thought. This tall woman with the broad shoulders, the harsh cheekbones and square jaw was the mother of the dainty Evita, with the perfect oval face of a porcelain doll. The second thought filled her with anguish. Evita had told her mother what a stupid girl she was: the girl from the other side who didn't even know the names of the colors.

She was so mortified that from then on she paid no attention to the conversation and only came out of her thoughts when María Eva re-wrapped the dress and got up to leave, saying, "Goodbye, *Doña* Anita, I have to go get supper. Lilia, whenever you feel like it, come and see me. I've got two girls helping me sew who come in the mornings, but in the afternoon I'm all by myself. Come and see me. You've got to start going out; otherwise, you will become a recluse."

"She will visit you," answered Mamá Anita. "I will make sure that she starts going out. She's going to go to Mass with me on Sunday. Now that Father Mirabal is back, we will have Mass again."

For two days and evenings Blanca Estela joined her mother in being a recluse, refusing to go out to play and finding excuses to avoid being sent out shopping. She had heard the children playing outside her window, but she did not recognize the games. Finally, on the third evening, she heard Mario again organize a game of Colors. Boldly, she marched out the door and went to join him.

"Will you let me play?" she asked him.

He looked at her with some surprise. "Sure," he said. "This time I'll be *La Vieja Inés*, and you can be my advisor."

She was relieved, for she had just realized that she had not brought a color sample.

They began to play. Mario asked for colors, without much help from Blanca Estela or from Mimi, the other advisor, and without much luck, either. Mimi spoke even less than Blanca Estela. During the day, Blanca Estela would spy Mimi scurrying about silently, as intent on her business as a little ant, and in the evening she limited her play to carrying out the role that others, usually her brother, allotted to her. Mario, in frustration, now turned to her and asked, "Mimi, can't you help me? Think of a color that the others are likely to have."

Mimi thought for a minute. "*Verde*," she finally said. "Ask for green."

Mario went through the routine again, knocking on the air, announcing who he was, and asking for the color green. The other team paused for a moment and looked at each other.

"What shade of green?" Evita's voice piped up, high and clear, with an undertone of satisfaction.

Mario retired to confer with Mimi, but she had no further suggestions to make. Next, he looked at Blanca Estela, without much hope. "What shade of green?" he repeated. "Dark? Light? Is that what she means?"

Blanca Estela remembered the pale green silk dress with the crystal beads, the dresses that Evita had claimed to be helping her mother to sew and which nobody was supposed to have seen. "*Verde Nilo*," she whispered in his ear.

"What? I have never heard of that!" he exclaimed, surprised.

"Just say that: Nile Green," she insisted vehemently.

He shrugged his shoulders, saying, "All right, I'll try that.... *Verde Nilo*," he announced loudly, as he approached Evita's group. For a moment nobody responded, and Mario was emboldened to demand, "Let me see. Open your hand, Evita."

"How did you guess?" Evita wanted to know, but he only shook his head and walked back to show his advisors the scrap of pale green silk that Evita had relinquished.

Blanca Estela did not press her luck with other games that evening. She stood in the sidelines and watched them play the games, trying to understand the words, not always being successful. But, no matter, she had won a victory that night, even if the others did not know about it. Still, she knew that she could not rest on her laurels. There would be other games and other words to learn if she wanted to avoid Evita's scorn or Mario's disappointment.

Later that night, as she was going to bed, Blanca Estela asked her mother, "Where is the River Nile?"

Mamá Anita heard her question and answered before Lilia had a chance to say anything. "In Egypt, of course. Don't they teach you geography nowadays?"

It was a sign of how things were changing that she was not abashed by her grandmother's scolding. But Lilia came to her defense. "She hasn't studied world geography yet, Mamá. She's still very young."

"Well, when I was a child we learned all that right away, in the first grade... at least I think we did. We studied the rivers of Mexico, and then the rivers of the world... sometime when we were in school anyway. I'll tell you what, Blanca Estela, tomorrow I will show you a book with pictures of far away places, a travel book. It used to belong to your grandfather. I'm sure that we'll find descriptions of Egypt and pictures of the River Nile."

"Why do you want to know?" Lilia asked her.

"Oh, I just wanted to see if it was really green."

# Chapter III

*¿Qué oficio le pondremos, Matarilerilerón?*

"*Mataril... Matariri, no... Matarilerile... rón...
Matarilerilerón.*" There, she had finally said it.
Blanca Estela gave a little hop of satisfaction. She
stood on the sidewalk with Mamá Anita, waiting for
Lilia to emerge through the door. Lilia finally came
out, looking very pale and nervous, but still very
beautiful, in a black silk dress with skirts that
swirled around her ankles as she walked. Over her
head she had draped a short lace *mantilla*, black as
her hair. Both dramatically framed her face and
showed it a translucent white.

As she stepped out in the sun, Lilia took out a
pair of dark eyeglasses from her shiny black handbag. Blanca Estela wished that her mother would
not cover her eyes with them. She delighted in contemplating the changing hues of her mother's eyes.
Sometimes they were deep green, with specks of
gold in them, sometimes gray, like a stormy sea,
made even darker by the long, dark lashes that shad-
ed them.

As Lilia put on her glasses, Mamá Anita pulled
the heavy doors shut and said briskly to Blanca
Estela, "Come on child, don't delay. It's almost time
for the third bell. I don't like being late for Mass."

They were on their way to church in their
Sunday finery—Lilia, quite elegant in her widow's

mourning clothes, Mamá Anita, very neat and crisp in a gray cotton dress, and Blanca Estela in the pale yellow frock that she had gotten for Easter two months before. Mamá Anita opened the parasol she was carrying and with it shielded Lilia and herself from the sun, which was already very hot at mid-morning.

Blanca Estela followed behind, skipping a step every so often, practicing under her breath the chant of the new game that she was learning.

Question: *¿Qué quiere usted, Matarilerilerón?*

Answer: *Yo quiero un paje, Matarilerilerón.*

Who was *Matarilerilerón?* He must be some powerful personage to come demanding a page. What was a page anyway? She had asked Mamá Anita why, when *Matarilerilerón* was asked what he wanted, he answered that he wanted a page. She had asked her what a page was, and Mamá Anita had pointed to a thick dictionary at the bottom of one of the stacks of books that covered a large table in the darkest corner of the parlor. The table was made of dark wood and had legs carved with lions' heads and other fanciful figures.

The dictionary told her that a page was a young boy who was learning to be a knight or who served a prince. Girls must also be pages, thought Blanca Estela, because Evita had said that she had been a page at her cousin's wedding and had worn a long gown, like the bridesmaids.

So why did *Matarilerilerón* want a page? Perhaps it was to give him an education. You were supposed to ask *Matarilerilerón* what occupation he would give the page, which also meant what the page wanted to be when he grew up. She continued to chant under her breath: *¿Qué oficio le pondremos, Matarilerilerón?* The only way she could say the word was to say it very slowly, breaking it up into syllables: *Ma-ta-ri-le-ri-le-rón.*

Mamá Anita stopped for a moment to ask her, "What are you muttering, child?"

"*Ma-ta-ri-le-ri-le-rón.*"

"She's learning to play that game, Mamá," Lilia explained.

"Oh, that's fine, but don't dawdle."

Blanca Estela did not think that she was dawdling. Rather, it was Mamá Anita who slowed down as they passed every open doorway to say "good morning" to the inhabitants within. When they went past María Eva's house and sewing workshop, María Eva called out that she would be in church later. Right now she was putting the finishing touches to the Christening robe for somebody's baby, who was being baptized that afternoon. Evita had already gone ahead of her.

The small procession of Mamá Anita, Lilia and Blanca Estela continued for three long blocks down the same street where they lived but in the direction away from the bridge and towards the center of town. Until now, Blanca Estela had not ventured farther away than Chabela's store, less than a block from the house. At the end of the third block they turned left and were soon in view of the town square, the plaza.

The plaza was guarded on the east side by an imposing church, of mission style, made of sandstone blocks and with a soaring bell tower. Facing the church, on the west side of the plaza, a pink, stuccoed, two-story building with a large clock on its face, looked almost playful in comparison, like the decoration on top of a cake. This building was the Municipal Palace, the seat of local government, Mamá Anita explained. Large stone houses, including one with two stories and adorned with ironwork balconies, lined the other two sides of the plaza. A gazebo and bandstand in the middle of the square looked almost diminutive surrounded by so many imposing structures.

The church itself was set back from the sidewalk and was shielded from the street by a high wall of bricks laid in a lattice pattern, which gave the wall an airy look. The small front yard, bare except for two date palms, was called the *atrium*, Mamá Anita told Blanca Estela, and it was here that people gathered for processions and special events.

On the steps of the door to the church they caught up with two gray-haired women who greeted Mamá Anita with little pats on the back. In high, fluting voices they told Lilia, and even Blanca Estela, how wonderful it was to see them and to have them visiting in town.

Suddenly Lilia cried out in vexation, "Oh, Mamá, I forgot to bring a veil or head scarf for Estelita."

"Don't worry. Father Mirabal doesn't care if girls wear a head covering. Let's go in. Mass is about to begin."

The double doors of the church stood wide open. They were even taller and heavier than those of Mamá Anita's house. These were varnished with a dark brown stain and had carved relief panels which were crowned by a bow-shaped transom through which light and air came in. And higher still, above the transom but below the belfry, there was a round window covered with amber and rose stained glass that glittered in the morning light like a jewel.

No sooner were they across the threshold than their path was blocked by a movable screen of fixed horizontal slats made of the same wood as the doors. It veiled the activities transpiring inside the church from the eyes of passersby or from any idler sitting on one of the benches on the plaza. Mamá Anita darted to the left and around the screen and hurried up the main aisle until she stopped before a pew, midway to the altar. She made a quick genuflection at the entrance to the pew and motioned to Lilia and Blanca Estela to follow her example.

They were just in time. They had just settled themselves in the middle of the pew when the tinkling of a little hand bell heralded the entrance of the priest to the altar, preceded by the altar boy. The congregation sprang up to its feet and then dropped to its knees, responding to the priest's greeting that the Lord be with all of them. Blanca Estela recognized only a few snatches of the Latin phrases of the Mass, such as the salutation of *Dominus vobiscum*, to which you were supposed to respond, *Et cum spiritu tuo*.

The majority of the people attending Mass were women, many gray haired and plump, like Mamá Anita. There were also six or seven girls who, one could tell, were just getting used to wearing high heels and putting on lipstick. Sometimes one of them would begin to giggle, and the others would quickly pinch her arm to hush her. On the front row Blanca Estela saw Evita, looking angelic in a white organdy dress, an image that was unfortunately marred by the piece of candy that she rhythmically shifted inside her mouth. Across the aisle from them were a man and a woman, flanked by a boy and a girl whom Blanca Estela recognized from some of their games. The boy and the girl were Jaime and Sandra, and they were the brother and the sister who were visiting their uncle, the doctor. That must be the doctor then, a man with a graying mustache and heavy eyebrows, tall, but with drooping shoulders, as if he were very tired. Blanca Estela could not see very much of his wife, even by leaning forward, except that she was fair skinned and slender and that her hair, where it was not covered by a white lace *mantilla*, glinted like dark gold.

Mamá Anita reached out and tugged gently at one of Blanca Estela's pigtails, pointing with her other hand at the altar to indicate where her attention should be concentrated. But she was so interested in everything around her that she barely registered annoyance or embarrassment at her grandmother's rebuke. Now the priest turned to face them, and he looked very handsome in his vestments of green, white and gold. He was strong and broad-shouldered with very dark, piercing eyes and black hair that curled all around the bald dome of his head.

"Pay attention to what Father Mirabal says," Mamá Anita admonished her.

The priest opened a little gate on the low altar rail and passed through it on his way down the altar steps. Blanca Estela wondered where he was going, but soon she saw him climb the wooden spiral staircase that seemed to wrap itself around a column. It ended in the ornately carved pulpit that towered above the congregation. When Father Mirabal was in the pulpit, you could only see him from the waist up. Resting his hands on the rim of the pulpit, as if suspended above them by levitation, Father Mirabal reminded Blanca Estela of a picture she had once seen of a man standing inside the basket attached to a balloon, floating over the people below. She wondered if they all looked small to Father Mirabal as he looked down at them from his elevated perch.

Father Mirabal began his sermon by reminding them that it was Sunday, the thirteenth of June, the feast day of St. Anthony of Padua, a great saint known for many things, besides being the patron saint of girls looking for a husband. The girls in the front pews giggled again. Blanca Estela could not understand all the rest of the sermon, since she did not know all the words he used, but, nonetheless, she was carried along by his voice, deep and melodious. Her spirits lifted when his voice gathered force in a crescendo, and she was soothed when he dropped it to a gentle murmur.

When the sermon was over, Father Mirabal returned to the altar. Blanca Estela came out of her trance as the congregation stood up to recite the Creed, which she knew only in parts. Then everyone knelt down again for the Offertory, following the cue of the altar boy's bell. Blanca Estela looked up at the altar when she was supposed to have her eyes closed in prayer and noticed that the altar boy assisting the priest was none other than Pedro, their playmate from their games at twilight.

She wondered at what time Pedro had to get up in the morning. Often, by the time she got out of

bed, Pedro had already come calling to deliver freshly laid eggs from his mother's hens, as well as
delivering the milk, still warm and frothy from the
cow. In the evenings, too, he helped his father bring
in the cows from the pasture for milking, and now
he was assisting the priest to say Mass.

Of her other playmates, Mario was not to be
found in church this morning, and only a very thor-
ough visual survey of the church revealed Mimi,
hidden in a dark corner lighted only by votive candles.

When it was time for Communion, Mamá Anita
got up and went to receive the host from Father
Mirabal at the altar rail. Blanca Estela looked inquiringly at her mother, but Lilia shook her head and
whispered, "I haven't been to confession." Blanca
Estela knew that she, herself, had not either, even if
she did not know exactly what confession entailed,
beyond the fact that its absence was obviously a bar
to receiving the host.

Mamá Anita came back from the altar with her
eyes downcast and her hands joined together in an
attitude of prayer. Blanca Estela noticed that the
doctor's wife had also received Communion, and as
she returned to her pew, Blanca Estela was able to
study her closely. She was much younger than
Mamá Anita, but perhaps older than Lilia. She had a
very pretty face, marred only by the fine lines that
ran down from the tip of her delicate nostrils to the
corners of her mouth. She kept her eyes downcast as
she returned to her pew, only raising them at the last
minute as she took her place again next to her husband. At that moment Blanca Estela saw that the

doctor's wife had eyes the color of turquoise. She also saw that her eyes were filled with sadness.

After Communion had been distributed, Father Mirabal wrapped up the Mass quickly, telling the congregation that the Mass had ended with a brisk, *Ite, Missa est.* People began to leave, stopping only at the end of their pews to genuflect in the direction of the altar as they left. Blanca Estela sank back on the bench and rubbed her knees gingerly. They were extremely sore from kneeling on the hard, wooden surface, particularly since both knees were also scraped from yesterday's fall, when she had attempted a long jump from the top of the steps of the entryway down to the patio. Looking at her knees, she decided regretfully that they were unquestionably knobby. Being thin and small like Evita was considered dainty, but she, herself, was growing tall and skinny, with arms and legs like matchsticks, she thought, full of self loathing for a moment.

"Estelita, stop daydreaming and let's go," Lilia said, prodding her on the shoulder. She jumped up and hurried after her mother and grandmother, forgetting to genuflect in her confusion.

Outside the church, in the atrium, people had stopped to chat with one another. Mamá Anita walked towards the doctor. He stood under one of the palm trees next to his wife, who held a white parasol above her.

"Doctor Marín, how are you today?" Mamá Anita asked him. The doctor, who had covered his head with a straw hat after coming out of the church, now removed it again in order to greet Lilia and Mamá Anita.

Blanca Estela could see why he needed to shield himself from the sun, for the top of his head was partially bald, and the scalp showed bright pink underneath. One could also see that by nature he was fair-skinned like his wife, but that long exposure to the sun had left his face burned and browned to varying degrees. His nose, for example, was dark red while his forehead was a pale tan.

"Do you remember my daughter?" continued Mamá Anita. "Rosalía, you do remember Lilia?"

"Of course I do," Rosalía answered, smiling sweetly and embracing Lilia.

"And this is my granddaughter, Blanca Estela."

"This is your daughter, Lilia? What a blessing that you were left with a child." Rosalía, saying this, reached down to enfold Blanca Estela in her arms. Blanca Estela found her face pressed against Rosalía's hair and inhaled the fragrance of orange blossoms that clung to her.

When Rosalía released Blanca Estela, she asked her, "Have you met Sandra and Jaime? They are my niece and my nephew, my sister Aurora's children," she added, addressing Lilia. "They come to visit us every year."

Blanca Estela glanced at her two acquaintances, and the three of them shifted uncomfortably. They had taken part in several games together, but the brother and sister had usually held themselves slightly aloof, as if they wanted to emphasize the difference between themselves, who came from the big city, and the country bumpkins with whom they were forced to fraternize during these visits. Blanca Estela felt that the two ranked her as even lower than the locals since she was ignorant of their games and frequently made mistakes when she spoke Spanish. It had never occurred to her that she could lord it over the other children by making a show of knowing English and of having come from the United States, or because of having known things that they did not have in Revilla. She suspected that in Mexico City, where Sandra and Jaime came from, they also had indoor toilets and refrigerators and telephones. To her, though, the fact that people in Revilla didn't have those things didn't mean that they had less—they just had different things. Their houses, for example, were so huge that you could play hopscotch indoors, and at night you could look up at the star-studded sky from the patio and fall asleep counting the stars above you.

"Jaime is thinking that he might want to be a doctor when he grows up, just like Filiberto," Rosalía said, smiling at her husband and then at her nephew. "Jaime will be starting high school next year." The boy scowled and said nothing. "Is your little girl already enrolled in school here?" Rosalía continued.

"No," answered Lilia. "She already finished school this year. You know, across the river the children finish the school year earlier: in May. They only go to school for nine months out of the year, not like here, where the school year lasts ten months."

"But in September, will she start school here?" Rosalía insisted.

"Aunt Rosalía, I'm hungry. I went without breakfast so I could receive Communion," Sandra interrupted fretfully.

"We'll go in a minute darling, and you can have dinner." After saying this, Rosalía leaned towards Lilia and added, "Aurora has two other children, younger than these two. She has not been in good health since her youngest was born. He's only a year and a half, and the other one is three. They were too close together, although she went more than five years without having a baby after she had Sandra. So, to help her out, I offered to give her a hand by bringing the two oldest to stay with us for several weeks. I enjoy these visits so much. Are you and Aurora of the same age? No, I think not. She is a little older than you and married before you did. She married a man who has a business in the capital, and we hardly ever see her. Do you remember Aurora?"

"Oh yes," responded Lilia. "She was very pretty: golden hair and rosy skin, like the morning light. She was very aptly named Aurora. Of these two children, Sandra takes more after her. Her hair is a pretty, golden brown, although they both have dark eyes."

"Yes, it's just like in our family: Aurora, Perla and I, all the sisters are blonde, like my mother, but my brothers, Juan and Leopoldo, have a dark complexion, like my father. I remember now: it was you and Leopoldo who were of the same age. And speaking of the devil, that's Leopoldo crossing the plaza and walking this way. He hasn't been in church since he made his First Communion, I'm sure, except for weddings of course. Not his own, though. He is still single. I always thought that he was sweet on you, Lilia, but you got married and went away."

"I think it is time that we went home, Rosalía," Doctor Marín told his wife.

"Yes dear, you are right, but here comes Father Mirabal. We must at least wait to greet him," she replied.

Father Mirabal had changed out of his Mass vestments and now wore black trousers and a loose white shirt, which was known as a *guayabera*. "Good morning, dear friends," Father Mirabal addressed them as he approached." I was so happy to see you all in Mass, especially you, Doctor Marín. I wish more men came to Mass."

Doctor Marín blushed and murmured that he felt the need to set an example for the young people. Mamá Anita, who had been quiet for longer than usual, said, "Doctor Marín goes to church because he already had the custom to do so when he arrived here. You have lived here among us, Doctor, for so long that most people have forgotten that you were not born in Revilla."

Doctor Marín smiled as he said, "I feel like one of you, *Doña* Anita. After all, I came here as a young doctor, to do some good, and I ended up falling in love and marrying here. And so here I stayed: how many years now? Twenty?"

"Don't talk about years, Filiberto. You make me feel old. We must go now, Father, and give these children their dinner. Goodbye, Lilia. I am so glad that you are here. Will you be staying now?" Rosalía did not wait for an answer but took her leave by embracing Lilia again and patting Blanca Estela on the head. She then hurried to catch up with her husband, who waited by a hump-backed gray car, not new but brightly polished, in front of the plaza, across from the church. Jaime and Sandra already stood by impatiently, watching the doctor talk with the man whom Rosalía had identified as her brother.

Father Mirabal, in the meantime, had embraced Lilia, saying, "Welcome home, my child. It is sad that I should see you again, like this. The last time I saw you was when I performed the marriage ceremony for you and Roberto. But it was the will of God. And this child... yours? She doesn't look like you. More like Roberto, especially those dark, deep-set eyes."

"She's going to be very pretty when she grows up," Blanca Estela heard her mother spring to her defense, and she felt a great wave of love wash over her, which she hid as she pressed her face against Lilia's side.

Father Mirabal laughed, "Listen to the lioness come to the defense of her cub. Nobody said she wasn't pretty. Of course she's pretty. Let me see you better, child," and he put out a large, brown hand and took her by the chin.

She felt herself blushing with anger and embarrassment. Blanca Estela looked up at him defiantly, and found herself looking into his smiling black eyes that held a great deal of eagerness, like those of a large, friendly dog.

"What is your name, child?"

"Blanca Estela," she answered in a clear voice.

"Well, Blanca Estela, we are going to be friends. Have you made your First Communion yet? If so, why didn't I see you at the altar this morning?"

She looked at her mother for help, and again Lilia came to the rescue.

"Estelita has not made her First Communion, Father. She was supposed to prepare for it this year, but with all the things that happened... we lived so far away from the church. It was different there, Father. For one thing, the priest didn't speak Spanish. He spoke English—and Polish too, I think—but that did not help me."

"There is a Catechism class that just got started for First Communion. She can join it. She has been baptized and confirmed, of course?" Father Mirabal asked as an afterthought.

"Oh yes, Father," Lilia hastened to assure him.

At that point, Blanca Estela decided that Father Mirabal must have eyes in the back of his head because, without turning to look behind him, he noticed that Mimi was quietly scurrying across the atrium on her way out. He called to her, "Mimi, where was your brother, Mario, today? He didn't come to Mass."

Mimi paused in midstep and stood on one foot, rubbing a new-looking shoe against the sock on her other foot. It was the first time that Blanca Estela had seen her wearing shoes. "He stayed up very late last night," she answered, faintly. "He had to help my big brother run the movie projector last night."

"Well, tell Mario that I expect him here for Catechism class next Saturday, if he is to make his First Communion next month. And you too, Lilia, send this child, as well, next Saturday afternoon, at three o'clock," Father Mirabal concluded.

"She will be here, Father," Mamá Anita intervened. "Poor children, Mimi and Mario, having to work nights if the rest of us are to have movies or electric light. Their mother's health has not been good lately," Mamá Anita added, looking after Mimi. "And now we must go. I am as hungry as that sulky child, Rosalía's niece. Poor Rosalía, too, how she has grieved at not having her own children. She has to make do, instead, with the visits from those two of Aurora's, and I don't think they are very pleasant. It's different when they're your own. Then you have to put up with them, but when they're not... well anyway, I'm rambling. Goodbye, Father. That was a beautiful sermon that you preached. You have always been a wonderful orator."

Mamá Anita opened the parasol, and the three walked on towards the street. The atrium was deserted now, and the doctor's car, too, was gone. As they reached the street gate a man stepped out to meet them from behind the wall. Blanca Estela looked up in surprise. There was something familiar about him, but she could not remember who he was. He had a dark, attractive face with a broad smile under a black mustache. He wore a khaki uniform, too, and for one wild moment Blanca Estela thought that he looked like her father's soldier photograph.

"Good morning, *Doña* Anita, Lilia," the man said.

"Good morning, Leopoldo. What a surprise to see you. You were not at Mass, were you? Did you know that Lilia and my granddaughter were here?" Mamá Anita responded rather primly.

"Yes, *Doña* Anita, I saw Lilia at customs the day she arrived." Then he added, with some confusion, "I did not know then, Lilia, what had happened... of your loss. Please accept my sympathy."

"Thank you, Leopoldo," Lilia answered, with a smile.

Blanca Estela remembered now. Leopoldo was, of course, one of the men who had chatted and joked with them at the customs checkpoint on the day of their arrival, when she had been so frightened after crossing the swinging bridge. Mamá Anita set off walking again towards home, holding the parasol at just the right height so as to menace Leopoldo with putting a spoke in his eye. He had to dodge his head from side to side to avoid this threat, which made Blanca Estela want to laugh.

"Are you working today, Leopoldo?" Mamá Anita asked.

"Yes, *Doña* Anita. I am just going to the next corner to wait for the car to pick me up and drive to the bridge. It's my colleague's car. My brother-in-law, Doctor Marín, was telling me that this is your daughter. Blanca Estela, is that right? It's a very pretty name."

Blanca Estela sent him a grateful look. Even if she did not much like her name, it was nice to hear somebody say that they liked it.

They were now approaching the corner where they were to turn right and return home the way they had come. An open Jeep, painted brown, waited there while a heavy-set man in a khaki uniform and military cap perspired profusely in the driver's seat, exposed to the full heat of the sun.

"That is my ride," said Leopoldo. "We are both on duty today. I would offer to drive you home, but you see how it is. It only has room for two people. *Doña* Anita, if there is any way that I can be of service, you only have to let me know. If you need anything from the other side—groceries, medicine, anything that we don't have here—just tell me, and

I will be very pleased to get them for you. I imagine Blanca Estela will miss things from across the river."

"Thank you, Leopoldo, but my granddaughter has adjusted very well to the way we live here. She is not one of those whining, spoiled children who always want the things they can't have."

Blanca Estela felt herself glowing with pride at this testimonial from her grandmother.

"Thank you, Leopoldo," Lilia added softly with a dazzling smile. "If we need something... something that we absolutely must have... we will ask you, as a favor, to get it for us."

"Of course, we would never ask you to bring anything that is not permitted to be imported," Mamá Anita was saying stiffly, but Leopoldo was not listening. He had jumped in the Jeep with a delirious smile on his face, saying, "Goodbye then. Until very soon, I hope."

The driver tipped his cap at them and drove off, slowly at first, so as to not raise the dust around them. Mamá Anita and Lilia walked on in silence under the parasol, treading carefully in their high-heeled shoes so as to avoid rocks on the street. Blanca Estela went back to pondering what occupation *Matarilerilerón* would assign to his page.

She had learned *carpintero, zapatero, marinero.* Most of the occupations seemed to end in *-ero.* Perhaps these were the occupations that the children knew. Carpenters and shoemakers existed in Revilla, but sailors, so far from the sea? What was Leopoldo's occupation? What did you call the uniformed men at the customs checkpoint? The customs office, she had learned, was called an *aduana*, so Leopoldo must be...?

"Look, Mamá, there's a car in front of the house," Lilia exclaimed, pointing ahead. They were a block away from the house, and a dark green pick-up truck was, indeed, parked in front. "That looks like your brother Raúl's truck," Mamá Anita said. "He said he might come to see us if he was in the area. Oh, I am so happy! Happy for me and because you will see him, too. It has been so long since the two of you were together. He went to see you in the United States several years ago, didn't he? But it's a long time, anyway. How I wish your two older brothers lived closer. You haven't seen them since your wedding. I hope Raúl went into the house; it's so hot outside. Do you see if he's in the truck?"

"Calm down, Mamá. We will see him soon enough. I believe if it wasn't for those shoes you're wearing, you would take off running." Lilia laughed, but she too, was excited.

Blanca Estela increased the pace of her steps to keep up with the two women, and soon they were stepping through the entryway.

"Raúl, *hijo*," Mamá" Anita called out, and a man came out of the bedroom door and walked across the patio, buttoning up his shirt as he approached.

He was tall and slender, with thick, black hair and eyes like Lilia's in a sun-browned face. He was handsome enough to be a movie star, thought Blanca Estela, remembering the collection of movie star cards that Evita guarded so jealously.

Mamá Anita ran to meet him and threw her arms around him. Her head barely reached his shoulders as she stood on tiptoe, embracing him. Raúl gave her a hug that lifted her off her feet and kissed her repeatedly. "Your prodigal son is back, Mamita," he said, laughing a deep, rich laugh. "And my little sister, my beautiful baby sister, Lilia, is here too?" With one arm he continued to hold Mamá Anita and with the other he embraced Lilia. Blanca Estela, alone, was left behind, standing forlornly in the entry. Suddenly, he spied her.

"Who is this? Don't tell me this is Blanca Estela! But it can't be. The last time I saw her she was barely walking." He came towards her, gently disengaging himself from the two women. He stood, towering above her, and then dropped on his haunches so they were face to face.

"You are my niece, Blanca Estela. I am your uncle, Raúl. You don't remember me, do you? No, you were too little when I went to see you and your mother. Do you know that you are my only niece? You are very special: the only granddaughter that Mamita has and my only niece. My two brothers who are older than me and who are married all have sons, five between the two of them, so you can imagine how excited Mamita was when you were born and she could sew and embroider pretty, frilly dresses for you. And I like having a niece. I brought you something—not a dress because I didn't know how big you were. I'll give it to you in a moment."

"Raúl, you just got here and you're already spoiling her," Lilia said, pulling him to his feet.

"You would like me to spoil only you, little sister?"

"Why don't you get married, so you can pamper children of your own?"

"I'm still running too fast for any girl to catch me," he laughed.

"Come on, all of you," Mamá Anita called from the kitchen. "Dinner is on the table."

"Tell me how you were so certain that I would be arriving today, Mamita? This is a feast that you have prepared. *Cabrito* is reserved for special occasions, so you must have known that the prodigal son would be arriving," Raúl said, smiling at the heaping platter of roasted young goat. "Did Manuel tell you I was coming today? I saw him in Laredo last week."

"He did say something," Mamá Anita admitted. "But I knew anyway. I dreamed about you two nights ago."

"Oh, well, your dreams are more reliable than letters or telegrams. We will be working around Laredo for a few weeks, doing some surveys for the new road that's going to be built. A paved road, Mamita, to take you quickly and comfortably to Laredo without having to go across the river first. It's high time, too," added Raúl.

"Your uncle is an engineer," Mamá Anita explained, and Blanca Estela added another occupation for *Matarilerilerón*: an *ingeniero*, which also ended in -*ero*. "He builds roads and bridges."

"Well, not by myself. The company I work for does. And you forgot to add building dams, Mamita. The dam that we are building on the Río Grande and which will affect our town."

Mamá Anita crossed herself. "Don't remind us of that. God willing, we will not see that."

"How long will you be in this area?" Lilia asked quickly, seeing her mother's distress.

"Several weeks, however long it takes to do the surveys. Then I may be back when the roadwork starts, but I don't know where they will send me next."

"I don't know why you want the life of a nomad, son, when you could be at home, taking care of your own land, your own cattle. It used to be that only those without land would leave home, but look at you."

"Look at my brothers, too, Mamita. It's what happens when the young people go away to study. When they get a professional education and see the big cities, it is difficult for them to come back home to be ranchers. My brother, Francisco, studied to be a lawyer and Rubén became an accountant, and they married girls from Guadalajara and Puebla, where they stayed. They both work in an office and wouldn't know how to work outdoors. I'm the only one who works outside, in the elements, but I don't like to be tied down to one place, and the ranch ties you down. And you, little sister, who would have thought that you would ever be a teacher and go so far away? You were the most awful little barbarian when you were six."

Blanca Estela opened her eyes wide. Her mother had been a teacher—when? She hastened to listen again to her uncle's conversation, suddenly seeing her mother as a different person, a stranger she had never met before.

"I remember when I was in the sixth grade," Raúl continued, "and we were supposed to draw all the countries of the Western Hemisphere for the final class assignment. I had drawn Canada and written across it: 'The Dominion of Canada.' You were a little brat and got hold of that map and drew a horrible monster all over the Canadian provinces.

I didn't notice it, and I turned in all my maps with your drawing on Canada. I got a failing mark on that map. Why did you do it, you brat?"

"Don't you remember? It was that story that Mamá used to read to me," cried Lilia. "It was about some children who came across the term, 'The Dominion of Canada,' and, not knowing what that meant, they began imagining what it could be. Finally, they decided that it was a personage so frightening, so awful—an ogre, perhaps—who had the imposing title of 'Dominion.' The 'Dominion' was so indescribably terrifying that the children could only get as far as imagining what his servants and emissaries were like, but never the Dominion himself. Oh, I must find that story and read it to Blanca Estela."

Blanca Estela continued gazing at her mother and trying to see her as a little girl of six or as a schoolteacher. A teacher was a *maestra*, or a *profesora*. Could either be made to fit the rhyme and the beat of *Matarilerilerón*? Perhaps *Matarilerilerón* and the Dominion of Canada were cousins, similar personages inspiring dread and obedience, demanding children to be their pages....

"Look, Mamá, I think Estelita is falling asleep. It's this big dinner and the heat."

"The cot is ready, so she can take a nap."

"I'll carry her to the cot."

Two strong arms picked her up, and her head was cradled against a hard shoulder while she inhaled the subtle scents of soap and tobacco, just as it had been with her father, long ago.

She woke up when the sun had already sunk behind the western wall of the house. Her mother and her uncle were sitting in the rocking chairs in front of the first window of the parlor, talking in the comfortable tones of people who have known each other all their lives.

Raúl was saying, "You don't have to go back, you know. You can stay here, with Mamá, and I would take care of both of you. I earn a good salary. You wouldn't even need your widow's pension. You could save that for Blanca Estela. Or, if you wanted to do something, you could teach in the school again, and Estelita would be there, too. I know it's too soon to think of these things, but I'm sure that if you wanted, you could marry again. Leopoldo has never married. I know he was in love with you before you married Roberto. Besides, by marrying you, he would also get land, because neither my brothers nor I are ranchers. He has always wanted to have a ranch and work for himself, but his grandfather sold their land and left the family to fend without it."

"You're going too fast, Raúl. And who are *you* waiting for? Why haven't you married? When you do marry and have a family of your own, you will need all your salary to support them. Don't you realize that I, like you and Francisco and Rubén, have been away to another country and would find it difficult to return here for always?"

"Children," Mamá Anita's voice interposed suddenly, "come and have your *merienda*. The coffee is ready, and there is fresh pastry that Raúl brought."

Blanca Estela turned her head and saw Mamá Anita standing in the doorway that led to the kitchen. "Look, my granddaughter is awake now.

Get up, darling, and come and have your bread and chocolate."

Children's voices and laughter burst out in the street and filled the room, which was now in twilight. "They're playing outside already," Blanca Estela said. "May I go play first? I'm not hungry yet. I'll have bread and milk when I come in." She looked at her mother pleadingly. Lilia nodded, and Blanca Estela ran outside. There, in the stretch of street between Mario's house and her own, Blanca Estela joined the group that was forming to play.

Jaime and Sandra were there. Mario was present, as always, as was Mimi, having changed again into her usual nondescript garb, and Evita, now transformed and looking more like an urchin than the angelic child who had been in church that morning. Pedro was there, as well, but in his overalls he did not look much different than he had in his altar boy vestments. He was still a pale, spindly boy with a chronic sniffle.

"Let's play *Matarilerilerón*," Blanca Estela whispered to Mario.

He thought about it for a moment before nodding, saying, "We really should be an even number to have two equal teams, but we can still do it."

"We'll play *Matarilerilerón*," Mario stated, forestalling Evita's own announcement. "Mimi, Blanca Estela and I will be *Matarilerilerón* first, and you four can select who will be the page."

Evita looked piqued, but she was not about to be done out of making a decision. "Pedro will be the page," she announced.

Each side joined hands and faced each other some twelve feet apart. The sun had now completely disappeared, leaving behind a sky painted with streaks of mauve and orange against a darkening gray background. Their faces, in the intervening distance, were no longer distinct. They were becoming silhouettes.

"Let's make him an *ingeniero*," Blanca Estela proposed, proud to be showing off her newly learned word.

"No, no," Mario objected. "First you give him an occupation that his team won't like. How about *barrilero*?"

"What is that?" Blanca Estela was discouraged. Here was still another thing that she had not learned yet.

"*Barrileros* are the men who drive those horse-drawn carts and go house to house selling water from the river out of the barrels that they carry on the carts. You have seen them go by the house," Mario told her.

"But my grandmother never gets water from them."

"Well, no, because you drink water from the *aljibe* and you get your water for washing from the faucet. But there are people who don't have faucets or cisterns and buy water from the *barrileros*. Also, sometimes the river is too low, and there is not enough water pressure for the faucets. My father knows all about that," Mario explained.

"We're getting tired of waiting," Evita's voice came out of the thickening dusk. "Let's start."

Mario, Mimi and Blanca Estela joined hands and marched towards the others, chanting an introduction and a greeting, "*Amó ató, Matarilerilerón.*"

Once they said this, they marched backwards, swinging their arms, to wait for the response.

The others imitated them, walking forward to meet them, chanting the question: "*¿Qué quiere, usted, Matarilerilerón?*" Then they retreated.

"*Yo quiero un paje, Matarilerilerón,*" Mario's team marched forward with their demand for a page and then retreated again.

"*¿Qué oficio le pondremos, Matarilerilerón?*" Evita's team demanded what trade or occupation they would give to the page.

"*Le pondremos barrilero, Matarilerilelerón,*" was the response.

A few giggles escaped from Pedro's teammates, and they promptly rejected the proposed occupation. "*Ese oficio no nos gusta, Matarilerilerón.*"

"Now what?" Mario asked his two companions.

"Let's make him a *lechero,*" suggested Mimi. "He won't mind that. Pedro's father is a milkman."

Blanca Estela was miffed that they would not use her contribution for an occupation, but she acquiesced, thinking that they would probably work up to *ingeniero* next. They marched forward, chanting, "*Le pondremos lechero, Matarilerilerón.*"

They had no sooner finished singing this when they heard Sandra's scornful laugh, followed by her comment, "Just like his father."

Someone gasped in the dark. Most of them were a little shocked. Pedro then broke loose from the hands holding him and ran away.

"See what you've done," Evita's voice sounded clearly in the dark, reproachful. "You have hurt his feelings."

"Well, it wasn't my idea to call him a *lechero*," Sandra was defensive.

"There's nothing wrong with being a milkman," Mario explained. "It's because you laughed and said that about his father that he was hurt. I think we had better play something else."

But Blanca Estela no longer felt like playing. "I'm hungry," she said. "I'm going home to eat. My uncle Raúl is visiting us. He is an *ingeniero*," she added. There, she had gotten to use the new word, after all. "He builds roads and bridges. He also brought me a present. I must go and see what it is." She withdrew, feeling herself enveloped in an aura of importance.

Inside the house she found the grown-ups still sitting around the dining table. Mamá Anita had placed the crystal lamp in the middle of the table, and its flickering light threw the three shadows against the wall, enlarging them to gigantic proportions.

"Come and have your bread and milk, Estelita," Lilia said. "Look, your uncle brought American milk from across the river. He kept it cold in an ice-chest so you can have cold milk, cool, anyway, and it is not boiled." She poured a tall glass for Blanca Estela, who drank it avidly, munching on the pastry, which Raúl had also brought.

"Here is something for you," Raúl said, getting a paper sack from a chair. He drew out a stuffed toy animal. It was a felt cat, black and white, with bright green buttons for eyes and a white mustache and whiskers that gave him a rakish air. Blanca Estela had never had a pet before, and the toy cat almost took life as she held it. She hugged it and put her face next to it.

"Oh, I love it!" she exclaimed. "What shall I name you? You are black and white. What shall I call you?"

"Since he is black and white, why don't you call him Domino?" Mamá Anita suggested.

"Yes, I think he will be Domino," she agreed after some thought.

"And now, I think it's time you went to bed," said Lilia.

"May I take Domino to bed with me?"

The grown-ups laughed. Mamá Anita said, "Well, since he is only a toy cat, I don't suppose that he will get the bedclothes dirty."

From bed she heard Mamá Anita washing dishes in the kitchen while Lilia and Raúl conducted a soft conversation in the parlor. She caught only fragments of sentences, isolated words which came drifting to her out of the clouds of sleep as Lilia tried not to disturb her.

"I have thought of being a teacher again... I only worked for a year before I married Roberto... In the United States... have to study... work... Estelita... born there... her home...

Blanca Estela found herself surrounded by cotton clouds, and then she was back in school, where her mother was the teacher. Lilia was showing her and Mario and Mimi and Evita pictures of the River Nile, pale green and serpentine. Then there was Domino, who was really the Dominion of Canada and who wore a jeweled turban on his head and had twitching white whiskers made of snowflakes. Finally, there was *Matarilerilerón*, draped in golden robes, with a lion's mane sprouting around his face, which was also Leopoldo's smiling face. *Matarilerilerón* said, in a deep voice, "I will take her home to be my page."

Blanca Estela asked him timidly, "Please, where is home?" She clutched Domino tightly against her and never heard the answer to her question.

# Chapter IV

*Hilitos, Hilitos de Oro . . .*
*Que manda decir el rey que cuántas hijas teneis*

Blanca Estela never thought that she would find herself longing to go to school. She had been relieved when classes had ended at her school, just before she and her mother had embarked on their journey to Revilla. And later, when they first arrived and she had been too scared to go even to Chabela's store for soda pop, she would have never believed that the day would come when she would wish to join her new friends at their school. Every morning, after breakfast, she would see Mario, Mimi, Evita and Pedro pass by her windows on their way to school while she stayed behind. María Eva had asked Lilia why she didn't send Blanca Estela to school with the other children, to give her something to do, but Lilia had pointed out that classes would be over in less than a month, which hardly made it worth the trouble for either Blanca Estela or for the teachers who now had to cope with preparations for final exams and assignments.

Thus it was that Blanca Estela waited impatiently on this Friday afternoon for her friends to come home from their classes, so they could all go to Sandra's birthday party. Rosalía and Doctor Marín had decided to hold the party on Friday, which was Sandra's birthday, rather than wait for the weekend, because Sandra and Jaime's parents were expected to arrive either Saturday or Sunday, and their visit would, naturally, keep the grown-ups busy. By four o'clock, then, Blanca Estela was waiting at the front door in the new dress that Mamá Anita had made for her. It was striped in green and white with a ruffle at the hem and little, puffed sleeves. In her hand she held a small package wrapped in pink tissue paper and tied with a white ribbon.

It was a birthday gift for Sandra, a hair bow shaped and colored like a rose, which had survived the journey south in Blanca Estela's suitcase. June and Linda's mother had given it to her as a farewell present, but she had never cared much for hair bows.

Shortly after four Mario and Mimi arrived breathlessly next door and called out to Blanca Estela from the sidewalk that they would be ready as soon as they had washed up. Evita followed a few minutes later, and from her own front door across the street, she announced that she would be out again in a short time. After what seemed an eternity, Mario and Mimi emerged from their house. Blanca Estela was surprised to see Mario wearing long khaki trousers, instead of his usual shorts, a starched white shirt, and lace-up shoes which looked recently polished. As he came out the door he looked down at his feet and grimaced, from which Blanca Estela deduced that the shoes were pinching him. Mimi, following him, wore the white shoes which she had worn to church and a smock dress printed with tiny yellow flowers on a brown background. She, too, carried a small package wrapped in tissue paper.

Evita then appeared at her front door, and, since her house lay in the direction towards Doctor Marín's house, she beckoned to them to join her. They crossed the street and stopped on the sidewalk where Evita stood, pausing before her for a moment, as she obviously expected them to do, to admire her new costume. With a well-developed sense of style, Evita (or perhaps María Eva, her mother, the dressmaker) had opted to wear, not the expected frilly party frock, but a simple navy blue dress with a pleated skirt and a sailor collar, encircled by a red tie. The three stood silently around Evita, feeling that compliments would be pointless when she was so clearly aware of her attractive appearance.

"What are we waiting for?" Mario asked gruffly. "Let's go, or the party will be over before we get there."

"There will be a *piñata*," Mimi interjected, surprisingly.

"I know," replied Evita, not to be outdone in having inside information. "Sandra thought that she was too old for a *piñata*, but the Doctor insisted on it because they also invited little children. Jaime did not like that. What are you giving her?"

Mario stopped to retie his shoe and did not answer, and Mimi said vaguely, "A bar of scented soap."

"Oh," said Evita, dismissively, and turned to ask Blanca Estela, "What about you? Did you get her something from across the river?"

Blanca Estela had noticed Mario's embarrassment and Evita's offhanded reaction to Mimi's reply. She now felt that it would be a good thing for

Evita to be snubbed, at least this time. She shrugged and answered with all the self-assurance she could muster, "I think Sandra should be the first to know what I am giving her."

"Oh," said Evita, this time sounding somewhat deflated. But after a moment, she added, "You are probably right. I was going to tell you what I have inside this box, but now I will give it to Sandra without telling anyone what is inside it."

Until that moment, Blanca Estela had felt no curiosity about the contents of the small box wrapped in silver paper that Evita carried in her hand, but now she suddenly regretted the moral victory she had achieved over her. To disguise her chagrin she turned to look behind them and asked nonchalantly, "Isn't Pedro coming, too? Wasn't he invited?"

"He had to go straight home from school," replied Mario. "He has to help his father with milking the cows."

"Doesn't he have other brothers to help, too?"

"He has two little brothers, but they're too small to help."

"When is your uncle coming back? He didn't stay very long last week," Evita interposed, feeling that they had discussed Pedro long enough.

"My uncle Raúl had to go back to work. He's building a road," Blanca Estela responded, trying to keep from showing how proud she felt to have a handsome and important uncle.

"My mother says that your three uncles were all very good looking," Evita said, as if she were imparting information that Blanca Estela could not have known otherwise. "It was a disappointment," she continued, "to the girls of Revilla when your uncles went away to study and married girls from the city. There are so few good matches for the girls here." She looked very seriously as she said this, but then she brightened up, adding, "Of course, your uncle Raúl is still a bachelor. It's too bad that my sister, Cristina, got tired of waiting and got married, though."

This last statement puzzled Blanca Estela. Was Evita suggesting that her sister, Cristina, had once contemplated marrying the idolized uncle that she, herself, had only recently got to know? She felt unreasonably angry and disappointed. She wanted her uncle to be her own, unique discovery.

Fortunately she was distracted from any more disquieting thoughts by their arrival at the Doctor's house. The heavy double doors stood open, and on the threshold they joined a woman who had two young children—a boy and a girl—attached to each of her hands. As they all entered, Blanca Estela looked around, full of curiosity, to see what the Doctor and Rosalía's house was like.

The house was laid out much like Mamá Anita's and the majority of the other big houses in Revilla. From the entryway, one stepped into a covered entrance that led directly to the patio. On one side, to her right, was the Doctor's office, or more precisely, the waiting room, since his office was beyond the waiting room. An old man and a woman with a young child in her arms waited there, sitting silently in dark armchairs. To Blanca Estela's left was the parlor. As she walked past the parlor door, she had a brief glimpse of a long sofa and several chairs covered in crimson cloth and of a low table with curving legs of dark wood and a white marble top, crowned with a large bouquet of wax flowers.

She could not see any more of the parlor because the shutters were half closed, leaving the room almost in darkness. Also, there was a young woman standing at the door, partially blocking it, while she kept the guests moving in the direction of the patio. Blanca Estela thought at first that it was Rosalía who stood there, but a closer look showed her that this was a taller, thinner and younger woman. Otherwise, the resemblance was great: the same fair skin and blue eyes, although the young woman's hair was a pale gold and stood around her head like the halo of an angel, whereas Rosalía's darker waves submitted to a more disciplined arrangement.

"Good afternoon, Perla," Evita said, addressing the young woman. She, in turn, smiled at Evita and then broadened her smile to include all the group then entering. It was a particularly encouraging smile, like that of a brisk teacher or nurse, and it kept them moving in the correct direction, but not before Blanca Estela had had the opportunity to look closely at her face and notice a small gap between the two upper front teeth, and a sprinkling of tiny freckles across her otherwise perfect nose. Blanca Estela felt reassured that the angel was human.

"Perla is Rosalía's youngest sister," Evita explained to Blanca Estela.

That explained the resemblance.

In the middle of the patio, milling about, and only occasionally pushing or pinching each other, there were some twenty children of various sizes. Sandra, the guest of honor, stood surrounded by several girls who wanted a look at the gold chain and heart-shaped locket that she wore around her neck and which had been her aunt and uncle's birthday gift to her. Jaime stood by himself at a distance from the group, feeling, no doubt, older and far more sophisticated than they. Only one girl, who seemed to be about his age, dared to approach him and tried to engage him in conversation, but he rebuffed her attempts.

Blanca Estela was surprised to see Leopoldo in the midst of the commotion, trying to suspend a *piñata* from a wire that stretched from one wall to a long pole stuck into the ground in the middle of the patio. Then she remembered that he was Rosalía's brother and, therefore, Sandra's uncle. Leopoldo was dark where his sisters were fair, but on his face was the same bright, cheerful smile that Blanca Estela had just seen on Perla. Leopoldo was undoubtedly handsome, but, comparing uncle to uncle, Blanca Estela thought that she came out ahead of Sandra. Her own uncle was even more handsome and charming than Sandra's uncle, Leopoldo. She wondered, though, if her own father had been with her, would she have had any attention to spare for uncles?

Rosalía came out of the house then, through what appeared to be the door to the dining room. A long table had been set just outside this room, in the patio. It was covered with an embroidered tablecloth, and on top of it, Rosalía and another woman began setting platters full of cookies and several pitchers of lemonade. Finally, there came a large white cake under a glass dome. The children began edging closer to the table.

Rosalía noticed this and called out in her high, sweet voice, "First the *piñata*, children. First break the *piñata*. Leopoldo, is the *piñata* ready?"

"It's ready," he replied, descending from a stepladder. "Sandra, it's in your honor. You go first."

"I am too old for breaking a *piñata*, Uncle," she responded, grimacing with embarrassment.

"Nonsense, you're never too old for a *piñata*. Let me blindfold you. I'll pull up the *piñata* quite high, so don't think that you'll have an easy time breaking it," her uncle told her as he turned her around three times before putting a stick in her hand. After doing that, he ran to pull up the cord from which the *piñata* hung. The *piñata* was circular in shape with a center made of clay and little cardboard spikes surrounding it to represent the rays of the sun. It was all covered in a fringe of white and gold tissue paper and had a painted smiling face which seemed to tease them all as it bobbed up and down above their heads, always out of reach.

Sandra swung her stick three times, each time finding only air because her uncle would pull quickly on the rope. The younger children howled every time she swung, some afraid of the crash that would follow the impact, but many out of frustration, fearing that they would miss their own chance at breaking the *piñata*. The rest of the older children (except for Jaime and the girl who had finally gotten his attention) followed Sandra, also failing to make even a dent in the clay face, or even the cardboard spikes.

Blanca Estela, who had wondered how all those children could miss hitting the *piñata* when it was so close to them, got to experience the complete disorientation of being blindfolded and then turned around several times. She heard the whoosh of the air around her stick as she struck out repeatedly and felt quite humbled as she took off the blindfold.

As the children lining up for the *piñata* got smaller, the *piñata* got lower, and the excitement rose higher. Finally, the last child was allowed to strike the clay center until he had cracked it. Candy began spilling out of the *piñata's* belly, and Leopoldo rushed to remove the stick from the child's hands to prevent him from cracking any skulls with it, as well. This was always the trickiest part, when the child who had broken the *piñata*, still blindfolded, continued to swing the stick, unaware that the other children were scrambling around him to gather the candy that spewed out.

Blanca Estela hesitated before joining the melee, but she saw Mimi and Mario dive into the crowd and scramble around on their hands and knees, scooping up little cloth pouches tied with ribbon. In the midst of the mayhem she also saw Evita, the sailor collar of her dress askew, jumping and whooping triumphantly as she clutched a handful of the candy-filled pouches. Then Blanca Estela, too, dropped to her knees and snatched away a little green sack from a small boy, who was in the act of picking it up. He let out a howl of outrage, but she ran away, still holding on to her prize.

At that moment Rosalía and Perla began clapping their hands, calling out, "Children, children, it is time to cut the cake. Line up in a single file. Sandra, come here and blow out the candles."

There was some quick shuffling while the children lined up, and Sandra, disheveled from the tussle like the others, approached the refreshment table. Rosalía put a match to the little pink candles which sprouted out of the white frosted top of the cake. Perla told Sandra to wish for something, and Sandra closed her eyes and held her breath for one dramatic moment while all the guests looked at her expectantly. She then opened her eyes, expelling her breath at the same time and blowing out all the candles at once. Polite applause followed while everyone waited eagerly for her to make the first cut in the cake.

After Sandra had cut the first slice, Rosalía took over, slicing quickly, and uniformly, which relieved the collective anxiety that there would not be enough cake to go around for all. Blanca Estela, who stood midway down the line, soon found herself receiving a slice of cake in a paper napkin from Rosalía. Perla, standing next to her sister, then nudged Blanca Estela towards the end of the table, which held the paper cups filled with lemonade and several platters of cookies.

Blanca Estela, her hands overflowing with cookies, cake and lemonade, walked towards a group which contained Sandra, Mimi and Evita, and joined them as they sat on a blanket, which had been spread on the ground. Sandra was telling the others that her parents and her little brothers were expected to arrive within the next day or two and that they, too, would bring her presents.

"What did you get today? Show us your presents," said a girl whom Blanca Estela had never seen before.

Sandra squirmed uncomfortably and answered evasively, "I don't know. I haven't opened them all yet. My aunt says I should wait until... until later."

"Why?" the girl insisted.

Sandra seemed at a loss for an answer, and Evita gave an audible sigh and looked witheringly at the girl. "It's so nobody will be embarrassed," she said in her high, clear voice. "In case somebody didn't give Sandra a good present."

Blanca Estela was amazed at Evita's great perception and store of knowledge about social conduct in Revilla. People's behavior here was obviously as subtle as the nuances found in the shades of color, as she had learned from playing the game about *Doña Inés*.

Perla approached them, saying briskly, "Children, if you have finished eating, there is time for some games. Nothing too rowdy because the doctor is still seeing patients in his office, and we can't disturb him or the patients. How about singing some *rondas*? Do you know *Mambrú se fue a la guerra?*"

Blanca Estela felt something tighten at her throat. She did not want to hear the song about *Mambrú* going to war and never coming back. She was therefore relieved to hear Sandra say, in the pouting voice that she usually found annoying, "No, Aunt Perla, I'm tired of *Mambrú*. Let's sing *Hilitos de Oro*." She turned to Evita for support. "You know *Hilitos de Oro*, don't you? It's the one about the king who wanted to marry one of the golden-haired daughters of the poor man."

"I like that one," said Evita, jumping to her feet. "It's so romantic! The daughters are just like your mother and your aunts. Do you think Doctor Marín is like the king? No, perhaps he is not rich enough. But maybe a king will some day ask for your hand in marriage, Sandra. It's too bad, though, that you don't have golden hair, like Perla. She looks like the picture of the guardian angel that my mother hung over my bed. Still," Evita concluded kindly, touching her fingertips to Sandra's hair, "your hair is a pretty golden brown, almost like golden threads."

Sandra looked pleased at Evita's qualified compliment. "All right," she said, "let's play *Hilitos de Oro*. Form a group to sing the king's role. Who wants to play the king?"

"I would rather sing the part of the poor man," responded Mario, who had come up to stand behind Blanca Estela.

She turned to him, whispering, "I don't know this game."

"It's easy," he answered. "It's just like *Matarileri-lerón*. One group walks towards the other, singing that the king wants to know how many daughters the man has. He is a poor man but very proud, so he answers that it's none of the king's business how many daughters he has. The king's people say that they have been offended, and they're going home. And then the poor man and his family say they didn't mean to hurt his feelings, and to go ahead and choose a daughter for a wife, and the king chooses one, the youngest daughter, I think. Stay with me, and you will catch on quickly."

They formed two groups, and Blanca Estela joined hands with Mario on one side and Mimi on the other. They were part of the poor man's family who got to tell the king to mind his own business. Evita, without having to think very much about it, joined the king's entourage. Sandra, after some consideration, concluded that she was meant to be the daughter who would be chosen by the king, and she had to link hands with Mario, who played her father, the poor but proud man.

Blanca Estela's group strolled towards the other as it sang its verses, Blanca Estela merely mouthing the words, since she was afraid of making a mistake. Blanca Estela's line then retreated to await the approach of the second team with its answer. When the king and his messengers finally announced that he would choose the youngest daughter, the one like a "newborn flower," Mario led Sandra by the hand to join the king's group, and they all applauded in recognition that Sandra was being honored through this game.

The doctor came out of his office, having finished with his last patient, and asked for lemonade. Rosalía brought him a fresh glass from the kitchen, and he wandered among the guests for a few minutes until several women stopped by the party to collect the youngest children. He was still chatting with the new arrivals when Blanca Estela, Evita, Mimi and Mario joined the stream of guests that was now steadily trickling out of the double doors, calling out their thanks and best wishes to Sandra.

As they walked home, the sun was putting on a final display of crimson and gold finery in the western sky before sinking behind the horizon. This was the time when they usually came out to play, but this evening they felt neither hungry for supper nor eager for more games. Evita was the first to arrive home, then Mimi and Mario, across the street and two doors down, and finally, Blanca Estela. When she crossed the threshold of her own house, she could hear Mamá Anita and Lilia conversing at the dining table. She called out that she was home, and Lilia asked her to join them.

"Do you want some supper, Estelita?"

She shook her head. The only thing she wanted was to take off her shoes that were beginning to rub against her heels. Either her feet had grown, or she had gotten out of the habit of wearing party shoes. In her hand she still had the little cloth bag filled with candy.

"Look what I brought you," she said to both her mother and her grandmother.

Lilia burst out laughing, "Thank you, my love, but I think I'm past the age for eating candy from a *piñata*. We'll save it for tomorrow, and you can eat it then. You look hot. Take off your dress and put on your nightgown... and your shoes, too. You look as if they pinched you. Did you enjoy yourself at the *piñata*? Tell us about it. "

"We had cake with white frosting, and we played *Hilitos de Oro*."

Lilia frowned, perplexed, "I don't think I remember that game."

"It's about the king wanting to marry the golden-haired daughter. Evita thinks that maybe someday a king will ask Sandra to marry him, but if I were the king, I would marry Perla instead. Her hair is like little golden threads, and it stands up around her head like the halo of the guardian angel."

"I think this child is rambling," Mamá Anita interposed. "Either she's falling asleep, or she got sunstroke. Let's get her to bed."

She did not protest.

The following day, which was Saturday, Mario came for Blanca Estela at four o'clock, after she had had her *merienda* of milk and bread, to go to church for Catechism class. Blanca Estela and Mario were both part of the class being prepared by Father Mirabal to receive Holy Communion. On the way to church, they stopped at Chabela's store, where Evita, Mimi and Pedro had congregated in the doorway after buying chewing gum. Those three had already made their First Communion the year before and felt slightly superior to the two who had not.

Neither Mario nor Blanca Estela felt great urgency to spend the next hour being drilled on the Ten Commandments by Father Mirabal and welcomed every opportunity to dawdle on their way to church. Comparing the movie star cards that came with the chewing gum was one way to postpone the religion class. They were just craning their necks to see the cards that Pedro held in his hand, when the unexpected and unusual sound of a car engine distracted them. They all looked up in amazement as a large car, cream colored and shiny with chrome, glided past them and came to a stop in the middle of the next block, in front of the doctor's house.

"What a beautiful car!" Mario exclaimed. "The engine is so quiet, but you can tell it's powerful. One of those V-8 engines," he added, reverently.

"Yes, but who is it?" Evita interrupted, impatiently.

The doors of the car opened, and two men came out from the front seat. As the driver got out he turned to open the door to the back seat, behind him. They could see that he was a tall, thin man who held himself very straight and wore a light gray suit. The other man was heavier and shorter, but they could not see him clearly because he was stooping down, as if getting something from the back seat. A little boy of three or four came out of the door which the driver had opened, while from the opposite side there emerged a woman with a child in her arms. The heavyset man helped her out of the car and up the sidewalk. She was small in height and a little plump, although they could not distinguish her features clearly from the distance of half a block, they could see the short, golden hair done in frizzy curls.

"I bet those are Sandra's parents," Evita said.

"But there are two men there," pointed out Mario. "Which one is the father?"

"Well, it must be the man holding the mother's arm. I think I remember him from the last time they were here... about two years ago," replied Evita.

"Then, who is the other one?" whispered Mimi.

"I... don't know," Evita admitted, "but I'll find out."

At this point, Mamá Anita came out of the house for some reason, perhaps responding to a presentiment that Blanca Estela and Mario had not made great progress on the way to Catechism class. Seeing them still standing outside the store, she raised her voice, "Blanca Estela, Mario, what are you doing? You are late already. Father Mirabal is going to scold you. Stop gawking and hurry up."

Blanca Estela and Mario broke away from the others, running lightly on the hot sidewalks that burned their bare feet. As they ran past Doctor Marín's house, they hoped to get a better view of the visitors, but the doors were just closing after them as Blanca Estela and Mario paused, for a moment, to gaze at the visitors from across the street.

On the following day, Sunday Mass had already started when Rosalía arrived in church, her high heels clicking intermittently on the tile floor as she vainly tried to tiptoe in silently. She was followed by her sister, Aurora, who led a young boy by the hand while Sandra flanked her on the other side. At the end, walking calmly but purposefully, came Perla carrying a little boy, between one and two, in her arms. The other parishioners turned to look at them, smiling, and greeted them with little nods of recognition.

Blanca Estela, who had been contemplating the wood carvings of the Stations of the Cross that adorned the top of the columns which lined the nave of the church, now turned her attention to the arriving women. The three were very much alike but also different from each other. Each one had hair of a different shade of gold, from the darkest of Rosalía's to the palest of Perla's. Perla was also the tallest and the most slender, as perhaps befitted the youngest. Aurora, Sandra's mother and the middle sister, was the smallest and the plumpest. Their demeanors and expressions were also varied. Rosalía had a sweetness tinged with sadness. Perla seemed so enveloped in serenity that you expected to find her dreamy and abstracted and instead, you were surprised by her competent matter-of-factness. Aurora's lips turned down at the corners, and little furrows marked her forehead, giving her a worried and discontented air.

Throughout the Mass the older of the boys beat a staccato with his feet against the pew, oblivious to his mother's whispered protests. Finally, his young brother burst out crying, out of either aggravation at his brother or frustration at not being able to also kick the pew. The three sisters then left hurriedly, just after Communion, leaving behind them the echo of two wailing children, and were followed by an embarrassed-looking Sandra.

After the Mass, Mamá Anita, Lilia and Blanca Estela paused in the atrium to chat with María Eva and Evita. "It's too bad that Aurora's children could not behave during Mass," said Mamá Anita without preamble.

"Yes, everybody was hoping to talk to Aurora after Mass," María Eva agreed. "She's looking tired. It's those two youngest children, so close together. She had a difficult time with the last birth."

"I wonder why Doctor Marín didn't come to Mass with them. Well, I suppose he had to stay at home to entertain his brother-in-law. Blanca Estela said they brought a guest with them, too," Lilia remarked.

"He's a friend or a business partner of Aurora's husband," María Eva said. "He's the owner of the car. I don't know why they came with him. Ramón, Aurora's husband, has his own automobile, but probably not as big or as elegant as this one. I have a feeling that the man really came for the dance. The Ladies' Club is having the annual ball next Saturday, remember? I have been making Rosalía's and Perla's ball dresses. Rosalía's is a very pretty lavender silk, but you should see Perla's. It's a sapphire blue taffeta. It will look beautiful on her. Actually, Rosalía picked out the fabric for her because Perla, as pretty as she is, is just not interested in clothes or cosmetics. She prefers helping the doctor with his patients, especially the children. As a matter of fact, when Aurora had her last child, and she was left so weak, Perla went to Mexico City to stay with her and looked after the three-year old, and even the baby. She stayed with them for about two months. We all wondered if she would meet somebody in the capital and get engaged there. She's already twenty," María Eva concluded her long commentary with a sigh.

"The man's name is Enrique Alemán, and he came to Revilla to dance at the ball with Perla," Evita said with the air of a conjurer pulling a rabbit out of a hat.

"How do you learn these things?" María Eva exclaimed and then answered herself. "I suppose it's the girls in the workshop. They like to pass on gossip, and this child is always listening."

"It's time that we went home to dinner," Mamá Anita said, squinting to look at the clock on the municipal building across the plaza. "Are you coming, María Eva?"

"No, *Doña* Anita, I have to stay and talk to Father Mirabal about some tablecloths for the altar. Evita, do you want to go ahead with them?"

Evita shook her head.

"She hopes that Father Mirabal will give her candy, as he sometimes does," María Eva explained.

"Mamá, perhaps I should stay to talk with Father Mirabal also, to see how Estelita is doing in Catechism class," Lilia said, hesitantly.

"Mamá, I'm hungry," Blanca Estela wailed in alarm. She did not want her lackluster progress in Catechism to be revealed in conversation with Father Mirabal. And, to Blanca Estela's relief, they went home to dinner.

Late Monday afternoon Leopoldo paid them a short visit. Blanca Estela went to answer the knocking at the door and found him rooting through a small metal ice chest in the back of his Jeep. He took out a paper-wrapped package from it, which he carried into the house. Mamá Anita came to meet him at the entrance, drying her hands on her apron.

"Good afternoon, *Doña* Anita," he said. "I hope you are well. Rosalía sends you a little something. It's some ice cream and cake. Yesterday afternoon she had a *merienda*, just for the family, to celebrate the visit of my sister Aurora and her family."

"Come in, Leopoldo. It is very kind of Rosalía to think of us. My granddaughter will enjoy eating ice cream. We don't have it here. And since we don't have a refrigerator, we'll have to eat it before it melts. Blanca Estela, take this to your mother and tell her to serve it in the little crystal bowls. You will join us, Leopoldo."

"Thank you, *Doña* Anita. I will stay for a little while, but I won't eat anything. I had a very late dinner."

Mamá Anita led the way across the patio and through the door into the kitchen, where Blanca Estela was already unwrapping the small container of ice cream. Lilia had set the large wedge of chocolate-covered cake in a porcelain plate. She smiled at

Leopoldo as he came in, pushing her hair away from her face with a nervous hand.

"Good afternoon, Leopoldo," she said. "You have brought us our *merienda*. Come and join us."

"Thank you, Lilia, but I just ate."

"You'll take some coffee, then."

"Thank you, that I'll do."

Lilia quickly poured him a cup of coffee and put the sugar bowl and a small pitcher of milk in front of him. She then began scooping vanilla ice cream into two delicate cut-crystal bowls. She passed one to Blanca Estela and the other to Mamá Anita, who pushed it away, gently saying, "You have the ice cream, Lilia. I don't like to eat very cold things. But hurry, before it melts."

Blanca Estela spooned the sweet, rich cream into her mouth greedily. She had almost forgotten how delicious it was. When she had finished, she looked longingly at what still remained in the ice cream container. Perhaps her mother wanted another serving, and Mamá Anita had not eaten any yet.

Lilia interpreted her look correctly and said, "Why don't you finish the ice cream, Estelita? Your grandmother doesn't want any, and neither do I."

Blanca Estela served herself again and went back to savoring the ice cream, but more sedately this time. As she finished the last of it, she looked up at Leopoldo, sitting across the table. He was smiling at her. She had not noticed how gentle his brown eyes were.

Lilia was slicing the wedge of cake. She cut four slices, distributed them into four small plates and asked, "Leopoldo, won't you have just a little cake with your coffee?"

Leopoldo did not answer at once, but he turned to gaze at Lilia with an expression that Blanca Estela could not fathom. Lilia held his look for a moment and then blushed and dropped her eyes. "Yes," he said softly. "I will have some cake."

Mamá Anita, who had been unusually silent, now cleared her throat and reached for the plate in front of Lilia, saying, "Here, Lilia, let me pass that plate to Leopoldo." After putting the cake in front of him, she continued, "Now, tell me, how is Aurora? I did not have the opportunity to talk to her after Mass. Are they staying long?"

"Aurora is well, but those two younger children wear her out. She and her family will be staying for at least a week. My brother-in-law brought a friend with him, too. They're business partners in a store that sells electrical appliances. Ramón, my brother-in-law, and his partner left this morning for Monterrey on business. They will be back in a few days. Aurora and the children are staying with Rosalía. Last night they stayed with us, but my parents are old now, and those two young children were too much for them, although Perla is very good at handling them."

"Where did the guest stay?" Mamá Anita asked.

"With Rosalía and the doctor. That's why Aurora and the children stayed with us last night, so it would not be such a burden on Rosalía to put up that many people."

"Are they all going to the ball next Saturday?" Lilia asked Leopoldo, still a little flustered.

"I think so," he answered, keeping his eyes on her. "At least I heard Aurora and Rosalía talking about ball dresses."

"Are you going to the ball, too?" Blanca Estela asked him and received a fulminating look from her grandmother, which meant that she was not supposed to take part in this conversation.

"I don't know," he answered, laughing softly. "I am not a very good dancer, but my sisters will probably insist that I go, even if only to dance with them. You remember, Lilia, how I used to step on your feet when I would dance with you? And you danced so well."

Lilia pushed the cake crumbs around her plate with her fork without looking at Leopoldo, but Blanca Estela noticed her mother's face turning very becomingly rosy, as if she had put on rouge. Mamá Anita cleared her throat again, and Leopoldo came out of the trance into which he seemed to have fallen as he looked at Lilia.

"I must go now," he said. "Aurora is waiting for some milk which I bought across the river. Her children don't like the milk straight out of the cow; it has to come from a bottle. If you ever need anything from the other side, just let me know."

"Yes Leopoldo, thank you for offering," Mamá Anita said, shepherding him out of the room as Lilia began to clear the table.

Blanca Estela was left sitting at the table, trying to remember the conversations she had overheard about her mother's friendship with Leopoldo. What was it she had heard? Something about Leopoldo being sweet on Lilia before she had gotten married. Blanca Estela thought that Leopoldo still looked "sweet" when he looked at Lilia. If he had married Lilia, Leopoldo would be her father. If he married her now, he would still be very nice as a father. But then Lilia would pay lots of attention to him. A sense of disquiet stirred in her. She did not want her lovely, wonderful mother paying attention to somebody else, just to her.

"Blanca Estela, what is the matter with you? You look as if you had been struck silly, with that spoon in your mouth. Come and help me wash these dishes," Lilia said, speaking to her more sharply than was her custom.

Blanca Estela felt hurt that her mother had scolded her, just when she was thinking how much she loved her. But then she told herself that there was no sense in worrying about things that might never happen.

On Saturday they had a very happy surprise. At about eleven o'clock Raúl arrived, unannounced. Blanca Estela was returning from the store with a kilo of tomatoes when she saw the pickup truck driving towards her and then stop in front of the house. She ran to meet him as he was getting out of the cab. When he saw her, he gave her a hug that lifted her off the ground and squashed the tomatoes against his chest. When he put her down, she ran inside the house, shouting, "Mamá, Mamá Anita, look who's here."

Both women came out of the kitchen, hurrying apprehensively and wiping their hands on their aprons. When they saw who it was, they broke out in smiles. They, too, were soon engulfed in his embraces. When she was able to speak, Mamá Anita told him to unload his suitcase and wash up because dinner would be ready at twelve, and he had better eat with them or she would be angry with him. Raúl laughed and said that even now, when he was at least twice as large as she was, his Mamita still struck fear in him when she scolded him and that of course he would eat with them.

While they were eating their dinner of stewed meat, beans in soup and guacamole with fresh corn *tortillas*, Raúl teased and joked with them. "You know, Mamita, I'm going to take you to a big city and open a restaurant where you will cook. Your *carne guisada* is the best I have eaten anywhere in the country."

Mamá Anita waved away his comments and told him not to be silly, that she only cooked for her family.

"Tell me, what exciting things have been happening in Revilla? What are people talking about?"

Lilia told Raúl about the arrival of Aurora and her family and about the Ladies' Club annual ball, which would be held that very evening. "Will you be going? Is that why you came today?" she asked.

"No, little sister," he answered, laughing. "I did not have the vaguest idea about the ball. I remember now that they always have it in the summer, but I haven't been to one in years. Besides, I did not bring a suit."

"You still have several suits here," Mamá Anita informed him. "I always keep them clean and pressed. All I have to do is air them out to get rid of the camphor smell. You haven't gained weight since you had the suits made, after you graduated from the university. I think you have *lost* weight," she added, accusingly.

"If I say that it is because I haven't been eating your cooking, you will insist that I move back home. You have me trapped," he responded, still joking.

"There is no reason for me to go to the ball," he added, more seriously. "All the girls I used to know and dance with are already married and have children. Who would I dance with? In the old days I could always dance with my baby sister, but now..."

Blanca Estela finally asked the question that had been troubling her. "Mamá, why can't you go to the ball? You would have two dancing partners—Uncle Raúl and Leopoldo."

Lilia blushed and looked at her plate while Mamá Anita turned to look at Blanca Estela with a shocked expression. Raúl put out a hand and touched her cheek very gently, without saying anything.

Finally Lilia, after taking a sip of lemonade, addressed her very quietly. "Estelita, I am in mourning... for your father. It is not proper—and I do not want to—go out to dances and parties. You see, I am sad, still sad, that he is... gone. That is why I wear black clothes."

"But then, I..." she stammered, "I am sad, too... because of Papá. But you do not make me wear black clothes?"

"No, children don't—shouldn't—wear black clothes. Children should be happy. I want you to be happy. Your father would wish you to be happy. But grown-ups are different."

"How long will you wear black clothes and not go to parties?"

"Oh, about a year, or whenever I feel that I am ready to enjoy those things again."

Blanca Estela fell silent. It was all very complicated. Whenever she remembered that her father was dead, she did feel sad, although she did not remember him very well. Other times she did not think of him at all, and she laughed and played quite happily then. Was this wrong? Her mother did not seem to think so.

Blanca Estela asked another question: "If I don't have to wear black clothes, can I go to the ball?"

Lilia and Raúl burst out laughing.

"Estelita," said Lilia, "you're not old enough to go to dances. Who would be there for you to dance with? Little boys don't go dancing. These are grownup parties."

She felt so dejected and looked so crestfallen that Raúl hastened to comfort her with a proposal. "I'll tell you what we'll do. Tonight, when the ball starts, we'll drive in the truck to the plaza, and from there you will be able to see the guests as they arrive at the Hotel Cañamar. That's where the ball will be, isn't that right, Lili?"

"Oh yes, that's where the balls are always held."

That afternoon, in spite of Raúl's protests that he had no intention of going to any dance, Mamá Anita took Raúl's dark suit from the wardrobe to air it out and ironed a fresh white shirt for him. She also found a tie for him in a drawer of the bedroom chest. It might have been an old tie of Raúl's or one of his brothers', but she declared that it would do very well, in any case.

Across the street, in María Eva's workshop, activity was also at a high pitch as women came to pick up party dresses that were just being finished. Even Evita was kept busy snipping loose threads and checking buttons and decorations. Blanca Estela, walking into the workshop at sunset, found Evita picking up pins and sticking them into a large pincushion. María Eva and her two workwomen were covering up the sewing machines as they finished the day. Evita had a serious and self-important air, and Blanca Estela, wanting to impress her, told her that her uncle was taking her in his truck to watch the arrivals at the ball. Evita was instantly alert and asked without preamble if she could go, too. Blanca Estela regretted her boasting then, but, having no alternative except to be unusually rude, said yes, of course.

When she left the workshop, she saw Mario and Mimi standing outside their house. Their father and older brother, who still intimidated her for some reason, were just getting into their old truck. She waited until they had driven away and then crossed the street to talk to her friends. "The Ladies' Club Ball is tonight," she announced to them.

"We know," Mario said. "That's why we are having electrical light tonight until two in the morning, instead of midnight. The ballroom will be ablaze with lights," he added, wistfully.

"Would you like to come with me to see how it looks?" she asked him. "My uncle is taking me to the plaza to look at the guests. Evita is going too. We're going in his truck."

"Sure," Mimi and Mario answered in unison.

Blanca Estela could barely eat her supper that evening. She wanted it to be dark, so her uncle would take her to the plaza to watch the arrivals at the dance. Her uncle kept teasing her, telling her that people wouldn't arrive at the Hotel Cañamar until nearly midnight.

"But the lights will go out at two in the morning," she cried out in disappointment. "It will be a very short ball. Mario told me about the lights, and he knows because his father and his big brother run the turbine for electricity."

At eight o'clock, soon after the electric street lights came on, they left for the plaza, Blanca Estela and Evita riding in the cab with Raúl, and Mimi and Mario in the back of the pickup. Raúl drove to the plaza and parked the truck facing away from the church, which stood dark and empty this evening, its doors already shut. Blanca Estela and Evita got out of the cab and climbed in the back with the other two, the better to watch the hotel. They faced the municipal building, which was also dark, except for the illuminated face of the clock. A few yards away from the Municipal Palace, the Hotel Cañamar blazed with lights, as Mario had predicted.

The hotel was a two-story building with a row of balconies in the upper floors, which were guarded by iron balustrades turned and shaped as delicately as filigree. The ballroom was upstairs, Evita explained to Blanca Estela, and it had floors of such highly polished wood that they reflected the light. She had been to several wedding receptions there and could attest to that fact from personal experience. From the ceiling beams there hung crystal chandeliers that sparkled like diamonds, and the staircase that led upstairs curved up most elegantly.

What was downstairs, Blanca Estela wanted to know. There were some guestrooms and a restaurant, they told her, but the hotel was mostly closed nowadays. The owners only opened it for great occasions, like tonight's ball and large weddings. They would be serving refreshments downstairs, in the restaurant, while the dancing went on upstairs.

"Look," cried Mario, "the musicians have arrived."

A bus had pulled up in front of the hotel, and some twelve or fifteen men got out of it, balancing instrument cases, and hurried inside.

"They also have a piano in the ballroom," Evita commented. "One of those big black ones with a tail."

Raúl got out of the cab and came to stand next to the bed of the truck. "We're taller than you are, Uncle," Blanca Estela teased him fondly, looking down at Raúl from her elevated platform.

"Indeed you are," he answered good naturedly. "You will have a better view of the ball. Tell me what you see."

Cars began arriving and parked first around the plaza and later along the side streets leading to it. They mostly carried women, who looked transformed this evening in their silk and chiffon dresses the color of gemstones and in soft pastels. Many of the men, especially the young ones, arrived on foot, looking hot and uncomfortable in their dark suits, for even after the sun had gone down, the temperature was still very warm.

Two automobiles drove up, one after the other, to the hotel entrance. The front one belonged to the doctor, who was the driver. Rosalía got out of the front seat, while from the back emerged Perla in the sapphire-colored gown described earlier by María Eva. Even from a distance the girl looked beautiful, tall and slender, the gold of her hair contrasting with the blue of the dress and—no doubt—of her eyes, also. A collective "Aahh!" escaped from the lips of Evita, Mimi and Blanca Estela. Leopoldo then followed Perla in getting out of the back seat of the car.

The second car, the cream-colored late model Ford that had so impressed Mario, contained its owner and driver, the tall visitor with the elegantly clipped mustache, and Aurora's husband, who held the back door open, so his wife could get out. Aurora was also in blue, but a pale *celeste*—as Blanca Estela had learned it was called—draped tightly around her like the dresses of the movie stars. No doubt her gown had come from Mexico City. Following Aurora came Sandra in a pink dress of what looked like organdy.

Blanca Estela and Evita were taken aback with surprise and chagrin.

"Why did *she* get to come to the ball? I thought it was only for grown-ups," Blanca Estela asked her uncle.

"I'm sure they made an exception for some reason," he answered, trying to pacify her.

"Well, they are leaving tomorrow or Monday," Mimi volunteered.

"That's true," Evita agreed and, after some consideration, added, "and she *is* older than we are, so maybe they're trying to teach her how to behave at a ball. Of course, she is not going to dance; she will just watch."

After escorting his sister into the ballroom, Leopoldo came out of the hotel and walked towards where Raúl was standing. The two men shook hands and embraced, and Leopoldo asked Raúl why he wasn't coming to the ball. Raúl answered with the same reasons that he had given to Mamá Anita, but Leopoldo persisted. "All my old sweethearts are also married," he said, and then stopped in confusion. "I mean," he continued, "that we are both of about the same age. We're probably the oldest bachelors here, so we'll be in the same situation. Don't let your mother's work go for nothing."

Raúl laughed, "All right, you have convinced me. I'll go home and put on a suit and tie and join you here, so we can watch the dancing. Perhaps your sister Perla will dance with me."

"She would like that. I think she's afraid that Enrique, my brother-in-law's partner, will insist on dancing all night long with her. He seems very interested in her, but there is nothing formal between them. I don't even know if she likes him."

Raúl told his passengers that it was time to take them home. Seeing Blanca Estela's disappointment, though, he promised that tomorrow he would tell her all about the ball.

"All right," she accepted, "but you must tell me whom you danced with and all about the dresses, and if Perla dances with the man from Mexico City. Don't you like her? Why don't you dance with her? She is beautiful. And," she added, "tell me about Leopoldo too, whom he dances with."

"Why about Leopoldo?" Raúl asked her, laughing. "Are you interested in him? He's a little old for you."

She bit her tongue and wished she had not said anything about Leopoldo. To cover up her confusion, she added, "But be sure to tell me about Perla. She looked so beautiful, just like the girl who married the king in *Hilitos de Oro*."

He promised that he would recount every detail of the ball, and thus reassured she went home and to bed, still hearing the strains of the waltz, played by the violins in the shining ballroom upstairs. She had been asleep for hours when her uncle came home. The electric lights went out throughout the streets of Revilla, leaving only the stars to sparkle above.

# Chapter V

*A la víbora de la mar, por aquí pueden pasar, los
de adelante corren mucho, y los de atrás se
quedarán . . .*

The following morning, Sunday, Raúl was still
sleeping as Blanca Estela, Lilia and Mamá Anita quietly got dressed and left for church, leaving Blanca
Estela with her curiosity about the ball still unsatis-
fied. Attendance at Mass that morning was, not
surprisingly, less than usual as the revelers from the
night before stayed home that morning to recuper-
ate from their exertions. The communal fatigue
even communicated itself to those who were in
church, filling them with an air of lassitude, and
even Father Mirabal was more subdued than usual
in his sermon, uttering only a half-hearted condem-
nation of those who would celebrate on Saturday
night and forget the Lord on Sunday.

Blanca Estela noticed that none of the golden-
haired sisters, as she called Rosalía, Aurora and
Perla, were in church, nor any members of their
family or their guests. María Eva and Evita were sitting in one of the front pews, and Blanca Estela
hoped to get some reports of the ball from them,
but when Mass was over, Mamá Anita hurried them
out, commenting to Lilia that they needed to get
home so Raúl could have his dinner before leaving.
Blanca Estela then looked for Leopoldo around the
plaza, but there was no sign of him nor of the Jeep

that took him to work. There was still more frustration when they passed Doctor Marín's house, where the doctor's old gray car and Enrique Alemán's gleaming new automobile stood empty, one in front of the other. The doors to the house, too, remained stubbornly closed, although the faint sound of voices came floating out to the street through the open shutters.

When they arrived home, they found Raúl drinking coffee in the kitchen. He was already dressed, and his suitcase stood ready by the parlor door. Mamá Anita immediately busied herself warming a pot of soup on the little kerosene stove while Lilia set the table. Blanca Estela stood by quietly, waiting for her uncle to say something, but he seemed abstracted and paid no attention to her.

Finally her patience evaporated, and she spoke to him. "Uncle, aren't you going to tell me about the ball?"

He paused in mid-sip, looking puzzled for a minute before responding. "The ball? Oh yes. Ah... it was very nice, very lively."

"Did you dance? Who did you dance with?"

"Yes, I danced a little."

"Did you dance with Perla? Did the man from Mexico City dance with her all night? Did he keep you from dancing with her?"

He laughed. "Yes, I danced with Perla once or twice."

"Did she look beautiful?"

"Yes, she's a very pretty girl."

"What else did you do? And Leopoldo, did he dance with his sisters like he said he would?"

"I believe he did dance with his sisters. I don't know if he danced with all three, but he did dance with Perla."

"I wonder if he asked for her hand in marriage?"

"Who? Who asked for whose hand?"

"Enrique Alemán. Evita said that he had come to dance with Perla and to ask for her hand in marriage."

Raúl shook his head, bewildered. "Blanca Estela, you know much more than I do."

Lilia stopped going to and fro from the stove to the table and joined Blanca Estela in questioning Raúl. "Couldn't you tell if Perla looked happy dancing with her suitor? Did they look as if they were engaged?"

Raúl threw up his hands. "I couldn't tell anything like that. Leopoldo and I spent most of the time in the restaurant downstairs, talking and drinking a few beers."

Lilia looked displeased and murmured under her breath, "I think it was more than a few beers."

Raúl did not seem to have heard her, but Blanca Estela did, and she looked at her mother with surprise. Even as a murmur, the tone of Lilia's words had been sharp, which was unusual for her.

Throughout dinner Raúl continued, distracted, saying hardly anything, and even Mamá Anita made only half-hearted conversation. As soon as they had finished eating, Lilia got up from the table and began washing the dishes, instead of lingering in after-dinner conversation, as was the custom. Raúl stood up, too, and announced that it was time for him to leave. Mamá Anita and Lilia followed him to the front door. Blanca Estela trailed behind them, feeling deflated, as if a party had ended too soon. She was disappointed that her uncle had not kept his promise to describe the ball in detail to her, and she was puzzled by the tension that she sensed in her mother. Before driving away, though, Raúl smiled his old smile and embraced his mother and his sister and then, spying Blanca Estela half-hidden behind the front doors, he retraced his steps until he stood before her. He surprised her by lifting her in his arms and giving her a quick kiss on the forehead. Then he was gone.

That evening at game time, Evita, Pedro, Mimi, Mario and Blanca Estela, pondered which game to play or which song to sing.

"We haven't played *La víbora de la mar* in a long time," Pedro said, his voice trailing off hesitantly, as it usually did on the rare occasions when he volunteered a statement.

"Yes, let's play *La víbora de la mar*," Evita supported him.

Blanca Estela turned to Mario with a question in her eyes, which he understood immediately.

"It's simple," he said. "Two people build a bridge with their arms, and the others line up, one behind the other, holding together with their hands to the waist or the shoulders of the one in front of them. Then the line passes under the bridge, except that the bridge falls down at the end of the verse and catches the last person."

She nodded with comprehension. It was like "London Bridge Is Falling Down." "But I don't know the words in Spanish," she felt obliged to warn him.

"Don't worry. Just listen the first time. We'll repeat the verses several times," Mario assured her.

Mimi and Mario held up their arms and locked hands with each other. Evita then lined up first, then Pedro put his hands on her shoulders, and finally Blanca Estela lined up behind Pedro with her hands around his waist. The first four chanted the verses while Blanca Estela listened, and the line passed under the bridge. The height of the bridge formed by Mario and Mimi's interlocked hands was sufficient for Evita, but Pedro and Blanca Estela, who were taller, had to duck to pass underneath it.

Blanca Estela listened to the words of the chant, wondering, first, why they invoked the snake of the sea. Why was the game called "The Snake of the Sea?" Perhaps because the line snaked around and under the bridge. The players also sang something about those who were ahead running very fast, and those in the back would be left behind. And just as they were singing *"Los de adelante corren mucho y los de atrás se quedarán..."* the bridge came down on the last word, just as Blanca Estela was passing underneath it. She was the one left behind, and she was out of the game.

She went to stand on the sidewalk and listened to the other verses that followed. There was something about a woman selling fruit: *"Una Mexicana que frutas vendía, ciruela, chabacano, melón y sandía."* She knew the words for melon and watermelon—*melón y sandía*—but she would have to find out what *ciruela* and *chabacano* meant. Pedro was caught next, leaving Evita as the winner, and they were about to reshuffle the positions to begin again when Sandra arrived to join them.

"We're playing *La víbora de la mar*," Mario told her. "Do you want to be part of the snake, or do you want to be the bridge?"

She shook her head. "I can't play. I have to go home right away. We're packing our suitcases. I just came to... to say goodbye," she added, shyly.

"Will you miss us? Will you remember us when you're in Mexico City?" Mario asked her seriously.

"Yes," she answered softly. "I think so."

"We won't forget you, and when you come back, you can play with us again," he reassured her.

"Don't forget to write to me," Evita reminded her. "Tell me which movies you see and if you meet any movie stars."

When Sandra had turned away to go home, all that remained with them of her was her white dress, reflecting the moonlight, growing fainter with every step she took away from them. Then Blanca Estela remembered that she had forgotten to ask Sandra to tell them about the ball.

The front door of Mimi and Mario's house suddenly flew open, and a woman's voice called out clearly, "Mimi, Mario, it's time to come in."

Mario let out a groan, "Oh, Nereida, it's still very early."

In the narrow opening of the door, Blanca Estela could see a room brightly illuminated by electric light and, silhouetted against the light, the figure of a tall, slender woman. She had on a dress of silvery material that clung to her waist and hips, and flared out around the knees. For a moment, Blanca Estela was reminded of the pictures of mermaids that appeared in her grandmother's fairy-tale books, the creatures called *sirenas*. Who could this person be?

It was not Mario's mother, who was always referred to as Delia by Mamá Anita and who was a small, thin woman who seldom raised her voice above Mimi's. She waited for Mario to say something by way of explanation, but he remained still, looking after Mimi as she slipped silently into the house.

"All right," he said in a placating tone to the apparition in the doorway. "I will be there in just *one* minute." He then turned to Blanca Estela, saying, "That's my big sister, Nereida. She's been away and just got back this morning while you were in church. She was visiting my aunt who lives in California. When she got there, Nereida decided that she wanted to be a beautician, and so she stayed six months to take some classes. She likes combing and cutting people's hair. I had better go inside before she comes to get me. She pinches awfully hard. Good night."

Pedro had already drifted up the street in the direction of his house, and Evita said she had better go to bed early since she had to go to school the next morning. Before she retired, though, she passed on additional information about Mario and Mimi's family.

"Nereida wants to open a beauty parlor," Evita said. "We don't have one in Revilla. She brought back from across the river a whole bunch of lotions and curlers to give permanents."

"How old is she?" Blanca Estela asked, impressed.

"I think she just turned seventeen. Yes, I think that's right because Tino, the brother, is the oldest, and he's twenty."

"Is that why she came back, to start a beauty parlor?"

"Well, no, she mainly came back because their mother is not in good health. She gets very bad headaches—migraines, my mother says they're called. Nereida is supposed to help their mother with the house, but she's also going to use one room for her beauty parlor, where she will cut hair and give permanents. I'll ask her to cut my hair soon, if my mother lets me. I had better go to bed now. You're lucky that you don't have to go to school."

But Blanca Estela did not feel particularly lucky about this, although reason and logic told her that she should. She merely felt left out because they went off to school without her. The following afternoon, however, she appreciated the benefit of being home, instead of at school, because she got to join her mother and grandmother and María Eva when they sat down for an early *merienda* and conversation.

María Eva arrived at three, bringing some fruit *empanadas* that she had baked, and Mamá Anita immediately put a pot of coffee on the stove to serve with the apple turnovers. Finally Blanca Estela got to hear the missing details about the ball. As María Eva settled down at the kitchen table to enjoy her *empanadas* and coffee, she began the conversation by saying, "Well, I can get some rest at last. The rush work of the ball dresses is over. The only thing I will have for the next month or so are perhaps some First Communion dresses and some baptism robes. Not that I'm complaining about having too much work. It's hard making a living as a widow..." She stopped suddenly and looked at Lilia in distress.

"I hear that your ball dresses were much admired," Mamá Anita interposed.

"People are kind to say so. Of course, so much depends on who wears the dress. I had told you about the blue dress I made for Perla Escalante. Well, of course the girl looked beautiful in it. She's young and has a good figure, and with her coloring, she was bound to do justice to the dress, which was made of very good fabric, by the way. And speaking of Perla..."

"Yes, do tell us about her and her suitor," Lilia broke in, expectantly.

"Well, I stopped by the Doctor's house yesterday after church, because I had to deliver some dresses that I was altering for Aurora. They needed letting out because she has put on some weight. Anyway, I took the clothes after Mass to Rosalía's house, and they were all there, all except Perla that is, who was at her parents' house looking after her father who had a flare up of his diabetes. Aurora was very upset because Perla had refused their guest's declaration of love."

"Aah!" Lilia and Mamá Anita exclaimed in unison.

"I thought she might," Mamá Anita began, but María Eva swept aside the comment and continued with her tale.

"You know that Enrique Alemán is a business partner of Ramón, Aurora's husband. They sell refrigerators and stoves and household appliances, things like that. He fell in love with Perla when Perla went to stay with Aurora more than a year ago, at the time that Aurora's youngest child was born. As a matter of fact, Enrique and Perla were the godparents at the baptism of the baby. However, Enrique did not declare his love for the girl then. He thought that she would feel that he was pressuring her because they had not known each other very long. But he began corresponding with her when she came home. He wrote to her every week. Armando, the mailman, remembers delivering the letters that came very regularly."

"And did the girl respond to his letters?" Mamá Anita asked.

"That I don't know. Armando remembers seeing a few letters addressed to a man in Mexico City, but not on a regular basis. I think he wrote much more often to her than she did to him. Anyway, he drove Aurora and Ramón and the children down here because he came to ask Perla to become engaged to him. And at the ball, he did ask her."

"How do people know that?" Lilia asked.

"Enrique danced with Perla almost all night long, except for one or two dances when she danced with her brother, Leopoldo, and, oh, one dance with your boy, Raúl, *Doña* Anita. A very handsome couple they made, I hear—Perla and Raúl. But towards the end of the ball, Enrique and Perla stepped outside on the balcony, and people could see that they were conversing seriously. Then Sunday morning it came out that Enrique had asked Perla, on the balcony, to become engaged to him. He told her that his intentions were to marry her, and that he would speak to her parents about it as soon as she gave him permission to do so. And she said 'No!'"

"Why? Did she give a reason?" Lilia wanted to know.

"She wouldn't give any explanation at first, especially not to Aurora, nor to their mother, who was very upset with her. But, finally, she told Rosalía

that she wanted to go away to study to be a nurse.
She said that while helping Doctor Marín, she had
realized that she would have liked to have been a
doctor, too, but since she had missed all the medical
preparatory courses of study, it was too late for her
to go to medical school, even if she had had the
money to do so, which I don't think her family has.
Still, since she received so much satisfaction from
helping others get well, she would study to be a
nurse, she said. It is not too late for that."

"And where is she going to study? We don't have
any nursing schools or hospitals here," Mamá Anita
commented, puzzled.

"She will go stay with her aunt in Monterrey and
study there. Doctor Marín assured her that he would
help her to enroll in the kind of studies that she will
need to be a nurse. You can imagine the upheaval in
that family! Doctor Marín and Rosalía say that they
will support Perla in her desire to study, while
Aurora, Ramón and *Doña* Luz, the girl's mother, are
angry that she is throwing away her best opportunity
for a good marriage. They say that Enrique is a
wealthy man, that he could offer Perla a very comfortable life, even luxury perhaps, the opportunity to
live in a great city, to meet important people... and
he's good looking, too. Anyway, Aurora and her
family and their guest all left this morning, most
upset with the girl."

"And what does Don Juan, Perla's father, say
about her refusal?" Mamá Anita asked.

"He says that it is up to Perla to decide her future,
that if she does not love this man, he would never
pressure her to marry him. He says that it does not

matter to him how much money Enrique has, that his daughter is not for sale."

"*Hilitos de Oro*," Blanca Estela murmured under her breath, but nobody heard her.

"My goodness, this is almost like a novel," Mamá Anita remarked and then added briskly, "Well, I hope the girl doesn't regret her decision later on. She may be giving up a life of security and comfort."

"I am glad that Perla did what she did," Lilia interjected with a touch of defiance. "After all, there is no guarantee that the man would always be rich, or even that he would be a good husband. He could be rich and still make her unhappy. It is far better for her to do what gives her satisfaction, and at the same time gives her the ability to earn a living, so she can support herself. After all, María Eva and I know what it's like to be left alone to raise a family and without the preparation to do so."

"Lilia, don't forget the child is here," Mamá Anita scolded her, indicating Blanca Estela with her eyes.

Blanca Estela had sat quietly, imbibing the fascinating revelations, hoping that neither her grandmother nor her mother would remember that she was present. Adults always wanted to exclude children from the most interesting conversations.

"Well, *Doña* Anita, Lilia, I think I had better be going. Evita will be home from school any minute now, and she'll be wanting a *merienda*. That child looks like a little bird, but she eats constantly. By the way, did you know that Nereida, Néstor Balboa's oldest girl, returned yesterday? She has been in California with an aunt, but her mother needs her at home to help her. Poor Delia, she'll have a good spell, but then a migraine will knock her down for days."

"Nereida is going to set up a beauty parlor in her house," Blanca Estela could not resist showing off her knowledge.

María Eva laughed. "Evita must have been talking to you. Evita *wants* Nereida to have a beauty parlor, so she can have her hair cut and set. Still, the girl—Nereida—has always had a talent for that sort of thing. She knows how to cut hair quite well, if you need her Lilia. She's a very pretty girl, too. Those Balboa kids all grew up like weeds, more or less, without much attention, but they have learned to take care of themselves and are all hard workers."

"María Eva, if you see the girl—Nereida—would you tell her that I want her to cut my hair, whenever she has time," Lilia said, touching her wavy black hair that almost reached her shoulders. She laughed, "My hair is getting so long and wild that I look like those hermits from the Bible."

"Don't worry, I'll tell her, or I'll send word to her with Evita. And now I really must go."

"But your hair is so pretty. I like it long," Blanca Estela lamented when María Eva had shut the door behind her.

"Thank you, darling, but I need to begin getting things in order."

"What things?"

"Oh, like my clothes, my hair, so that I can..."

They were interrupted by a shrill whistle outside the door. Lilia and Blanca Estela were still standing in the entryway while Mamá Anita went to hang a wet dress on the clothes line at the back of the patio.

"That's the mailman," Lilia remarked, suddenly alert. "Let me see what he has."

Blanca Estela was surprised, for on the infrequent occasions when the mailman brought them letters, it was she, Blanca Estela, who was usually sent to the door to receive them. Lilia opened the door, quickly took what appeared to Blanca Estela to be two envelopes and thanked the mailman. She said, "A letter from my brother, Raúl," and disappeared into the dimness of the parlor, where the shutters had been closed to keep out the afternoon heat.

The following afternoon, just as the parlor clock was chiming four, there was a knock at the front door, and Blanca Estela went to answer it. A young woman stood on the sidewalk with a barber's white cloth draped over her arm and a pair of scissors and a comb in her hand.

"I've come to cut your mother's hair," she said, stepping over the threshold with the same confident air as Mario.

"You must be Nereida," Blanca Estela said, although in the harsh glare of the sun, the young woman did not look like the mermaid that she had resembled in the moonlight.

She was quite tall and slender but "well developed," as Mamá Anita would say, referring to the bosom and hip area, all of which was emphasized by her dress, a faded cotton print which seemed too short and too tight for her. Blanca Estela gazed with interest at Nereida's face, trying to sort out the family resemblances. In coloring she was more like Mimi. She had light brown hair, like Mimi, although Nereida's curled in soft ringlets around her ears and down the nape of her neck. Her eyes were golden amber and tilted up at the corners, like a cat's and not like Mimís'. When she smiled, showing her perfect teeth, she had the same joyful air as Mario.

Lilia came hurrying out of the parlor, her wet hair wrapped in a towel, turban-like. "Thank you for coming, Nereida. I just washed my hair, so I'm ready. What do you say if I bring out a chair here, to the entryway? We will have the best light, and it's still hot enough that I won't catch a chill with my hair wet. Blanca Estela, do you think that you can carry one of those chairs from the parlor and bring it over here?"

Blanca Estela nodded and returned shortly with one of the ladder-back chairs that had once belonged in a dining set but now lined the walls of the parlor. Lilia sat with her back to the patio, where the light came from, and Nereida draped the sheet around her shoulders, asking her how much she wanted cut. Lilia indicated with her three middle fingers the length that she wanted cut off, and Nereida began to snip at the two-inch lengths that protruded through the teeth of the comb.

Blanca Estela sat down on the top step from the entry to the patio and watched with dismay as her mother's full mane of hair was reduced to only a fragment of its former glory.

"I will feel much cooler with shorter hair," Lilia was saying, oblivious of her daughter's disapproval.

"Short hair is more stylish, too. In California, where I was, they were wearing it short. I cut mine, too, when I was there," Nereida agreed.

"Do you want to go back there?" Lilia asked her.

"As far as wanting, yes, but I don't know if I will be able to, at least for now. My mother can't cope by herself, as long as Mario and Mimi are still young and in school. So I'll stay here for a while, but I will not be wasting time. I will arrange a room where ladies can come to get their hair cut or to have a permanent. I brought the latest products to give hair permanents without having to use those horrible electric curlers that burn your hair."

"But if you could go back...?"

"Oh, I would go back. There is so much more of a future there. More work opportunities and education, too. Of course I would miss my family. People are more loving and closer to each other here, but still..."

"Yes," Lilia said, almost under her breath, but Blanca Estela heard her, nonetheless. "There is the future to think about."

There were no games after sunset the remainder of that week because all the children (with the exception of Blanca Estela, of course) were preparing their end-of-the-school-year assignments: writing compositions, coloring maps, and, in particular, finishing their projects for manual arts. For manual arts class, which was held on Friday afternoons, the boys usually did woodwork and the girls embroidery.

Pedro surprised Blanca Estela by showing her, with a great deal of stammerings and blushings, a handsomely carved and varnished picture frame, which was his class project. He later planned to give it to his mother, so she could put in it her wedding portrait, which had remained unframed for more than ten years. Mario had made something practical, a shoe-shine kit box, which he said he would later put to use when he started his shoe-shine business. Mimi had embroidered some daisies, rather haphazardly, on a dishtowel, but Evita had outdone herself with a set of napkins, which she had embroidered in a dainty cross-stitch. Blanca Estela was surprised at the abilities of her friends, as well as dismayed at her own dearth of talents. Evita, sensing her discouragement, offered to show her how to embroider after school let out. For the first time, Blanca Estela felt a surge of warmth for Evita and ceased to feel jealous of her.

Friday was to be the last day of school, and Blanca Estela awaited the day with almost as much impatience as her friends, but on Thursday she woke up to a sight that drove all other thoughts from her mind. Since early morning, while she was still half-asleep, she began to hear voices and shouts in the street, accompanied by rapid thumping sounds. Curious, she got up from her cot and opened the window shutters to peer outside.

The street, which at this time of day—or at any other time for that matter—usually saw only a few pedestrians, such as children going to and from school, and women visiting each other or doing their grocery shopping, now seemed to be full of horses. They were beautiful, powerful, quivering creatures with black or gold manes, which fluttered in the breeze when they tossed their heads. And on the horses there were riders wearing cowboy hats and bandanas around their necks, trotting or galloping the animals, sometimes stopping to show off their mounts as they pranced and pirouetted in front of a house.

Several times before, Blanca Estela had seen a few men dressed like these, wearing rancher hats and even leather leg coverings, which Mamá Anita had told her were called *chaparreras*. The men rode rhythmically on their mounts, the reins in their left hand, the right hand resting casually on their leg, as they went on their way to or from their ranches. Mamá Anita had explained that there were no roads to those ranches in the brush, only paths or *senderos*, and therefore, people had to travel on horseback. Or, if the *sendero* was wide enough, they could travel by wagons pulled by horses or mules. But today it seemed to Blanca Estela as if all the ranches must be empty because the horses and riders had all congregated in town.

She ran to the kitchen, where Mamá Anita was cooking flour *tortillas*, calling out to her, "Mamá Anita, come and look out the window. There are so many horses outside. You have never seen so many horses before, I'm sure."

Mamá Anita burst out laughing delightedly and was still chuckling when Lilia came in from the patio and asked, "Why are you laughing, Mamá?"

"This child, she thinks I have never before seen as many horses as there are outside today. Bless you, child. In the old days there used to be many more. Not everybody has a horse nowadays."

"But... why?" Blanca Estela asked, growing more confused by the minute.

"Today is June 24th. The feast day of Saint John the Baptist. It is a custom in Revilla to promenade on horseback on this day. It is also a custom to go bathing in the river early in the morning, but at my age I don't do that any more. Not even the young ones do it very much anymore, although going to the river on the morning of St. John's feast day, *la mañana de San Juan*, is a very old custom, coming probably from Spain. It's a shame how things change."

The galloping continued most of the morning until the riders went home to dinner. Blanca Estela watched them in fascination from the safety of the embrasure of the window. The horses looked so large and powerful that she was afraid to go out on the sidewalk for fear that one might charge into her. She was not completely confident that the riders could always control their mounts, especially the young boys. She noticed that the riders were mostly men or boys, except for the occasional instance where a horse carried two riders: a man in the saddle and a woman seated sideways behind him with her arms around his waist.

Late in the afternoon, after the heat of the day, the riders returned to promenade on their mounts on the street. Several impromptu horse races took place before Blanca Estela's amazed eyes. Sometimes the races were evenly matched, but other times one horse would gain the lead immediately and leave the competitor far behind, hidden in a cloud of dust. By the time the sun went down, the riders finally began going home, but the dust that the horses' hooves had raised remained in the air for several hours, spoiling the neighbors' enjoyment of sitting before their open windows or on the sidewalk, and spoiling their children's games too.

After dusk Mario came looking for Blanca Estela. He found her sitting in the entryway with her mother and grandmother, behind the closed front doors, sipping lemonade and fanning themselves with fans made of dried palm leaves. He said good evening very politely to all of them and then said that he had come to invite Blanca Estela to accompany him and his family to a picnic on the river on Saturday morning. He added that, because his father and his brother had to work on repairing the turbine at the electrical plant on the river, the entire family had decided to go along, especially since they had missed the early river bathe on the morning of St. John. They were taking meat to grill over coals and other food already cooked.

Blanca Estela looked inquiringly at her mother, but Lilia acted doubtful and did not respond at first. "I don't know," Lilia finally said, hesitantly. "Blanca Estela, you don't know how to swim, and I don't want to place the responsibility for looking after you on Delia. She has enough worries of her own. Your mother is going too, Mario?"

"Oh yes, and she would like it very much if you would join her, too," Mario responded, gracefully including both Lilia and Mamá Anita.

"I can't go," Mamá Anita said quickly. "I have to visit a friend of mine who has been ill, but you, Lilia, should go. The fresh air will do you good, and I am sure that Delia will welcome your company."

Lilia finally overcame her reluctance, and it was agreed that they would all ride in Néstor Balboa's truck on Saturday morning, just after breakfast. Blanca Estela was too excited to wait till the following day to plan for the picnic and immediately went off to find the only playsuit that she had brought with her and which she had not had an opportunity to wear yet. The playsuit would have to do because she did not have a bathing suit, and she wanted to go in the water.

The evening before the picnic, though, a thought filled her with anxiety as she was going to bed. What her mother had said earlier was true: she did not know how to swim, although she had enjoyed playing in the shallow end of the swimming pool back home. Now, they were going to the river, that frightening, sullen river that slithered over rocks and churned in brown pools. It would suck her in and drown her, surely. She asked her mother timidly if they were going to have the picnic under the swinging bridge that they had crossed on the day of their arrival.

"Oh no, darling, we're not going there at all. I forget that you still don't know your way around here very well. The river we crossed when we arrived was the Río Grande. Tomorrow, we're going to the Río Salado. It's a much smaller river and closer to town. Revilla is really built on the Río Salado, not on the Río Grande. The water that people use here is from the Salado, and that's where the electrical plant is. This is our own river, although after it passes Revilla it empties into the Río Grande. We share the Río Grande with the United States, so it is not all ours. It used to be all ours... when the land across the river also belonged to Mexico."

Blanca Estela had not bargained for a lesson in history and geography when she had asked the question about where they were going to swim, but since it had turned out that way, she thought she might as well get something else clear. She asked her mother, "So that's why people here, like Evita, say that somebody is from 'across the river,' or that something came 'from the other side' instead of saying 'the United States?'"

"Yes, although I had not thought about it before. I suppose I say things like that, too, without realizing it."

Saturday morning, right after breakfast, the truck belonging to Néstor Balboa, carrying him and his wife, Delia, Tino, Nereida, Mimi and Mario, stopped in front of the house to pick up Lilia and Blanca Estela. Néstor drove, and Delia and Lilia rode in the cab with him. Tino, Nereida, Mimi and Mario were standing in the back, holding on to the wood railings around the bed of the truck. They helped Blanca Estela to climb up to them. Mamá Anita stood in front of the house, calling out to Blanca Estela to remember to wear her straw hat and asking Lilia if she had remembered to take the parasol. They assured her that they had, and the truck drove off slowly, making a right turn at the corner of Mamá Anita's house.

Blanca Estela had not yet explored the town in this direction, except as one of two routes to go buy fresh eggs from Pedro's mother, and that was a trip of only two blocks. They traveled downhill along a very rocky, narrow street, and as they got closer to the river, the houses got smaller, although they were still made of stone. They finally came within sight of the river, which they could glimpse from the height of the truck bed, over the tops of the green rushes that lined the banks. The river was green, Blanca Estela noted with satisfaction, perhaps not Nile green, but at least green and not brown.

Néstor turned the truck to the right again, and drove a short distance to a spot where the rushes were cleared. A large willow tree grew at the water's edge, close to a square concrete building. Néstor pulled the truck to the side of the squat concrete box and stopped. While Tino jumped off the back of the truck, Mario explained to Blanca Estela that the turbine was "in there," pointing to the building. From where she stood Blanca Estela could also see, on the far side of the structure, a channel leading from the river to what looked like a swimming pool, which in turn, was linked to the turbine room by a concrete trough.

The two men, Néstor and Tino, disappeared into the building while Delia and Lilia got out of the cab holding on carefully to a couple of clay pots, one containing rice and the other beans, and to a basket with beef ribs, which they planned to grill over the coals. Mario then jumped off the truck and followed the men into the turbine room, leaving Nereida, Mimi and Blanca Estela to scamper off the truck last.

Blanca Estela noticed how carefree and pretty her mother looked that morning. She still wore black clothes, but it was a dress of thin material with short sleeves and cut low around the neck. On her feet she wore rope-soled canvas espadrilles, and her legs were bare and very white. Lilia had put on her sunglasses, but with her hands occupied with the pots, she had no use for the parasol and offered up her smiling face to the sun while the wind played with her recently shorn hair.

A short distance away, Nereida, in a white cotton dress with a short, full skirt that barely covered her knees, stood with her hands on her hips, calling out, "Mario, Mimi, you had better go gather firewood right now, so we can start the fire. It will take a long time to make coals."

Mario came out of the turbine room, grumbling about bossy sisters and motioned to Mimi to follow him. Lilia turned to Blanca Estela, who stood by the truck, uncertain of what to do, and told her she could go gather firewood with the other two, but to be sure to wear her hat and wear her blouse over the playsuit.

The playsuit had been a point of contention with Mamá Anita. It was composed of two parts: short pants that stopped a couple of inches above the knees and a sleeveless, smocked top that left her midriff exposed. Mamá Anita had commented that she wasn't sure if the garment was proper for a granddaughter of hers to exhibit herself in public. Lilia had responded that children in the United States wore clothes like that quite frequently with their parents' approval. Mamá Anita had changed her tactics then and told Blanca Estela that she would suffer a severe sunburn on her exposed skin, and all three had finally agreed that Blanca Estela would wear a loose blouse over the top, which she would remove, of course, when she went in the water.

Under the supervision of Nereida, the three of them began to gather twigs and small branches that were lying on the ground. "Stay close to me," Mario told Blanca Estela while with a hatchet he hacked off small limbs from a mesquite bush. "We have to be careful of snakes. Have you ever seen a snake?"

She shook her head.

"Well," Mario continued, "if you hear a hissing or a rattling sound, look around you quickly.

Actually, we hardly ever see any snakes around here, but you never know. Sometimes snakes come out of the river, but not usually around the turbine room."

When each had gathered an armful of twigs and small branches, they returned to where their mothers waited for them under the willow tree. Mario and Nereida then busied themselves building a small fire inside a circle of stones. While the fire burned down to coals, Delia and Lilia spread out a quilt under the willow and composed themselves on it, enjoying the breeze in the shade and watching the campfire from there.

"Let's go swimming right now," Mario said, "because after we eat they won't let us go in the water."

The river was much friendlier than the Río Grande, being green and placid, but Blanca Estela still did not feel confident to go in it and said so, although she was ashamed to admit her fear. "Oh no, we don't go in the river," Mario reassured her. "We swim in the holding pool. The sluice gate to the turbine is shut now, so it's like a swimming pool."

Relief made her lighthearted again as she heard this.

"Nereida and Tino are very good swimmers, and they sometimes go in the river, but Mimi and I are not allowed to do so," Mario continued. "Nereida," he called out to his sister, "we're going swimming in the pool."

"Wait for me," she answered. "I'm going in the water with you. Mother would worry if you go in alone. If the pool is full, the water comes up over your head, and you're not as good swimmers as you think."

Nereida told Delia and Lilia that the children were going in the pool and that she was going in with them. Lilia told Blanca Estela to stay close to the edge, and Nereida promised that she would stay with Blanca Estela. Blanca Estela took off her blouse and left it with her mother. Mario in turn, pulled off his T-shirt, keeping only his shorts, and Mimi removed her skirt, revealing underneath it a pair of cotton shorts like her brother's, while above her waist she wore a T-shirt that also matched his.

Nereida, for her part, retired to the truck, and when she emerged she had changed out of her dress and into a swimsuit of dark green material that draped and gathered in folds from the right shoulder to the left hip. She ran lightly on her bare feet over the hot sand and pebbles until she reached the edge of the pool. There, she stood for a moment, poised as if about to dive in, and Mario called to her anxiously, "Don't dive in; it's too shallow."

She flashed him a smile, saying, "I know. I was just pretending," and she jumped in, feet first, and ducked completely under water. She surfaced a few seconds later and pulled herself out of the pool, shaking the water out of her hair, like a dog will do when it is wet. "Come and get in the water, you chickens," Nereida called, walking towards the three who still stood under the willow tree, as if mesmerized by her vision.

Blanca Estela marveled at the beauty of Nereida's long, slender legs and at the golden sheen of her skin, now dappled with brilliant drops of water. Suddenly, for no apparent reason, she remembered something that she had meant to ask her mother. Turning to Lilia, she asked, "Mamá, what does *chabacano* mean—in English?"

"What a strange question," Lilia said, a little annoyed. "Let's see, it's a fruit, like a peach, but I don't know how to say it in English."

"Apricot," Nereida said, pronouncing the 'a' like a Spanish sound. "I learned some English when I was away up north," she explained, looking shyly at Lilia.

Of course. Blanca Estela had seen apricots in the stores when they had lived across the river. A honey-colored apricot, that's what Nereida reminded her of with her golden legs and arms and the green bathing suit.

"Come on, time to get in the water," Nereida repeated, taking Mimi by the hand.

Mario followed, and Blanca Estela came last. At the edge of the pool Mario and Mimi jumped in the water and began thrashing their arms and kicking out with their legs like a pair of tadpoles. Blanca Estela, seated at the edge of the pool with her feet in the water, still hesitated until Nereida, standing in chest-deep water, took her by the waist and pulled her in.

Blanca Estela had a moment of panic when it seemed that the water would come over her head, but it actually reached only her chin. She tried to stand on tiptoe, but the water, pressing and swirling around her legs, robbed her of control over them. Nereida told her to face the edge of the pool and hold on to it with her hands. Then she told her to let her legs float behind her.

Blanca Estela raised one leg first, skeptical that it would float. When she felt it drifting upwards, she was so delighted that she willed herself to let the other one go too, and it rose like a balloon set free. Soon she began to kick her legs behind her, splashing water on the others.

Nereida placed her hands under Blanca Estela's stomach and told her to let go of the edge of the pool. Blanca Estela hesitated again, wondering if she dared to abandon herself to the promise which the girl held out. She finally released her grasp, one hand at a time, and soon found herself borne towards the center of the pool, still kicking her feet and flaying with her arms, telling herself that she was swimming. Nereida then led her back to the edge and told her that she was going to let her go. Blanca Estela grasped the edge of the pool again, but this time with only one hand. Nereida then told her to put her arms around her neck and that she would carry her piggyback across the pool. A little shyly, Blanca Estela locked her arms around Nereida. They crossed the pool in this manner, with Blanca Estela holding on to Nereida's neck, kicking her legs and splashing the other two, still pretending that she was swimming.

Suddenly Mario and Mimi ceased their wild somersaults in the water and simultaneously extended their arms towards each other, locking their hands together and forming a bridge while they chanted, *"A la víbora de la mar, por aquí pueden pasar."* Without warning, Nereida threw back her head and took a deep breath before arching her back and plunging underwater, like a dolphin, to pass under the bridge. Blanca Estela convulsively tightened her grip around Nereida's neck as a green wave rushed over her head and enveloped her, shutting out daylight and air in one terrifying moment. It seemed to her that she was underwater for an age, wrapped in a roaring darkness, while she wondered why no one realized that she was drowning.

A lucid part of her mind, however, noted that almost immediately after their dive, Nereida had kicked out strongly and flayed her arms, gathering impetus for surfacing again. When they broke the surface, Nereida paused to take a deep, shuddering breath while Blanca Estela, clinging frantically to her, coughed up water. Nereida quickly led her to the edge of the pool and disengaged herself from the arms that still clutched her around the neck.

Blanca Estela hung onto the edge of the pool while her arms and legs trembled. She looked in the direction of her mother. Lilia was deep in conversation with Delia under the shade of the willow and never once looked in her direction. Glancing quickly over her shoulder she saw that Mimi and Mario were now playing water tag. Nereida lay floating on her back in the middle of the pool, a splash of dark green and gold on the opaque surface of the water, completely withdrawn from them all, but especially from Blanca Estela.

She had not cried out in fear. For that much she was grateful. She had not shamed herself before the others, but the shame was there, nevertheless, because she had sensed the disappointment in Nereida. What a stupid, cowardly girl she was; that had been Nereida's unspoken message when she left her at the edge of the pool. And her mother had been oblivious to her anguish and her silent cry for help, wrapped up in her own grown-up concerns. She told herself to be sensible, that surely she had not been in any danger of drowning with so many people, especially grown-ups, around her. But it was still frightening to realize that, even surrounded by people, no one had sensed the sheer terror that had suddenly seized her, no one, not even her mother, had noticed it, except for the siren who had led her into and out of fear.

Gripping the edge of the pool, she threw one leg over it and pulled herself out of the water, shivering as the wind blew over her wet body. She felt very chilled and alone.

# Chapter VI

*Tengo una muñeca vestida de azul . . .*

Monday morning she woke up with a sense of foreboding. It seemed to her that it was very dark, both in the room and outside. Perhaps it was still nighttime, but her mother's cot was already empty, and the faint sound of voices reached her from the kitchen. The window shutters were partially open, and through the gap between them Blanca Estela caught a glimpse of gray, swollen clouds in the sky. It was the first time since her arrival in Revilla that the sun was not shining when she woke up. Perhaps this was the reason for this feeling of heaviness in her chest and the dull ache in her head. Except that this vague sense of desolation had been with her since Saturday afternoon.

The picnic on Saturday had been, according to everybody, successful. Delia and Lilia had both returned home with better color and spirits than before. The two women had clearly enjoyed conversing with each other. The meat cooked over coals had been delicious and enjoyed by all. The men had repaired the trouble with the turbine. And the three friends, under Nereida's supervision, had played until they were tired. Blanca Estela knew all this and felt that it would be ungracious of her to spoil even the recollection of the outing by dwelling on her own anxieties. Therefore, she had resolved to put out of her mind the brief moment of terror when she had believed that she was drowning and did not mention the incident to her mother on that afternoon—or even later—and had played continuously with Mimi and Mario until it was time to go home.

After eating they had packed up the picnic dishes and put up the leftovers, folded the quilt and doused the campfire. Then they got back in the truck and returned home to spend the hottest part of the day indoors, where they could also take a brief nap. It was quite a brief one in the case of Blanca Estela, for by three o'clock Mamá Anita had already seen to it that she had changed into a dress and had dried and combed her hair in preparation for the regular Saturday Catechism class. Mario, too, showed the results of having changed into clean clothes and combed his hair as he waited for her at his front door. The two of them were rather subdued, though, as they made their way to church, running part of the distance but saying little.

Father Mirabal was already in the church when they arrived, as was the rest of the class: three boys and a girl. Blanca Estela had not paid much attention to them before, but today she observed them with a heightened attention that she could not explain. The boys came from families that she had heard described as not "belonging to the town." What that meant was not clear to her, since the boys lived in town, but she sensed that it meant that they were not considered suitable to be her friends. She attributed this to the fact that they were often not very clean and had rough manners.

The girl did belong, but in an undefined way. Her name was Aminta, and she lived with her

grandparents in one of the smaller houses that started some two blocks past the doctor's house. Blanca
Estela had seen the girl in Mass before with her
grandmother. Mamá Anita would say good morning
to the grandmother and add a few words about the
weather or inquire after somebody's health, but not
converse with her at length. Aminta was small and
thin, with a rather sallow complexion and dark,
lank hair that she pushed behind her ears. Blanca
Estela had seldom heard Aminta say anything, even
in class. In all, grandmother and child were politely
treated, but not noticed very much by the people
who usually gathered to chat after Mass in the
church atrium.

Father Mirabal began the class with the basic
question of "Who made you?" They all knew the
answer, which was simple: "God." The follow-up
question was also a repeat from previous lessons:
"Why did God make you?" This was slightly more
difficult, but they still managed to come up with the
correct reply: "God made me, so that I may love
and serve Him." Every time she gave this answer,
Blanca Estela had a moment of rebellion. Was it
quite fair of God to create people solely in order to
be loved and served by them? Wasn't it rather selfish
of Him? But she had never dared to voice her reser-
vations to Father Mirabal, and he went on, unaware
of her doubts, to drill them on the Ten Commandments.

The three boys, whose names she still had not
learned, fell by the wayside with the Ten Commandments, unable to recite more than half of them.
Father Mirabal had rapped them all on the head
with his knuckles and had sent them to a distant

corner with a dog-eared copy of the Catechism book, which contained the Commandments. He ordered them to not return until they had memorized all ten of them. The lesson then continued with only Mario, Aminta and Blanca Estela.

Mario had tripped up on reciting the Commandments of the Church, which were in addition to the Ten Commandments of God, and only the two girls were left. They both recited correctly the Apostles' Creed, but when it came to the Salve Regina, Aminta's thin, reedy voice was the only one heard. Father Mirabal had praised the girl for being the only one who knew the entire lesson and dismissed them all with instructions to go home and study, so they would be ready to receive their First Communion the following month.

On the way home, Blanca Estela commented to Mario that she had been surprised that Aminta could recite all the prayers, adding, "She had never said very much before."

Mario shrugged indifferently, and said, "Well, she ought to know the Catechism. She's been through it before."

"But why hasn't she made her First Communion, then?"

"Her grandparents took her to the ranch or somewhere before she finished the class last year. She's weird," he added.

This comment, coming from Mario, surprised her. "How is she weird?"

"Oh, I don't know... just odd." Mario would not elaborate any further, and they parted at Mario's doorstep.

When she had crossed the threshold, she was met by the unusual sound of raised voices. It was Lilia and Mamá Anita who were sitting at the kitchen table, finishing an early supper. When they heard her footsteps, their voices ceased suddenly, and Lilia rose to meet her, saying in a tremulous tone that betrayed the strain behind it, "Estelita, do you want some supper, my love? Shall I warm up some of that meat that we brought home from the picnic?"

She shuddered at the thought of a heavy meal and shook her head.

"No, of course not, Lilia," said Mamá Anita, going to the stove. "The child will want something light. Here is some rice pudding that I made for you, Blanca Estela," she added, placing a small bowl before her.

Blanca Estela looked at the mound of rice and milk, sprinkled with sugar and cinnamon flakes, grateful to her grandmother for disguising the taste of boiled milk in the pudding. She ate it in silence. After she finished eating, she felt sleepy, and her grandmother, as if reading her thoughts, soon made up the cot for her. As she felt sleep closing in over her, she had a moment of panic. Sleep felt so much like the green wave that had washed over her in the pool. She thought that she had cried out, but if she did, no one heard her. Her mother's and her grandmother's voices had resumed rising and falling, and reached her from the other end of the house, and then from far away and then not at all.

The next day, the three of them attended Sunday Mass, as Blanca Estela had already become accustomed to doing. It seemed such a natural part of her life now, to go to church on Sunday morning with her mother and her grandmother and, after Mass, to linger behind, listening as Lilia conversed with María Eva and Mamá Anita exchanged news with other gray-haired women like herself. Today, though, María Eva and Evita were absent, gone up to Laredo to visit the older married sister, the one who might have married Raúl, if he had asked her. It was, perhaps, their absence that broke the pattern, because this time Lilia and Mamá Anita did not stay to chat after Mass let out, nodding only on their way out to Rosalía and Doctor Marín and then hurrying home.

Almost immediately after dinner, Lilia set to ironing clothes that she had washed the day before, while Blanca Estela had been at Catechism. Mamá Anita, apparently infected by this fever of activity, began to air out and rearrange the contents of the two large wardrobes. Blanca Estela at first watched as her mother maneuvered, not the electric iron with which Blanca Estela was familiar, but a larger implement made of cast iron. This iron had a hinged lid that opened on top to receive within it, glowing chunks of coal from the fireplace (where the beans had cooked earlier). These coals heated the iron with which Lilia now pressed black gabardine skirts and starched cotton blouses.

Lilia ironed with such determination, her forehead furrowed as perspiration beaded on her face, that Blanca Estela felt strangely inadequate and superfluous to her mother's labors. She wandered off to watch Mamá Anita, instead. The scent of camphor balls and lavender sachets greeted her when she found her grandmother. She was bending down behind a stack of bed linens and garments from long ago, handling them lovingly.

Suddenly Mamá Anita exclaimed in surprise, "Why, here she is!" She lifted out a doll from her swaddle of white tissue paper. It was an object of perfect beauty, as only a doll can be: golden hair, pink porcelain face, blue eyes, a delicate rosebud of a mouth, and it was dressed in an opulent frock of sapphire blue satin. Blanca Estela wondered briefly if Perla had copied her ballgown from this doll. On her feet, the doll wore dainty slippers of white kidskin. Lilia, coming into the room at that moment with an armload of ironed clothes, paused to contemplate the vision of spun gold and satin in her mother's arms. She, too, exclaimed, as if meeting an old friend who had been given up for lost.

"There she is... Amilamia... Amaranta... Amalia... no, no. Aminta. Her name was Aminta."

Blanca Estela mouthed a silent "No" and unexpectedly asked her mother, "Are you sure that is her name?"

"Yes, I remember now, that was her name."

Blanca Estela was certain that the blue doll had not been named after the awkward, sallow-faced girl from Catechism class, but she wanted to hear her mother's reasons. "Why did you name her that?" she asked.

Lilia carefully laid down the ironed clothes on the bed and placed her index finger on her chin, frowning in an effort to remember. "Why did I? I was very young, about your age, so what could I have been thinking of?... I know, it was the little girl in the picture album. A very pretty little girl, sitting on a small sofa with her doll sitting next to her. The little girl's name was Aminta. I named my doll after her."

"Who was she?" Blanca Estela inquired, increasingly curious.

"The little girl? I don't remember. It was in that old album of yours, Mamá. Do you remember the photograph, a little girl about two or three, with curly hair, sitting next to a golden-haired doll?"

Mamá Anita only shook her head.

"I remember now," said Lilia. "She was your niece, Mamá, the little girl who died of scarlet fever."

Mamá Anita said, "Oh yes, I had forgotten. My sister Rosa's oldest child. She would have been some fifteen years older than you. My sister was almost ten years older than me."

Blanca Estela did not want to hear about a little girl who had died long ago, so she was relieved when her mother went on to remember happier things.

Lilia asked Mamá Anita, "Remember how I learned the song about the doll dressed in blue?" She began to croon softly: *"Tengo una muñeca vestida de azul, con zapatos blancos y su manto azul.* My doll never had a blue mantle, but it does have white shoes and a blue dress. And that is how I first learned to add and multiply, by learning the second part of the song. How does it go? '2 y 2 son 4, 4 y 2 son 6, 6 y 2 son 8, y 8, 16.' Estelita, you must learn this song, too. All the children in Mexico learn it, even before they go to school. Repeat after me..."

And Blanca Estela repeated the words and the tune after her mother until she memorized the song, including the arithmetic. She even learned the last two verses, which she did not like because they brought up again the disquieting subject of death. The complete song first described the doll dressed in blue and then went on to relate how the doll had gone for a promenade and caught a chill and died.

*Tengo una muñeca vestida de azul,*
*con zapatos blancos y su manto azul.*
*La llevé a la plaza y se me resfrió,*
*La llevé a la casa y la niña murió.*

She hurried over those two last verses and with relief reached the part with the addition. After she finished, she asked her mother timidly, "Can I play sometimes with your doll?"

Lilia seemed to come back from far away before she answered her, "Yes, darling, but you must be very careful with her. She is made of porcelain, and she is very delicate. I never really played with her. Mamá would only let me touch her gently and perhaps display her in the parlor. For playing, I remember that I had a rag doll. I don't know what happened to it, probably ended up in shreds. Let's put her up now, wrapped again in tissue paper, and we'll place her inside the wardrobe, on the top shelf. That's where she was, isn't that right, Mamá? When you want to take her out, you ask your grandmother, and she will let you play with her."

Blanca Estela nodded seriously, conscious of the care and ceremony that had to be taken when handling such a beautiful thing. But as she was going to sleep that night, a thought surfaced briefly in her mind: Why did Lilia say that she must ask Mamá Anita for permission to take out the doll if the doll belonged to Lilia? Before she could think of an answer, she was asleep.

The next morning, Monday morning, she woke to a dull heaviness left behind by half-remembered dreams of a doll taken for a promenade in the plaza. The doll was left behind, abandoned on a bench in the rain. The rain swelled up the river, which then rose to cover up the plaza and carried away in its current a drowning doll. She swung her legs over the side of the cot and stood up uncertainly. The clock in the parlor chimed the half hour, and she peered at its face through still sleep-leaden eyes. It was already eight-thirty, later than she usually woke up.

She made her way to the kitchen, following the murmur of voices and clattering of dishes that originated there. Lilia was already at the table, finishing a plate of *machacado con huevos* and refried beans. Mamá Anita stood in front of the kerosene stove, turning a flour tortilla that puffed up on the hot griddle as she said, "You need a big breakfast because you don't know at what time you will eat dinner."

She stopped suddenly when she caught sight of Blanca Estela standing at the door. Lilia, too, looked up quickly and pushed back her chair to approach her. She put her arms around Blanca Estela and kissed her forehead as she held her tightly against her.

Blanca Estela was surprised at the intensity of the embrace and pushed her mother away, saying, "I'm hungry."

Lilia released her and said, her voice a little tremulous, "Breakfast is ready, darling. Come and

eat. Your grandmother just scrambled some eggs
with some very good dried beef."

Blanca Estela sat at the breakfast table silently
while her mother placed the promised *machacado*—
the dried beef with sautéed onions and tomatoes and
scrambled with eggs—in front of her, along with a
still steaming tortilla. After she did so, Lilia continued to stand before her, as if searching her face for
some response, a comment about the food perhaps,
but Blanca Estela ate in silence.

Lilia then began a nervous monologue. "Did the
thunder wake you up? There was some thunder and
lightning last night, but very little rain. You know,
Mamá," she added, turning to her mother, "it's a
good thing that you didn't sleep outside, in the
patio. You would have gotten wet. I don't think it's
good for your rheumatism to sleep outside. Even in
dry weather the dew gets all the bedclothes damp,
and dampness aggravates the rheumatism."

Mamá Anita, still standing by the stove, made no
reply, but it seemed to Blanca Estela that she stared
intently at Lilia, her lips tightly compressed, as if to
hold back a remark. The silence lengthened, and
finally, a sigh escaped from Mamá Anita who then
said, "It's fortunate that those children from next
door left on yesterday's bus. Today, if it rains hard,
the road may be impassable."

Blanca Estela recalled suddenly the reason for
the dejection that she felt just under the surface:
Mario and Mimi had been taken by Nereida to visit
an aunt in Saltillo, up in the mountains past
Monterrey. Mario had told her on Saturday, after
Catechism, that they were going to Saltillo, where it
was cool even in the middle of summer. Evita was

gone, too. It seemed that everyone had taken flight as soon as school was over, and now she had no one to be her friend.

Something stirred in her memory, and she turned to look into the bedroom behind her. There, on the bed, was the large suitcase that she had only half-noticed in passing on her way to breakfast a short time ago. It must mean that they, she and her mother (or was Mamá Anita included too?), were going somewhere, perhaps to see her uncle, Raúl, who was supposed to be somewhere near Laredo.

She turned to her mother and asked, "Where are we going?"

Lilia pulled out a chair and, resting her arms on the table, leaned forward towards Blanca Estela. "Estelita," she began and paused to clear her throat. Her voice did not seem to be fully under her control, for she had to make several attempts before she could speak again. "Estelita, I have to go away," she said quickly. "Just for a little while. I have to go take care of some things across the river... look for a job to support us and other things. You will stay here with your grandmother for a short time, until I come back."

Blanca Estela continued to chew on her food, which had developed the consistency of an expanding wad of paper that she found difficult to swallow. She concentrated on chewing, not seeing Lilia in front of her, but noticing Mamá Anita in the background, moving about like a gray shadow in the kitchen.

Outside there was an occasional roll of distant thunder. She finally swallowed the food and took a sip of pale coffee and milk. Then she repeated, in a conversational tone, the remark that she had just heard Mamá Anita express: "If it rains, the road may be impassable."

A little choking laugh escaped from Lilia, "Oh, darling, you sound like your grandmother. I'm going in Manuel's car, only across the bridge. The road on the other side is all paved. The bus will pick me up at the store. Do you remember Dolores, the big woman at the store, and Chucho, her son, who helped us with the luggage?"

"She doesn't know where you're going. Tell her where you will be," Blanca Estela heard her grandmother's voice float out of the shadows by the cold fireplace.

"I am only going to San Antonio, Estelita. That is not so far away. It is much closer, much closer than where we were before."

But she did not want to hear where her mother was going, if she was going without her. She pushed her chair away from the table and got up, feeling her limbs strangely stiff as she went to find her clothes, so she could change out of her nightgown. She was already dressed by the time the car stopped outside the house, and Manuel knocked on the door.

Lilia checked to make sure the catch was securely fastened on the suitcase and then pulled at her stockings, snapping the garters that held them up. Mamá Anita led Manuel inside the house, so he could carry out the suitcase to the car. The big man came in with a smile on his brown face, wishing them good morning and saying cheerfully, "Well, it looks like St. John brought us rain, after all, not on his feast day exactly, but close enough. The ranchers will be happy, and the river will carry enough water for the turbine to make electricity. I bet Néstor is happy that he fixed the turbine before the river rose."

Mamá Anita nodded absently and pointed to the case. With Manuel and Mamá Anita leading the way, Lilia stopped to look back at Blanca Estela who stood motionless in the parlor, holding on to the back of a chair.

"Estelita, aren't you coming out to see me off?" She took her by the hand and led her outside. Out on the sidewalk, Lilia dropped down on one knee so she could look at Blanca Estela, face to face. Blanca Estela looked over her mother's shoulder and past her to the closed doors and windows of María Eva's empty house.

"Estelita, listen to me," Lilia pleaded, her voice taking on a frantic edge. "I am coming back soon, and I am taking you back with me, so you can start school across the river in September. I don't want you to lose the advantages that you can have over there, but I must find a job first. I will miss you very much, and I will write often. Please be good and mind your grandmother."

Blanca Estela still said nothing, and Mamá Anita reached to touch Lilia's shoulder, saying, "You must leave now *hija*. It is starting to rain again. Have a safe trip, and God bless you."

Lilia put her arms around Blanca Estela and kissed her on the cheek. Then she quickly got to her feet and also embraced her mother and hurried inside the car. Heavy drops of rain began falling as the car pulled away. Lilia's face was blurred behind the rain-splattered glass and the tears that suddenly clouded Blanca Estela's eyes.

She made a desperate dash to follow the receding car, but Mamá Anita snatched at her dress and pulled her back, putting her arms around her. Blanca Estela remained like that, with her face buried against her grandmother's apron, inhaling the smell of soap and sun-dried clothes that was a part of Mamá Anita, until she had her tears under control. Then she pushed away from her, saying gruffly, "I have to go to the bathroom," and she ran in to hide in the stifling cubicle of the outhouse.

She heard the rain beat down on the tin roof of the privy and endured the nauseating vapors that rose and stagnated in the humid air trapped inside with her. She waited out the rain, and still she would not come out until she felt her conscience nudging her, telling her that Mamá Anita might worry that she had fallen in. But if she worried, why didn't she come looking for her? She finally emerged, half-suffocated, walked gingerly across the muddy patio and entered the house through the kitchen.

There she found Mamá Anita seated before a small mound of pinto beans, which she was engaged in cleaning. Mamá Anita looked up and said matter of factly, "My eyes are not very good anymore, and it's so dark outside, Blanca Estela. Come and help me sort through these beans. Pick out the pebbles and any little bits of twigs or dirt. I need to set the beans to cooking."

Mamá Anita vacated the chair and indicated to Blanca Estela that she should take her place. She moved on to the fireplace where she began to arrange small, foot-lengths of firewood, which she set ablaze, and then began to do her daily chores while the wood burned itself down to coals. When Blanca Estela finished cleaning the beans, Mamá Anita washed them and then put them in a clay pot, which she filled with water and, after adding salt and spices, she set on a trivet over the coals.

The beans simmered over the coals, and Mamá Anita busied herself around the house dusting tables and sweeping floors, folding linens and plumping up pillows on the beds. Blanca Estela remained sitting at the table as if the mound of pinto beans were still before her. Silence hung over the house as heavily as the clouds outside. Finally Mamá Anita returned to the kitchen, carrying a tin box about a foot long by about three quarters as wide. She deposited it on the table before Blanca Estela. The box was cream-colored with a hinged lid on which was depicted a boating scene. The illustration showed a narrow waterway, crowded with boatmen standing at the oars while spectators looked on from a bridge, which spanned the canal, or leaned out of windows from the houses lining the shores.

Blanca Estela looked at the box and then at her grandmother with a question in her eyes, but she said nothing.

Mamá Anita said, "Open it."

Inside, Blanca Estela found a profusion of buttons. For a minute, Blanca Estela was reminded of a scene in a movie she had seen where somebody—a pirate maybe, had opened a treasure chest and had been dazzled by the golden coins and the jewels inside it. The buttons glittered like so many gems and coins. There were glass buttons the color of emeralds and rubies, there were gold buttons like ancient coins, and there were even delicate, smooth pearls.

"I need twelve buttons," Mamá Anita said, "twelve pearl buttons. There are many pearl buttons in there, but they are not all alike. The twelve must all be the same. Will you sort through the box and find me a dozen pearl buttons? "

Blanca Estela said nothing as she looked at the treasure trove before her, wondering if there were twelve identical buttons of any kind at all. Why didn't her grandmother just buy a package of buttons?

Mamá Anita seemed to read her thoughts. "I don't like to waste anything," she said. "Throughout the years I have been saving buttons from dresses and shirts and leftover buttons from packages that I buy for a particular garment. These in the box are all fancy buttons. The plain white ones from shirts and the like, I keep in a jar. So now, when I need buttons for a dress, I seldom have to buy them. It will take you some time to sort through so many buttons, but don't worry. Take as long as you need. We can eat on the other side of the table."

Blanca Estela contemplated how to best approach her task. A quick survey showed her that there were at least two or three styles of pearl buttons, and she must find twelve of the same size and shape. She began by picking out all the pearl buttons and setting them aside. Then she began to sort them by size and shape. As the minutes passed, she developed four or five piles of pearl buttons, adding to one or another every so often after inspecting each button closely to make sure that it was a perfect match to its companions. Gradually, she began sorting buttons of other types until she had several stacks of gold or silver metal buttons or of colored glass.

She was surprised when her grandmother interrupted to say that it was time to eat. More than three hours had passed while the beans simmered, her grandmother cooked and she sorted buttons. She noticed, also, on looking out, that the clouds were parting, and the sun had begun to show through the breaks every so often. It surprised her too, that she was hungry and that she could enjoy the food that Mamá Anita placed in front of her.

After she ate, she was sleepy again, but she felt that she must push on to finish her sorting task. Mamá Anita noticed her drooping eyelids and suggested that she should go lie down; the cot was still set up in front of the window. The buttons would wait—today or tomorrow, there was no hurry. And so, although it was still daylight, she took off her dress and took Domino, the toy cat, to bed with her. She slept till the following day, dreamlessly and deeply, as if she had been anesthetized.

The days passed with an aching monotony. The clouds left, and the sky was clear again. The sun beat down on them with greater ferocity, and a hot, dry wind picked up handfuls of dust and scattered them indoors through the open windows. The mournful cooing of the turtledoves and the whirring of the cicadas were the only sounds to be heard outside in the middle of the day.

Inside the house, it was silent too. Gone were the sweet ripples of the sound of Lilia's voice and the little laugh that sometimes caught in her throat. Blanca Estela, herself, felt no desire to speak now in either her still awkward Spanish or the now receding English. Perhaps this was what Mamá Anita had predicted for girls like her who knew neither language well: they would end up mute.

Mamá Anita did not force her to speak, either. Whatever she said seldom required a spoken reply. Blanca Estela realized that Mamá Anita had lived alone for so many years that silence no longer disturbed her. But she was kind to Blanca Estela, remembering to disguise the taste of boiled milk with chocolate or cinnamon, washing and combing her hair in the long afternoons, braiding her pigtails with different colored ribbons and reading to her from the magical tales of the Arabian nights. All this was balm on the raw-skinned grief that she felt at being left behind, abandoned, as she saw it, by her mother. She wanted to be angry at Lilia, but all she could summon when she thought of her was a crying ache, a longing to see her flower face, to stroke the raven wings that rose from her temples, to hear the sound of her voice like running water and the reassuring rustle of her skirts when she approached.

And throughout those days, the button box remained on the table with its treasure spilling out of it while the small mounds of buttons grew slowly. She began to lose track of the days and had to consult the calendar on the kitchen wall, which she normally avoided because it had a colored picture of a boy and a girl crossing a rickety bridge over a raging torrent. The picture always caused her anxiety, and she was not reassured by the presence of a blue and mauve angel hovering over the children. This morning, the calendar told her it was Saturday, and this afternoon, therefore, Mamá Anita would expect her to go to Catechism class.

Blanca Estela averted her eyes from the angel
and the children in the storm. Father Mirabal had
been telling them about angels and archangels, and
her grandmother had taught her a short prayer to
her guardian angel. The calendar picture was called
precisely that, "The Guardian Angel," and the idea
was that he was watching over the children as they
encountered danger. The angel would make sure
that no harm came to them. But Blanca Estela had
also overheard one of Mamá Anita's friends say that
when children died, they became angels, so that the
angel in the picture was a dead child. What was the
point of having a guardian angel, then?

Perhaps the bridge in the picture was about to
collapse, and the children would be swallowed up
by the angry river, and later they would join the
company of angels. Perhaps she ought to ask Father
Mirabal if it was a good thing to have a guardian
angel watching over you. But Father Mirabal would
probably view her question as proof of a lack of
faith and would prevent her from making her First
Communion. She was in the throes of these doubts,
still staring at the picture on the calendar, when her
grandmother hurried into the kitchen, waving a
paper in her hand and saying, excitedly, "Blanca
Estela, look, a letter from your mother."

A beating of wings stirred in her chest and
became trapped in her throat as she turned away
from the picture on the wall to face her grandmother. She could not speak, but her hands fluttered as
she held them out towards the letter. Mamá Anita
did not see her gesture because she was peering at
the writing through her eyeglasses.

She intermingled reading and commentary: "It says here that she arrived safely that same day, in the evening. Blessed be God and the Virgin Mary for that—although she had already sent word by telephone, long-distance, to Dolores at the store across the river, and she relayed the message to Manuel, who gave it to me the following day.

"But here it says that it was already dark when she arrived. Fortunately her friend, a very nice woman whose husband is in the military, was there to meet her at the bus station and take her home. She also says that she talked on the telephone with my *Comadre*, Lupe's sister, who lives there with her son and his family. Thank goodness for that. At least she's in contact with somebody from Revilla. Her friend may be very nice, but it is not the same as someone from Revilla, from your home town, where you know who people are.

"She says that she has started looking for a job, but it is difficult for a woman like her, with no education in English, to find decent work. Still, she is not discouraged, and look, Blanca Estela, she says that she loves you very much and hopes to see you soon. She says: 'Estelita, you must remember that I love you with all my heart, and I keep you in my memory and my prayers. Be good with your grandmother; don't give her any cause for worry. I hope to see you soon. Study hard in your Catechism class, so that you will be able to make your First Communion. I would give anything to be able to see you receive Communion, but I must stay here until I find a job. When I do, I will go back for you. Have you thought whom you would like to have as your godmother for your First Communion?'"

Mamá Anita folded and put away the letter in its envelope and asked her, "Well, have you thought of whom we should ask to be your godmother?"

Blanca Estela frowned, puzzled, and shook her head. She had no idea that one needed a godmother for a First Communion. "Well, you don't have to decide this moment," said Mamá Anita. "We can talk about it later. Right now, what we should do is eat dinner; then this afternoon, you must go to Catechism. You'll have to walk to church by yourself because Mario and his sisters are not back yet. I am sure that you miss them and Evita. I know that I miss María Eva. She is such a good neighbor, but I think she'll be back next week. Now, help me set the table."

Shortly before three o'clock, Blanca Estela set off for church, wearing sandals and carrying a small, pink parasol that Mamá Anita had disinterred from the bottom of a trunk. That afternoon, she entered the church atrium at a sedate pace, twirling the open parasol, the shaft resting against her shoulder. She had not met anyone on the street at that unfriendly hour, when the sun heated the sidewalks like griddles for *tortillas,* and the stonès of the houses turned the interiors into ovens.

Only Rosalía, the doctor's wife, had looked out of one of her windows as Blanca Estela passed and waved at her with a gentle smile. Blanca Estela had wanted to call out to Rosalía, knowing that Rosalía would understand and share in her joy, "My mother has written a letter to me, and she says that she loves me and misses me, just like I miss her." But she had said nothing, merely waving back, and had continued on her way to Catechism.

However, Blanca Estela carried with her to church a little worm of regret that bored into her happiness. She should have stopped to talk to Rosalía. Rosalía was so kind and pretty, but there was always something sad about her. Probably she missed Sandra and Jaime, now that they were gone and that she was left alone. Mamá Anita had remarked once that Rosalía spent a lot of time by herself because Doctor Marín was out visiting sick people a great deal of the time. The next time that she walked by the Doctor's house, she would stop to talk to Rosalía, Blanca Estela resolved. She liked Rosalía very much.

Now, as she entered the cool dimness of the church, she paused to let her eyes adjust after the glare of the sun outside. The only light inside came from the clerestory windows above, close to the ceiling, and from the red votive candle that burned on the altar in the distance. She could barely make out the shapes of the three rowdy boys and the girl, Aminta, as they sat in the front pew, the boys at one end, laughing under their breath and shoving against each other, while the girl seemed to cringe against the bench at the other end. Father Mirabal came down the steps to the altar, spying Blanca Estela as she approached hesitantly, clutching her closed parasol.

"Come on, child, come here to the front," the priest called to her, to her great embarrassment. She was forced to go to the front pew where Aminta reluctantly moved a mere fraction to make a space for her, leaving her wedged between the end of the pew and her unsympathetic neighbor.

Father Mirabal began the class as he usually did, with a review of subjects from previous lessons, in this instance with the Ten Commandments. He reminded them that the first group of Commandments was couched in the affirmative, as in "Do this, do that: love God, love your neighbor, observe the Day of the Lord, honor your parents." As children, the Fourth Commandment, was one of the most important to them. It meant that you, as a child, should love your parents, and you demonstrated your love by obeying them and being respectful of them, as well as being affectionate to them. This commandment extended to the duty owed by children to grandparents and other elders who looked after them. You must love your parents, Father Mirabal, continued, even if they scold you or punish you for misbehavior.

Blanca Estela kept her eyes fixed on her hands, which gripped the handle of the parasol. She had the sudden conviction that Father Mirabal was speaking directly to her, remonstrating with her, because he knew that, deep inside her, she was not only sad because her mother was gone. She was also very angry with Lilia, and the anger sometimes also spilled over to her feelings for her grandmother who was, after all, not to blame for Lilia's departure or for her decision to leave Blanca Estela behind.

In truth, she felt much gratitude and tenderness for Mamá Anita when she saw her grandmother seek out the treats to present before her: the honeycomb still dripping with honey that the milkman had brought in the morning, the ice cream from across the river that, overcoming her scruples, she had asked Leopoldo to buy for her. She thought of her grandmother also reading stories to her at night by the flickering light of the lamp, peering through her eyeglasses at the yellowish page of the book—all to help her go to sleep. And yet, all those times Blanca Estela thought that it should have been her mother who ought to have been with her, but her mother had gone away in the black car. Now, all she could remember was Lilia's face bending forward, like a beautiful blossom on a slender stalk, from behind the car window that was quickly clouded over by the raindrops. She had tried to run after the car that took her mother away, but Mamá Anita had held her back. Mamá Anita was her jailer, and she was angry with her, too.

All this Father Mirabal must know, and that was why he was saying those things about the duty to love your parents and your grandparents. Blanca Estela made herself listen to him again and was surprised to hear that Father Mirabal was now talking about the Commandments that said "Thou shalt not." He was saying that they all dealt with clearly forbidden acts, terrible acts, such as "Thou shalt not kill." Was there anything about those Commandments, he asked, that they did not understand? Blanca Estela felt a stirring among the three boys at the other extreme of the pew and heard Father Mirabal ask one of them, "Yes, Eusebio, did you have a question about the Commandments?"

There was some more shuffling among the trio and an audible gasp before the one addressed finally responded. "I don't understand, Father," he said, "that one about fornicating."

Blanca Estela glanced at the speaker, looking past Aminta's slightly open mouth, and noticed that the boy, who seemed to be the oldest of the three, was trying, not very successfully, to hide a smirk.

"The Sixth Commandment forbids fornication," Father Mirabal retorted sharply and then paused, as if considering further replies. "I think, Eusebio," he continued, "that I should speak to you after class. You will stay behind this afternoon after the others leave. Now, I must remind you all, dear children, that you will make your first confession before you receive Communion. When you confess you will admit to the priest, and through the priest to God, that you are sinners, and you will ask for God's forgiveness. And how have you sinned? By disobeying God's Commandments, the ones that you have been studying. Have you been disrespectful to your elders? Have you disobeyed your father or your mother? And what about the sins that nobody sees: your thoughts? Have they been thoughts of anger?"

Father Mirabal continued, but Blanca Estela no longer listened. Yes, she had been angry—at Nereida for nearly drowning her, at her mother for leaving her, at her grandmother for holding her back, but she could not make herself feel sorry about feeling that way. She was a sinner without repentance. She became uncomfortably aware of Aminta close to her. Why wouldn't the girl move away? She looked down and saw a bead of perspiration running down Aminta's leg and also noticed the white, salty trace, like a snail's trail, that the already dried sweat had left from the girl's knee down to her ankle. Blanca Estela felt a shudder of revulsion pass through her. As she tried to pull away from her neighbor, Blanca Estela realized with something akin to panic that the back of her knees was stuck with dampness from her own perspiration, or perhaps from Aminta's who had sat in that space before her, to the varnished surface of the pew.

It was fortunate that Father Mirabal chose that moment to dismiss them, forgetting, however, to hand out to them the hard candy with which he usually rewarded their attendance at class. Perhaps he was still upset with Eusebio. Blanca Estela jumped to her feet, dropping the parasol, and had to suffer Aminta picking it up and holding it out to her with an expectant smile. She took it promptly, barely remembering to say "thank you," and tried to escape, but the girl would not let her go so easily. She followed her to the exit, where they both made a quick bob of a genuflection, emerging together into the blinding sun. Blanca Estela opened the parasol and found that Aminta moved close to her to share in the shade. It was impossible to push her away, though she would have liked to do so.

The girl was chattering without pause in her thin, sing-songy voice. "I hope that Father Mirabal punishes Eusebio. He's such a nasty boy. He always tries to look at the girls' underpants when the wind blows up their skirts."

Aminta continued telling stories about Eusebio and his friends, but Blanca Estela barely heard her. She was trying to guess when the girl would finally remove herself from under the parasol and go on her way home. Perhaps when they turned the corner past the plaza, but no, Aminta continued, attached to her. She was supposed to live some two blocks up the sidestreet that bordered the doctor's house. She would certainly turn off there, but they passed the doctor's house, shuttered and silent in the late afternoon, and Blanca Estela still could not shake loose of her companion. She realized that Aminta was asking her a question.

"You live with your grandmother, don't you?"

"No," Blanca Estela retorted angrily and then felt ashamed that she was, in some way, denying her grandmother. "I am staying with my grandmother," she tried to clarify, "while my mother is away."

"I live with my grandparents," Aminta volunteered. "My grandmother and I come and stay in town while my grandfather is at the ranch. Sometimes we all stay at the ranch. My mother is dead," she added, matter of factly, "and my father is away... but we don't know where. Do you know where your mother is?"

"Of course," Blanca Estela responded, marveling that this girl could say so many things that made her angry. "I just had a letter from her today," she added, triumphantly.

"Your father is dead, isn't he?" Aminta continued, relentlessly. "That makes you an orphan," she concluded. "I am an orphan, too, since my mother died. I wonder what's worse, for your father or for your mother to die?"

Blanca Estela was horrified at this ghoulish speculation. She was sad when she thought of her father dying, but his was a very dim memory, a less than shadowy presence. Whereas, if she thought that her mother might die, that she might not return, a sense of horror and anguish enveloped her. She wanted to strike out at the awful girl who had voiced the possibility. She realized that they had reached Mamá Anita's house—her own house now—and Aminta showed no signs of departing. She pushed open the door and walked in, pointedly not inviting her to enter, but the girl followed her in, anyway.

She found Mamá Anita in the bedroom, mending some pillowcases. She looked at Blanca Estela and her companion with a question in her eyes, but said nothing and waited for Blanca Estela to speak. Blanca Estela cast about her mind in vain for some way to convey to Mamá Anita that she had not invited the unwelcome guest and finally said feebly, "We just got out of Catechism class. I guess I... I guess we... are going to play for a while."

Mamá Anita did not respond immediately. She finished snapping off a short length of thread with her teeth and then said slowly, "Yes, why don't you return to the patio and play with your jacks? I think you left them there."

Blanca Estela turned around and motioned for Aminta to follow her. They walked into the parlor and crossed the long room towards the patio. On the walls flanking the door between the parlor and the entryway were hanging the heavy, ornately carved wood frames that contained the portraits of the ancestors, as Blanca Estela thought of them collectively. One was the man with the fierce mustache, Mamá Anita's beloved departed husband, Blanca Estela's own grandfather. The other was an elderly couple with a rather severe expression who were Mamá Anita's dead parents and her own great-grandparents. The third and smaller portrait was of a wistful-looking young woman in a white dress who was Mamá Anita's oldest sister, who had died very young,

As they passed the portraits, Aminta paused before them and contemplated the faces, curiously intent. Suddenly she turned to Blanca Estela and asked, almost eagerly, "Is this house haunted?"

Blanca Estela felt a chill go through her, followed by a sense of outrage. "Of course not," she protested. But the strange thing was that when she walked under those portraits, especially at this time of day, when the shadows in the room played on the faces that looked out from the frames, she always hurried and averted her eyes because she could not be sure, in the gloom, that they were not looking at her. She was also secretly relieved that a tall, hinged screen hid her cot from the entrance to the parlor, so that she need not fear that the ancestors were keeping a watch over her while she slept.

"Do you ever hear something like... like the sound of somebody chopping wood, especially in the middle of the night? Or like somebody is dragging chains, or strange sounds between the walls?" Aminta continued, very seriously.

Blanca Estela was shaking her head, vigorously, while inside her a voice was saying, "Well, of course you've heard the sound of chopping wood... when somebody was chopping wood, but in the middle of the night? No. But how did she know that it wasn't so? She was asleep then.

"When you hear those sounds, it means that the house is haunted, usually by someone looking for buried treasure." Aminta pursued her topic relentlessly. "There was once a man who was killed by robbers in his house. The robbers wanted the gold coins that he kept under his bed. Years later another man owned that same house, and he fell asleep with his arm hanging down from the bed, and at midnight the dead man came out from under the bed and pulled the sleeping man down. And in the morning they found the owner of the house, dead, on the floor by the bed, and a gold coin was lying on the floor by him."

Blanca Estela cast about in a panic for something that would stem the tide of horrific tales from Aminta and found herself saying what she had never intended to say: "I have a doll, a beautiful doll, dressed in blue satin. Would you like to see her?"

Aminta stopped her recital in midstream and responded eagerly, "Let me see her. Where is she?"

"In the wardrobe. I... I have to ask my grandmother to take her out."

She ran back to the bedroom and said, breathlessly, "Mamá Anita, please may I have the blue doll, so I can show it to... to her?" She finished nervously, pointing back to the parlor.

Mamá Anita finished folding a pillowcase and walked slowly to the wardrobe, as if giving her time to change her mind. She opened the wardrobe and deliberately unwrapped the tissue that surrounded the doll. She looked intently at Blanca Estela, and Blanca Estela realized that she was asking her silently if she was sure that she wanted to entrust the doll to the other girl. It was impossible for Blanca Estela to explain to her grandmother the desperation that had led her to take this step. She took the doll from her grandmother's hands and carried her gently to where Aminta waited.

The girl's eyes lighted up greedily. "Oh, what a beautiful doll" she exclaimed, reaching out to take it. But Blanca Estela continued to hold on to the doll. "What is her name?"

Blanca Estela rebelled at the thought of giving the girl the satisfaction of knowing that she shared the same name as the beautiful object. Better to violate the Ten Commandments and lie. "She... doesn't have a name... yet."

"Let me baptize her and give her a name," Aminta pleaded, still holding out her hands. "Let me be her godmother."

"No... my mother is going to give her a name, when she comes back," she continued to lie.

"Please, let me hold her for a minute," Aminta wheedled and, in a surprise move, grabbed the doll from Blanca Estela's arms.

A red wave of anger washed over Blanca Estela, and she shouted, trembling with fury, "Give me back my doll," and snatched her from Aminta's hands. She heard a sickening ripping sound and realized in horror that the lovely blue satin dress now gaped open with a tear in the back.

"Go away," Blanca Estela shouted, clutching the doll to her chest. "Go away, you horrible, ugly girl. Go home and leave me alone. I hate you. I hope you... I hope you die."

The moment she had finished uttering these dreadful words, she was horrified at what she had said, but before she could retract her curse, Mamá Anita had hurried into the room. Her glance took in quickly the tears streaming down Blanca Estela's face and from there passed on to Aminta, shrinking back from the fury that she had provoked.

Mamá Anita addressed herself briskly to Aminta, saying, "I think it is time that you went home. Your grandmother must be expecting you for supper."

The girl seemed relieved to be dismissed and melted out and away through the open door. Mamá Anita then turned to Blanca Estela and gently pried the doll from her hands. "Let me see," she said, examining the doll. "It's only the dress that got torn. We can repair this. I will mend it with very fine stitching. You will hardly notice the mend."

"But my mother... my mother," Blanca Estela sobbed loudly now. "What will I tell my mother? It was her doll, her beautiful doll."

Mamá Anita put her arms around Blanca Estela and crooned softly, "Hush, hush child. Your mother will understand. Besides, she is your doll now. Your mother gave her to you, don't you remember? You will help me mend the dress, and we will take very good care of her in the future. What is her name? I have forgotten."

Mamá Anita paused, as if trying to remember, but Blanca Estela would not bring herself to say the name which had such unpleasant associations.

Mamá Anita continued after the pause. "I think that we—that *you*—should give her a name. She is your doll now. But there is no hurry. You will name her when you are ready."

# Chapter VII

*Doña Blanca está encerrada*
*en pilares de oro y plata...*

María Eva and Evita returned bearing gifts from Laredo. They arrived late Sunday afternoon on the daily bus that left Revilla early in the morning and made the return trip by six o'clock in the evening. But Mamá Anita would not allow Blanca Estela to rush across the street to welcome them immediately. First they had to be given the opportunity to unpack, air out the house, which had been shut up for over a week, and get some rest, Mamá Anita explained. The following morning, however, María Eva and Evita came to visit before Mamá Anita had even finished her housework. This was a sign that they were so eager to see their neighbors that they had overlooked the local proprieties, which limited visits to afternoons (after the siesta but before supper) or to evenings, after people had finished eating, as Blanca Estela had learned when she had first arrived in Revilla.

María Eva brought with her a large, brown paper parcel, and Evita a much smaller one, no larger than five or six inches square. Evita opened hers first, saying to Blanca Estela, "Look what I got for you." It was a pair of hairclips, two narrow, gold-colored bars outlined with little pearls. "They're very simple," Evita pointed out, "but simple things are always more elegant. If you decide to cut your hair, you can use them to hold it in place. Right now, you can still wear them, if you let your hair loose, or even if you wear it in braids."

Blanca Estela was slightly taken aback, not being aware that cutting her hair had been under consideration, but she felt very touched that Evita had thought of her while shopping in the city. "Thank you, very much," she said, shyly. "The clips are very pretty."

María Eva and Mamá Anita, in the meantime, had already made their way to the bedroom, and María Eva had begun to unwrap her package on the high, four-poster bed. She spread out on the blue coverlet a length of delicate white silk. "What do you think?" she asked Mamá Anita. "It's very good quality, very fine silk. And here, I also bought some white cotton batiste for the slip underneath, and this narrow lace edging for the collar and the sleeves."

The two women bent over the cloth and fingered it gently. Mamá Anita nodded. "Yes, very good indeed."

"Do you like it?" Evita asked, and it took Blanca Estela a minute to realize that she was being addressed.

"Yes, of course," she finally answered.

"Do you like the style, too?" Evita continued, and Blanca Estela felt completely bewildered.

Mamá Anita turned to answer instead. "Blanca Estela doesn't know anything about it, yet. It was to be a surprise. It's for your First Communion dress, child. Do you like the fabric?"

"Oh, yes, it's so delicate and light," she answered, overwhelmed.

"María Eva is going to help me make the dress for you. The style is very simple, no frills. The fabric and the cut will do it all. María Eva is going to cut the pattern; she is an expert seamstress, not like me. However, I will sew it, with her help."

"*Doña* Anita, you are too modest. You always made Lilia's dresses before she got married, and she had beautiful clothes," María Eva protested.

Mamá Anita took a measuring tape from one of the drawers in the cabinet of the sewing machine that stood by the bedroom window. "Now, child, stand still so we can measure you."

They encircled first her chest and then her waist with the tape while Evita called out the numbers that the two women had difficulty reading. María Eva wrote them down in a little notebook. They also took measurements around her neck and the length of her arms and the distance from the back of her neck to her waist and then to her knees. All this was written down.

María Eva then said, "Well, *Doña* Anita, I am glad that you are pleased with the fabric that I brought you. I thought you would be since it's very good silk. Now let me go home and cut the dress pattern on paper from these measurements. If you like, later we can also cut the pattern on the fabric on the large table that I use for cutting in my shop. I don't know if your dining table will be large enough to work on it. I will let you know when I am done with the paper pattern. We're going now, so you can get on with cooking dinner."

"Again, María Eva, thank you for doing us this favor. Just let me know when to bring the fabric," Mamá Anita replied.

María Eva and Evita then left, and Mamá Anita found a bed sheet to wrap around the length of silk. "This is to protect it from dust," she was saying as she folded the material carefully. Blanca Estela could only nod, overcome by a myriad of emotions that she found difficult to sort out: excitement at the thought of having a new dress, the most beautiful that she had ever had, deep gratitude to her grandmother for going to so much trouble for her, sadness that her mother was not with them to share in all the plans. But, underneath it all, there was a gnawing anxiety at the prospect of the ordeal which she would undergo before wearing her beautiful new dress: her first confession.

The next day, Evita came to tell them that her mother had finished cutting the paper pattern and would they bring the fabric later that afternoon. Blanca Estela relayed the message to Mamá Anita, and at three-thirty in the afternoon the two of them crossed the street to María Eva's workshop. Mamá Anita carefully carried the length of silk, still wrapped in the sheet, to protect it from the sand that collected in little drifts against the high sidewalks and which their footsteps and the hot wind picked up and sent swirling through the air.

Blanca Estela had sometimes looked inside María Eva's workshop through the door and windows, which were kept open all day long, but she had never actually been inside it, deterred by both her shyness and the reluctance to disturb the noisy work that went on there. Now she saw that it was a large room and that four sewing machines were set up, each one in front of a window (two facing the street and the other two the patio), with a very long table in the middle. She later noticed a fifth sewing machine, shrouded in a protective cover, against a far corner of the room. Three young women sat in low-backed chairs, each in front of a sewing machine.

Blanca Estela was amazed at the speed and coordination they demonstrated, pushing the large metal pedal at the bottom of the machine that turned a belt, which turned a large wheel at knee level. The belt passed through the interior of the polished-wood cabinet that housed each machine and emerged above where it turned a smaller wheel. This wheel on the head, or top, of the machine controlled the thread that went through the needle, which moved with piston precision over the cloth.

Blanca Estela noticed that the three young women were embroidering, rather than sewing. They pushed pieces of fabric, stretched tightly in round hoops, back and forth under the needle, creating designs of flowers and fruits in bright-colored threads of every hue: red, purple, yellow, orange and green.

María Eva addressed Mamá Anita, raising her voice to be heard above the whirring of the machines, "We're back to embroidering. Right now I'm the only one sewing. I have to make several dresses for Perla. Did you know that she will be moving to Monterrey to study nursing?"

"Where will she live?" Mamá Anita asked.

"She will live with her aunt, her father's sister. She needed some new clothes, not many because I imagine she will wear a uniform most of the time. Until the next wedding or dance comes along, there will not be much call for new clothes, so the girls are embroidering again: pillowcases, napkins and things like that for the buyers in the big cities."

Mamá Anita responded, also raising her voice to compete, not only with the whirring of the machines, but now also with the conversation of two of the girls and with the singing of the third one. "I wish you would let me pay you for your work, María Eva, and for all the trouble I'm giving you."

"Nonsense, *Doña* Anita, it is no trouble at all, and, besides, like I told you, I have nothing urgent right now. You see, even Panchita," María Eva here motioned with her head towards the singing worker, "who usually helps me with sewing is now embroidering linens. I hope that I will soon be getting an order for blouses from Guadalajara. Those we cut and sew and also embellish with a little embroidery, and the profit is somewhat better. Now, let me show you the pattern."

They moved towards the cutting table while the three girls, in unison, broke out in a song which Blanca Estela had often heard them sing in the long afternoons when she lay drowsily on her cot in front of the window. It was called *"Dos arbolitos,"* according to Evita, and it was about two trees that grow side by side, providing each other company, and the singer envies them because they have each other while he is alone.

Blanca Estela followed her grandmother, peering around her as the two women spread the length of silk on the table surface. María Eva then placed some pieces of brown paper, cut in different shapes, over the cloth, trying first one arrangement and then another until all the parts fit on the material.

It was like the pieces of a puzzle, Blanca Estela decided.

María Eva seemed to notice that she was there and sensed that she was curious, but feeling a little superfluous and said, "Blanca Estela, Evita was just finishing having her bath. She will be out here in a minute and play with you."

And, indeed, Evita appeared almost simultaneously, her short curls still wet, wearing a dress of blue and white gingham checks and smelling of soap and scented powder. She had what looked like a coloring book in her hand, but she shook her head when Blanca Estela asked her if that was what it was. It turned out to be, instead, a book of paper clothes for the cardboard dolls, which Evita also produced, along with a pair of scissors.

They settled themselves on the floor, but before doing so, Evita also brought out a large shopping bag stuffed with pieces of cloth of all colors and textures, leftovers from her mother's sewing.

"Instead of just cutting out the paper patterns and pinning them on the dolls, which isn't very interesting, we'll use the paper clothes as patterns to cut clothes for the dolls out of these cloth remnants," Evita explained.

They occupied themselves in this manner for some time while Mamá Anita and María Eva worked at the cutting table. When they had cut several patterns, Evita got up and, after some rummaging in the drawers of the idle sewing machine, came back with two needles and a spool of thread and showed Blanca Estela how they should sew the doll's dresses by hand.

"Why can't we use the sewing machine?" Blanca Estela wanted to know.

"I'm not allowed to sew on a machine yet. If you don't know how to use it, you can run a needle through your finger. It happened once to a girl who worked here before," Evita replied.

At that moment, Blanca Estela pricked her finger with the needle, which she wielded awkwardly as she tried to stitch together two pieces of dark blue velvet. She gave a little cry of pain and said, resentfully, "Look what happened. I just got the needle in my finger, anyway."

"Yes, but you don't have the needle sticking right through your finger. That was just a little prick, and it happened because you're not using a thimble. Here, put this little bit of cloth over it, so you don't drip blood on the rest of the fabric," Evita said, very matter-of-factly and, in Blanca Estela's opinion, quite unsympathetically.

After this mishap, she did not feel like sewing anymore and was glad when Mamá Anita announced a short time later that they were finished cutting the dress according to the pattern, and that they were going home. Mamá Anita then gathered the different pieces of silk, wrapping them inside the sheet, and they made ready to leave at the same time that the sewing girls covered up their machines in preparation for going home to supper.

Late Thursday, Mario and Mimi came home from their trip with Nereida. Blanca Estela expected that they would be eager to relate all the details of their journey, but when Mario came to fetch water from the cistern the following day, he limited himself to a brief description of the mountains they had seen, especially the Saddle Mountain in Monterrey, and to telling her that they had gone for a promenade around the Alameda in Saltillo, which, he explained, was a very large park with a lake in the middle. Mimi said even less, confining herself to answering Mamá Anita's questions, saying yes, they had enjoyed the trip; everything had been very pretty, but it was cold in Saltillo at night.

Blanca Estela had also expected that now that they were all back they would, again, play games in the evening. Mario pointed out then that Pedro was still away, helping his uncle to pick crops at the ranch, and Blanca Estela was ashamed to realize that she had not noticed his absence. Which crops, she had asked, embarrassed at her ignorance. They had just picked the watermelons, Mario explained, and now they were getting ready for the corn. Cotton was also coming up very soon, Mario added, and they—he and Mimi and other kids on vacation— would be going out every morning to pick cotton for a man who had a plantation on the outskirts of town. Who else was going, she wanted to know. Was Evita going, too? She might, Mario answered. Evita liked to earn spending money, just like they did. They got paid for picking cotton? Well, of course, he replied, a little scornfully. That was the reason they did it.

Blanca Estela pondered for a few moments, digesting Mario's information, and then asked, "Can I go with you when you go to pick cotton? I would like to earn money, too."

"Maybe," Mario said, not very encouragingly, "but you wouldn't earn very much, not at first, anyway, because you get paid by the sack, and you don't know how to do it."

She was stung by his assumption that she would not be very useful in the cotton fields and pretended to lose interest in the matter, saying, "I don't know if my grandmother would let me go. She needs me to help her sew my First Communion dress. You're going to have to catch up in Catechism class," she added, a little spitefully, "if you want to make your First Communion. You missed class last week."

"I'll be there tomorrow," Mario answered, unconcerned.

And, indeed, he was, together with Blanca Estela. In class, Father Mirabal explained again the significance of confession and the importance of repentance to achieve forgiveness. Blanca Estela was invaded again by a feeling of embarrassment, remembering her angry outburst at Aminta the Saturday before, but she questioned whether she was truly repentant for it.

She had wondered, on her way to church, what she should say or do when she faced the girl in class, but, on arriving in church, she discovered, to her relief, that Aminta was absent, and the problem was postponed. Perhaps, when she confessed her sins, she could ask Father Mirabal if she needed to apologize to Aminta. This solution struck fear in her immediately, though. What if Father Mirabal did tell her that she must ask forgiveness from the girl? She could not do that. The thought of speaking to Aminta still filled her with loathing; she disliked her so.

But wasn't this dislike a sin? The Ten Commandments said you had to love your neighbor, but even if

Aminta qualified as a neighbor (Father Mirabal had explained that your neighbor didn't have to live close to you, that all people, including those in China, were your neighbors), the Ten Commandments didn't say anything about *liking* your neighbor.

Father Mirabal also explained on this occasion about the miracle that happened before Communion, during the Consecration, when the host and the wine turned into the body and blood of Christ. She frankly did not understand how this happened, but she assumed that the miracle took place when everybody had bowed their heads and closed their eyes. The altar boy rang the bell just before Father Mirabal raised the host during Consecration, and the congregation bowed their heads and looked down or closed their eyes at this point. The reason for not looking at the altar at that moment must be so that the miracle could happen in secret. As for the wine being turned to blood—well, all she could think of was that she was glad that she was not expected to drink from the chalice. That was something only the priest did, and whether he drank wine or blood was something that only he knew.

Sunday Mass was moved back an hour as the summer heat gathered strength with the approach of the dog days of mid-July to late August. Since daybreak now came before six o'clock, Mass was at seven, which enabled the parishioners to walk to and from church while it was still relatively cool. It also made it easier for those receiving Communion to remain fasting until after Mass without risk of fainting from weakness, since they could still eat breakfast before nine o'clock. Mamá Anita planned to receive Communion on this particular Sunday, so she gave Blanca Estela bread and milk to tide her over until they returned from church while she, her-self, made do with a few sips of chamomile tea. Blanca Estela wanted to fast, also, even if she wasn't taking Communion, just to see if she could go with-out food until after Mass, to start training for her First Communion, as it were, but Mamá Anita would not hear of it, saying that bread and milk was already a very light breakfast, almost a fast.

Blanca Estela tried to concentrate on following all the parts of the Mass, as befitted one who would very soon be a full participant in the rites of the Church, but she still found herself looking around her to see who was there, rather than watching the altar. María Eva and Evita were present, as were Mimi and Mario, with Nereida, the three of them looking very sleepy, no doubt from having stayed up late the night before, helping their brother run the movie projector. They got to see so many movies that way while she, herself, had not watched a movie since she had been in Revilla. Perhaps Mamá Anita would let her go to the movies the next time they showed one. Since Mamá Anita did not go to the movies, neither did Blanca Estela, but Evita did, so her mother must take her. Perhaps she could go with them. Mamá Anita did not like for her to stay up late at night, though, and movies in Revilla were shown only on Saturday nights, and not every week. She would have to figure out a way to go to the movies.

Her gaze continued to sweep over the congrega-tion after a quick look at the altar, where she noticed an unfamiliar boy helping Father Mirabal. Pedro must still be at his father's or his uncle's ranch, picking crops. There was Doctor Marín, sitting next to Rosalía, and to her sister, Perla. Blanca Estela wondered if Rosalía missed Jaime and Sandra, who were now back in Mexico City with their parents. Doctor Marín looked tired, as if he, too, had stayed up late the night before, and Rosalía looked sad, a little bit like the Madonna at the foot of the crucified Christ. Blanca Estela remembered Mamá Anita saying that Rosalía wished that she had her own children. If Blanca Estela had not had her own lovely mother already, she would have chosen Rosalía for her Mamá. Suddenly, Blanca Estela knew that she would like to have Rosalía be her godmother for her First Communion. She would ask Mamá Anita if they could approach Rosalía to ask her for this favor; perhaps they could ask her after Mass.

When it was time for Communion, and Mamá Anita and Rosalía and many of the women present got up to go to the altar to receive the host from Father Mirabal, Blanca Estela took the opportunity to look behind her and confirmed that neither Aminta nor her grandmother were in church. She felt relieved, as on the day before, but also a little puzzled. Why would the girl miss Catechism class and Mass when it was so close to the time for their First Communion?

After Father Mirabal had given them the final blessing and told them to go home, Mamá Anita remained kneeling a few minutes more, praying silently. Blanca Estela waited until Mamá Anita had crossed herself and they were walking out before whispering to her that she wanted to ask Rosalía to be her godmother.

Mamá Anita thought for a moment and then nodded. "We'll ask her now, if they are still outside," she said. "We can't wait any longer; the day is so close, already."

Doctor Marín and Rosalía were just saying goodbye to Perla, who was going on ahead of them, when Mamá Anita caught up with them. After wishing them a good morning, Mamá Anita addressed Rosalía. "I know that there is not much time before the children make their First Communion, Rosalía, but Blanca Estela just told me that she wants you to be her Communion godmother. I know that Lilia would be very pleased if you agreed to do it, and I will too. We had left it to the child to choose her godmother, and she wants you to be it. Of course, she did not realize that you have to ask with plenty of time. I should have reminded her to ask you earlier, but I have been worried about Lilia since she left."

"Oh, don't worry, *Doña* Anita," Rosalía exclaimed, and, smiling sweetly at Blanca Estela, told her, "Of course I will be very happy to be your godmother. Do you have your dress already?"

"I am sewing it," Mamá Anita answered. "María Eva cut it for me from some silk that she brought back from Laredo."

"And the veil for the head?"

"One of María Eva's girls will make the headdress from Lilia's wedding veil. Lilia told me that she wanted it done that way."

"How is Lilia?" Rosalía asked. "My brother, Leopoldo, said that he had heard that she was in San Antonio."

"That's right, she is there, and she is well. I just wish that she was still here."

"That's natural. I will be so happy to be her daughter's godmother; it will be a bond between us." Rosalía turned to Blanca Estela and said to her, "I will give you your prayer book."

At this point Doctor Marín, who had been speaking to Father Mirabal, interrupted his wife's conversation to ask, "Rosalía, will you walk home? I am going ahead in the car to see that child. She is no better this morning."

Rosalía's face clouded over with a sad expression, and Mamá Anita asked quickly, "Who is sick, Doctor?"

"*Doña* Petra's granddaughter, the little girl, Aminta."

Blanca Estela thought her heart had suddenly stopped, and she heard the rest of the doctor's words as if they came from far away.

"They took her to the ranch last week," he continued. "There they get their drinking water from the ponds where the cattle drink, too. We haven't had enough rain in some time now. The water in the ponds is stagnant, contaminated, and they didn't boil it. The grown-ups are probably immune by now to all the germs in that water, but the poor child developed a bad stomach infection. And then they waited to bring her to town until yesterday. She was almost dehydrated by then. Now I am going to their house to see her again. I'm afraid that she is so weak that she may not have much resistance in her."

Blanca Estela looked at her grandmother, trying to divine from her expression whether Mamá Anita knew, as she herself knew that Aminta was sick because she had cursed her when she had said, "I hate you, and I hope you die." What would Doctor Marín do if he knew the real cause of Aminta's illness? Should she tell him? But he was already hurrying away, and Mamá Anita and Rosalía were now also walking home, talking about Aminta's grandparents and other people that she did not know.

While Mamá Anita cooked dinner, she sent Blanca Estela to buy corn *tortillas*, which she had not had time to make at home because of going to Mass and eating breakfast late. Blanca Estela met Mario sitting outside his house, mending a large burlap sack with a long needle. She asked him what the sack was for, and he explained that it was used for putting the cotton bolls inside it when he went picking cotton.

"We're starting tomorrow," he added. "By six o'clock the big truck will come to get us, and we'll come back in the late afternoon. They keep track of how many sacks we fill, and they pay us by the sack."

"Is Mimi going, too?"

He nodded.

"And Evita?"

"I don't know. She might. Last year she went a few times, but she didn't like it much. Do you want to go?"

She did not answer at once, and Mario added, "I can show you how to do it."

"All right," she answered, doubtfully, "but... when?"

"After dinner. While your grandmother is taking a nap, I will come and show you how to fill the sack with cotton. We'll be quiet, so we won't disturb her."

She agreed, feeling as if they were both accomplices in an activity that must be kept from her grandmother.

Mamá Anita was quiet during dinner, her forehead furrowed, as if she were thinking of something that worried her. Blanca Estela was relieved at not having to make conversation, since her own thoughts weighed heavily on her: should she seek out Doctor Marín and tell him what was the real cause of Aminta's illness? It was her curse, of course, and not the germs in the water. And what about Father Mirabal? What punishment would he give her when she made her confession to him? Perhaps he would not let her go through with her First Communion, and she would have to tell Rosalía that she would not be her godmother, after all.

She was glad that Mario was coming after dinner, during the time for the siesta. She might tell him then about her predicament. On the other hand, it would probably be better to say nothing. He would, at least, distract her with his lesson on picking cotton.

She helped Mamá Anita to wash the dishes and clean the kitchen after dinner, and they both lay down for naps, each on a canvas cot. She lay very still and waited until she heard Mamá Anita's soft snoring before getting up quietly and tiptoeing to open the front door softly. She sat down on the steps from the entryway to the patio to wait for Mario.

He arrived in a short time, also taking care to not make any noise. He sat next to her and held the burlap sack open at his side.

"See," he said, whispering, "you tie the sack with this rope around your waist, and you reach down for the cotton boll to pull it out whole and put it in the sack. After a while you get tired of bending down, especially at first, but you can stop to rest a little and drink water. Oh, and remember to wear a hat to protect yourself from the sun."

"Do we come home for dinner at noon?" Blanca Estela asked.

"No, of course not. You have to take food with you, but don't worry. I can take enough for both of us. Just bring a water bottle. Did you already ask your grandmother for permission?"

She shook her head, and at that moment they heard Mamá Anita's cot squeaking, followed by the sound of her clearing her throat. Mario stood up and quickly let himself out through the door. Mamá Anita called out, "Blanca Estela, where are you?"

She ran inside where she found her grandmother sitting on the edge of the cot. Mamá Anita was rubbing her eyes and her forehead. Her gray hair, which was always pulled back in a neat bun or, at night, plaited in the back, was falling around her face. Blanca Estela was shocked to notice that her grandmother looked old, not old as she had seemed when she first saw her, the day of their arrival in Revilla, but older than she had appeared earlier that morning. Anxiety grasped her. What if something were to happen to Mamá Anita? What would happen, then, to her? Her mother was far away. She would be left alone.

"Was there somebody out there with you?" Mamá Anita asked.

"Yes, Mario was here," she was glad to answer truthfully.

"What did he want?" This was more difficult to answer.

"We were just talking... He showed me the burlap sack where he will put the cotton bolls when he goes out to the fields." She made herself tell her grandmother all this, but still stopped before adding that she, too, wanted to go with the harvesters.

"I hope those children don't get sick out in the sun in this heat," Mamá Anita said in a tired voice, unlike her usual brisk tone. Blanca Estela decided to put off asking for permission to go out with Mario and the other cotton pickers.

In the morning, shortly after sunrise, she was awakened by the rumbling and the groaning of a truck passing in front of the house. She jumped out of bed and looked out the window and saw Mario and Mimi and other older boys and girls standing on the bed of the truck, holding on to the high wooden railings around it. They did not see her looking after them, and she concluded that Mario had realized that she would not be going with them that day. She could already hear Mamá Anita cooking breakfast in the kitchen and went to join her there.

Mamá Anita turned to greet her saying, to Blanca Estela's surprise, "Good morning, my love."

This sounded so much like Lilia that Blanca Estela felt a knot in her throat from longing for her mother. Mamá Anita was usually not so openly affectionate, although the warmth and the love were still there, underneath. Mamá Anita seemed to realize that she had acted unlike her usual self and added, briskly, "When you have gone to the privy, wash your hands well and fetch some water from the *aljibe*. Remember to be very careful and don't get too close to the opening."

Blanca Estela nodded and went to do as she had been told.

Soon after breakfast María Eva came in, looking very somber, and said without preamble, "That poor child, *Doña* Petra's granddaughter... Doctor Marín could not save her. She was already too sick when they brought her to town."

Mamá Anita gave a little gasp, "Is she...?"

María Eva nodded.

Blanca Estela looked from one to the other, her heart pounding and her eyes frozen, seeing again the ungainly and unlikeable girl clutching at the beautiful blue doll. The doll in the song had died after someone took her to the plaza. Was Aminta dead, too? Why didn't María Eva or Mamá Anita say the words, so she would know for sure?

Instead, Mamá Anita turned to María Eva, staring very hard at her, and asked, "Is Evita at home? I think that Blanca Estela should go play with her."

"Yes," María Eva agreed. "Evita is making clothes for those dolls she got in Laredo. Why don't you go help her, Blanca Estela?"

She wanted to hear more about Aminta, but she was also relieved to be able to escape from the cloud of gloom that seemed to have descended on the house with María Eva's arrival. Blanca Estela ran out of the house and across the street. In María Eva's workshop she found the sewing girls bent over their sewing machines, their songs silent this morning.

Evita was leaning over the cutting table, standing on a footstool, pinning paper patterns on cloth scraps that appeared to have been left over from Perla's bright blue ball gown. She looked up briefly when Blanca Estela walked in, but then returned to frowning as she tried to make the pattern pieces fit on the scraps of cloth.

Blanca Estela suddenly felt awkward and murmured, "Your mother said to come and help you."

Evita looked up again and nodded. "Yes, she went to tell your grandmother that Aminta died last night. She was in your Catechism class, wasn't she? Last year, too, and at the last minute they took her to the ranch, and she didn't make her First Communion then, either. This time she had her Communion dress already made, so they will bury her in that."

This was too much for Blanca Estela. She choked back a sob and ran out of the workshop and back across the street. Outside her door she paused, longing for Mario and Mimi, wishing that they had not gone picking cotton, so she could hear their conversation about movies and motors and, doing so, forget the awful news about Aminta's death.

She could not think of any place to go where she could escape her grim thoughts, so she slipped back into the house and sat down on the steps from the entryway to the patio. From this spot she could hear María Eva and Mamá Anita's voices drifting out of the kitchen in unintelligible murmurs which were pierced suddenly by isolated words like knives: "coffin," "burial," "mourning."

"I will see to it about ordering two wreaths," María Eva's voice suddenly said clearly, directly behind her.

Blanca Estela turned around and saw that María Eva was saying this to Mamá Anita as she let herself out the door. Mamá Anita, following behind, found Blanca Estela still sitting on the steps. She did not seem surprised to see her there, as if she had forgotten that she had sent her out of the house.

"Come, child," Mamá Anita said in an attempt at her usual bustling manner. "We're already late with our housework this morning. You must clean the beans and, afterwards, I need you to go to Chabela's and buy some tomatoes and onions."

The morning passed this way with the usual housecleaning of sweeping and dusting and preparing the main meal. After dinner, which was a very tasty stew of meat and squash with tomatoes and onions—one of Blanca Estela's favorite dishes, but which this day she barely noticed—they lay down for their naps. Blanca Estela was sleepy because she had awakened earlier than usual that morning, but she could not go to sleep. She lay on her cot with her eyes closed, seeing the sallow face of Aminta with her mouth slightly open, her beady eyes gloating over the doll in blue. She tried to imagine Aminta in repose, eyes shut, clothed in her Communion dress. A shudder of fear ran through her, but she forced herself to continue thinking of Aminta, dead, buried in her Communion dress. This terror was a way of doing penance, of atoning for the sin of having wished her dead.

Blanca Estela herself would get to wear a beautiful silk dress that only lacked a row of pearl buttons to be sewn to it and the lace edging around the collar. But perhaps she would not get to wear this dress, after all. If Father Mirabal denied her forgiveness when she went to confession, she would not receive Communion and would never get to wear the dress. People would find out why she had been denied Communion, even if Father Mirabal never told a soul and kept the secret like priests were supposed to do. It would be better for her if she never tried to make her First Communion. She could go away—but where? She could leave early tomorrow morning with the cotton pickers and not return home. That was it. That was the solution. She felt herself relax and was soon asleep.

The cotton pickers returned home as the sun was going down. She heard the truck stop next door, and she ran outside in time to see Mimi and Mario slip down from the truck bed, which was now piled high with woolly cotton balls that clung to the children's clothing and drifted out from under the tarp to be carried like plump snowflakes in the wind. The two were flushed and grimy, and Mario was more subdued than she had seen him before. She told him that she would join them to go picking cotton on the following morning.

Mario nodded faintly and said in a tired voice, "You must be ready when the truck comes; it will not wait."

"How early should I get up?" Blanca Estela asked him.

"You have to get up before the Morning Star sets," he answered.

"The Morning Star?"

"Yes, the bright star that you see in the sky before the sun rises. Haven't you ever seen the Morning Star?"

She hung her head to hide her shame at her stupidity, but, fortunately, Mario seemed not to notice and merely said that he was going home to wash up and eat.

She had heard somewhere that if you concentrated hard enough, you could make yourself wake up at a particular time without an alarm clock. Mamá Anita did not have an alarm clock, only the pendulum clock on the parlor table that chimed the hours and struck once on the half hour. Even if she had had an alarm clock, setting it would have been impractical because it would have awakened Mamá Anita, as well as Blanca Estela, since they both slept in the same room.

Blanca Estela told herself as she lay in her cot in the dark to wake up before the Morning Star set. The problem was, at what time did that happen? She had trouble going to sleep, partly, no doubt, because she had had a long nap that afternoon, but also because she kept remembering the story that Aminta had told her about the dead man under the bed who had pulled the sleeper down. She was afraid to let her arm hang down over the side of the cot, fearing that Aminta would be waiting to pull her down and drag her away with her to her grave. Before Mamá Anita had put out the light, Blanca Estela made sure that the space under the cot was empty, but Aminta would have only returned in the dark, anyway.

Sleep finally overcame her, but she slept restlessly, dreaming that Aminta was pursuing her and that she kept running from her, saying, "If I can reach the Morning Star I will be safe." Blanca Estela woke up suddenly and jumped out of bed and ran groggily to look out the window. The sky was a whitish gray, and the stars grew paler by the moment. She did not know where to find the Morning Star. Mario had said that it set when the sun rose, so it must be in the east. She ran out to the patio and scanned the sky in the direction from where the sun rose. The horizon there was a faint pink, and the stars had already dimmed their light, except for one point of brightness which faded away, even as she gazed at it.

A cry of dismay escaped from her, and, as she turned away, she saw Mamá Anita standing on the patio steps in her night clothes, looking at her with consternation. "What is it, child? Why are you up so early? Are you feeling sick, Blanca Estela?"

She shook her head. "No," she said, forlornly, "I was looking for the Morning Star. Mario told me to look for it. I had never seen it before, and I missed it."

She kept listening for the sound of the truck that would pick up Mario and Mimi while she helped Mamá Anita to prepare breakfast, and later as they ate, but it never came. She had tried to think of a way to get the message to Mario that she would not be going with them, after all, without alerting Mamá Anita to what she had been planning to do, but no opportunity presented itself. Finally, she concluded that the truck had come when she had been in the privy and that it had left with her friends, who must now be disgusted with her for failing to keep her appointment with them once again.

After breakfast, but while they were still at the table, Mamá Anita said, "We are going to put off doing any housework until we finish your Communion dress. All it needs is sewing on the buttons. Remember those twelve buttons that you found for me? They are going down the back of your dress. They have to be sewn on by hand. Come and help me. You can hand them to me as I sew."

Blanca Estela shook her head. Something inside her chest could no longer be contained, and, putting her head down on the table in front of her, she broke out in sobs.

"What is it, child? Blanca Estela, what is the matter?" Mamá Anita cried out, alarmed. "Are you sick? Is it your stomach? Does your head hurt?"

She could not speak. She could not stop sobbing. At last she was able to shake her head, and her grandmother, understanding that it was not physical pain that brought the tears, put her arms around her and made cooing sounds until Blanca Estela calmed down.

"Now, tell me, what makes you cry?" Mamá Anita coaxed, sitting down next to her. "Is it... is it your mother? Do you miss her very much?"

Blanca Estela nodded, taking in a big gulp of air that sent a shudder through her body, and finally said, "Yes, I miss my mother, but it isn't that. I... I... I can't make my First Communion."

"Why not, child? Don't you want to?"

"Oh yes, I want to very much, but I can't. I will have to go to confession and tell Father Mirabal what I did, and he won't let me receive Communion."

Mamá Anita seemed completely nonplussed. "What could you have done, child? Tell me about it."

Blanca Estela swallowed hard and, taking a deep breath, she blurted out her confession. "I cursed Aminta. I told her that I hated her and that I wished she would die. And now she's dead, and I never asked her for forgiveness. It's too late now."

Mamá Anita shook her head and seemed about to smile but checked herself. "Bless you, child. Is that what has been troubling you? You did not cause that poor girl to die. It was an infection that she got from drinking bad water. Doctor Marín said so, don't you remember? But if you are sorry that you were angry at her... was it about the doll?"

Blanca Estela nodded and then decided to confess all. "I just didn't like her, and then she told me scary stories and wanted to keep my doll... my mother's doll..." She threatened to break out in sobs again.

Mamá Anita hastened to reassure her. "It's all right. We don't always like everybody. And, if you were angry with her... you are sorry about it now? You wish you hadn't said those things?"

Blanca Estela nodded again.

Mamá Anita continued, "Well, that's all it takes to be forgiven. You tell Father Mirabal that you are sorry, and he will give you absolution. You would not have said those things again if she were alive, would you?"

Blanca Estela shook her head, a little doubtfully this time, and asked something else that had been bothering her, "Will she become an angel?"

"Who?"

"Aminta. Didn't somebody say that when children die they become angels? Will she be a guardian angel?"

"Why do you ask?"

How to explain to Mamá Anita that she was concerned that Aminta might end up being assigned to be a guardian angel to her, Blanca Estela. Even as a guardian angel, she didn't think that Aminta could ever be very good company. How could she tolerate her by her side, night and day?

Mamá Anita responded slowly, as if she were giving the matter great consideration. "I think guardian angels are... older... than Aminta was. And now, we must finish your dress soon because we still have the housework to do afterwards."

They sewed the buttons on the dress, and then Blanca Estela tried it on. It was so light and pretty that wearing it Blanca Estela felt that she was enveloped in a cloud. She took it off carefully, and then they hung it up in the wardrobe to await the following Sunday, which would be her First Communion day.

They did the housework and cooked and ate their meals almost in silence, exhausted from the early morning storm. As the sun went down, she waited for the cotton truck to return Mario and Mimi home, so she could apologize for having left them waiting, but, again, she never heard it. At dusk, Mamá Anita showed her a long, white nightgown that she had made for her.

"I had some cotton batiste left over from the slip for your dress, and I made this nightdress. Put it on, even if you are not ready to go to bed. It will be cooler than what you're wearing."

She did as Mamá Anita said and looked at herself in the mirror, waving her arms at her sides and attempting a little pirouette, as if she were dancing.

It was then that she heard the voices out in the street. She ran to the window and looked out, pressing her forehead against the iron bars that still retained the warmth of the sun which had touched them earlier. Out in the street, in the thickening light, she could see Mimi, Mario, Evita and Pedro. None of them looked hot and tired, as they would be if they had just come back from the cotton fields.

"Did you just return from the harvest?" she called out, puzzled.

Mario turned around to reply. "We didn't go. Mother said it was too hot to be out in the fields. We spent the day helping my brother oil the turbine. That was in the shade, though."

"I hardly ever go pick cotton," Evita volunteered. "Look, Pedro came back from the ranch. He was with his uncle. They brought back some watermelons."

"Why don't you come out to play? We're trying to decide on a game," Mario told her.

Blanca Estela turned to her grandmother. "May I go out to play?"

Mamá Anita nodded, smiling.

"But," Blanca Estela paused on her way out, "I need to change again," she said, looking at her long white dress, regretfully.

Mamá Anita chuckled softly. "No, it's already dark. Nobody will remark on what you are wearing. Go on, child."

Outside, a crescent moon hung crookedly on the darkening sky. Blanca Estela's white gown stood out against the shadows of the houses and the dark sand underneath their feet. Mario, looking at her, said to the others, "Why don't we play *Doña Blanca*? We haven't played that game in a long time."

Blanca Estela remembered the children singing about *Doña Blanca*, the lady who was encircled by pillars of gold and silver, from her first night in Revilla.

"I don't think we have enough people to play *Doña Blanca*," Evita pointed out. "We need somebody to be *Doña Blanca* and stand in the middle. Then we need several people to encircle her and somebody to stand outside the circle to try to break in. We need at least six people, and there's only five of us."

"Why don't we get Nereida to play, too?" Mimi suggested.

Mario ran to the door of his house where Nereida, who no matter what she wore always seemed to shimmer in the moonlight, stood outlined against the light of the room behind her. He tugged at her hand and pulled her towards the group in the middle of the street.

"We're going to play *Doña Blanca*," he told her, "and we need to have you stand outside the circle to break in. Don't push too hard, though. Remember, you're much bigger, and it isn't fair."

Evita seemed ready to take her place in the middle of the circle when Mario said, "Blanca Estela will be *Doña Blanca*. She has the same name, after all, and she's dressed in white."

Evita appeared ready to protest, but then she gave way, saying generously, "That's right, it's her turn now. She has never been *Doña Blanca*."

Blanca Estela found herself as in a dream in the moonlight, surrounded by her friends who sang that they would break down a pillar to see *Doña Blanca*. *Doña Blanca* was the favored personage. She was at the center of the game, surrounded by pillars of gold and silver. Blanca Estela, like *Doña Blanca*, felt safe and loved inside the circle of friends. Unlike her first night in Revilla, tonight she felt that she was home.

# Chapter VIII

*Naranja dulce, limón partido, dame un abrazo*
*que yo te pido.*
*Si fueran falsos mis juramentos, en otros tiempos*
*se olvidarán.*

"Don't move, just stand like that for a minute." Doctor Marín peered through the lens of his camera for what seemed to Blanca Estela like a very long time, during which she tried to hold a smile while Mario, standing next to her, continued to look calmly into the camera. They were posing for their First Communion pictures, and they both looked quite magnificent. Mario wore a short-sleeved white shirt and long white trousers, both impeccably starched, and held before him, for the photo, the white Communion candle. Blanca Estela, for her part, looked as pretty as she felt in her white silk dress with the long row of pearl buttons in the back. On her head she wore a white lace veil that floated around her like a cloud, anchored by a headband which was also covered in white silk and embroidered with tiny pearls. Panchita, María Eva's best embroiderer, had fashioned the headdress, embroidering the band and attaching the veil to it, which was particularly precious to Blanca Estela because it had been cut from Lilia's wedding veil. Even her feet were well shod in brand new white shoes, which had been bought with money sent by her uncle, Raúl, as his First Communion gift to her. What princess could be better outfitted than this? Posing for the photograph, Blanca Estela held in one hand the Communion candle, like Mario's, while in the other she displayed a dainty prayer book covered in mother of pearl, the gift from her godmother, Rosalía. Blanca Estela wanted Doctor Marín's camera to capture every important detail of their First Communion regalia, although she realized that Mario's gift from his godfather, Doctor Marín, was probably too heavy to hold in one hand (it was a book with colored illustrations depicting the lives of the Apostles), and that must be why Mario had left it on the parlor table. To complete the cycle of photographs, Doctor Marín asked his brother-in-law, Leopoldo, to hold the camera while he, Doctor Marín, and Rosalía posed with their godchildren, Mario and Blanca Estela.

When they were finished recording the event, they went into the dining room for the Communion breakfast, which Doctor Marín and Rosalía were giving. There were several people already there waiting for them to arrive, so they could sit down to eat. Father Mirabal had been invited, of course, and there was Mamá Anita, as well. Mario's mother, Delia, was there, too, although it had been uncertain whether she would accompany them because she had had a migraine the day before and was still looking weak. Nereida and Mimi were there, too, as was Pedro, who had assisted Father Mirabal at Mass. María Eva and Evita had also been asked and were there, as was Perla who, as usual, was helping Rosalía attend to the guests. Leopoldo came in last, still holding the camera.

The large dining table was covered with a long white tablecloth on which rested platters of little pastries: fruit-filled *empanadas* and shortbread cookies, like those made for weddings. A round, silver tray was also piled high with tamales, and a large, porcelain pitcher, decorated with blue flowers, held steaming, hot chocolate. A silver pot at the other end of the table held coffee. Blanca Estela gazed at the laden table and was surprised to note that she was not as ravenously hungry as she had expected to be after fasting for Communion. Perhaps it was all the excitement that had made her forget her hunger.

Doctor Marín came up to her and, putting a hand on her shoulder, said softly, "When the photographs are developed, we'll save some prints to show your mother how pretty you look today."

Blanca Estela felt a knot at her throat and quickly looked down, so no one would see the sudden tears that trembled on her eyelashes. She nodded, not trusting herself to thank this kind, gentle man who had divined her feelings. How she longed for her mother to be with her now. Instead, she would write to Lilia and tell her about the flowers and the candles on the altar in church, about walking up the aisle to the altar, side by side with Mario, to receive the host. It had been only the two of them because the three rowdy boys had not shown up, after all, for some reason, and Aminta... well, better not to think about her.

The day before receiving Communion, they had also made their first confession. Father Mirabal had sat in a little chair inside the confessional, which looked like a large wardrobe. To each side of Father

Mirabal were purple curtains that shielded the prie-
dieu where you knelt to confess. She had had a
moment of panic when she had stepped inside the
little recess, which was suffocatingly hot and
smelled of the dust that clung to the curtains. She
feared that she was going to faint, even more so
when she heard Father Mirabal's voice behind the
little mesh-covered screen, asking her if she wanted
to confess. She could not remember the words that
she was supposed to say. Father Mirabal had cleared
his throat and prompted her, "My child, what do
you want to confess?"

Then she remembered to cross herself and say,
"Bless me Father, for I have sinned."

Beforehand she had made an inventory of her
transgressions, debating with herself as to their fre-
quency and degree. Had she been disrespectful to
her mother or her grandmother? She couldn't really
remember having been particularly bad in this area,
but it was probably safe to say that, at some time or
another, she had talked back, or argued with them.
What about lying? She had not exactly lied to
Mamá Anita about planning to go picking cotton;
she had just not told her the complete truth. Better
put that in, so she could be forgiven for doing whatever wrong that had been. What about being angry?
Which commandment did that go under? Probably
the one about loving your neighbor as yourself.
That's where Aminta came in.

Once she was in the confessional, however, she
had forgotten her inventory and began pouring out
to Father Mirabal the story of the quarrel with
Aminta and then, somehow, that led to realizing that
she had also been angry with her mother for going

away and with her grandmother for holding her back when she had wanted to run after the car that was taking away her mother.

Father Mirabal had listened without interruption until she had exhausted herself and then asked, "But you repent, my child, for having been angry with your mother and grandmother and with your friend?"

She had answered, "Oh yes, Father," without even pausing to realize that, in this manner, she had admitted that Aminta had been her friend. Then Father Mirabal had told her that she was forgiven, but that she had to do penance by saying one "Our Father" and one "Hail Mary" before going home. She had done so, willingly, and then gone home feeling strangely light and clean, as if she had just bathed. And now, here she was, not only confessed and absolved, but also a first-time communicant, which Father Mirabal had explained meant being part of a community.

As they were getting ready to sit down to breakfast, Leopoldo said, "Wait, Blanca Estela, I have a surprise for you, a gift."

She looked at Mamá Anita with a question in her eyes, but her grandmother merely smiled. Leopoldo brought out a square package some twelve inches in size. It was wrapped in brown paper. Leopoldo showed her that it was addressed to her but in care of Dolores Guerra, the big woman who ran the store across the river. Then she noticed the return address. Her mother's name was on it. All of a sudden her heart was pounding and her hands trembled as she tried to tear the paper. Leopoldo took out a small pocket knife and tore off the wrapping. She quickly opened the box, completely at a loss as to what her mother could have sent her. Inside the box, cushioned in tissue paper, was a white handbag, a small one but with a handle that you could put over your arm—a grown-up handbag, like her mother carried, only smaller, of course. She looked up at all the guests around the table, and they smiled at her, expecting her to say something, but she could not find her voice.

Rosalía took the bag from her, saying, "Let me see. Oh yes, it is a most elegant handbag, and it is so useful. Look, we will put your prayer book inside it." She opened the bag and, after depositing the prayer book in its interior, she snapped it shut, commenting, "It has a very good clasp," and gave her back the handbag.

"Do you like it?" Evita asked from the other end of the table.

"Oh yes," was all she could say, but her eyes were shining.

"Lilia sent it in care of Dolores because she knew that it would reach you faster that way than by international mail. When I was at the store yesterday, Dolores asked me to deliver it to you. I'm very happy I brought it, especially since it has made you so very happy," Leopoldo concluded, smiling at her.

Blanca Estela put the handbag in her lap and kept it there throughout breakfast, during which she ate a remarkable number of tamales and pastries and drank two cups of chocolate. She had not realized until then how hungry she was.

Three days later they received a letter from Lilia. It was only a short note, but it contained wonderful news. Lilia said that she would be coming home soon, in two weeks or less, and she would tell them then about all the things that she had been doing. Blanca Estela was wildly happy: her mother was returning to her. Now they would be together again, the two of them, no, the three of them, because now Mamá Anita was part of her life, too. She promptly went out and told all her friends that her mother was coming home.

Waiting, though, was agony. Two weeks was such a long time, but perhaps it would be less. Perhaps Lilia would arrive sooner. Every day Blanca Estela would wake up to the happy possibility that she would see her mother that very day. By Saturday, she was so impatient waiting for her mother's arrival that even Mamá Anita seemed to wish for something to distract them from counting the days until Lilia's return. Perhaps that was the reason why she agreed so readily to let Blanca Estela go to the movies that evening with Mario and Mimi. Nereida was taking them, and, at the last minute, Evita went along, too.

Going to the movies in Revilla was different from what it had been like in the United States. In Revilla, they showed only one movie, on Saturday night, in a building next to the church which was referred to as the "old school" by some people and as "the theater" by others. When she had first arrived in Revilla, Blanca Estela had thought that the building was abandoned, because it had a padlock on the massive doors. Now she realized that it was only open when there was a movie to show or when there was some kind of theatrical presentation.

When they walked into the theater, she saw by the yellowish light of the bulbs that hung from the high ceiling that there was a raised platform, like a stage, at the opposite end of the room. A white screen had been placed in the center of this platform, in front of some draperies that hid about half of the stage from them. In the seating area there were rows of wooden seats that folded up and were bolted to each other like those in real theaters. They chose to sit in the middle of a row, fairly close to the stage. Behind them, in the back of the room, there was a small wood cubicle raised several feet above the floor, with little openings for windows cut at various levels.

"That's where the movie projector and the projectionist are," Mario told Blanca Estela, pointing to the cubicle. "The projectionist is my brother, Tino," he added. "Nereida sometimes helps him." And, indeed, Nereida got up then and left them to go inside the little room with her brother.

Blanca Estela noticed another difference between the movie theater in Revilla and the ones back home—no, not back home, she corrected herself. Revilla was home now. Here there was no concession stand where you could buy popcorn or candy. As if reading her mind, Leopoldo suddenly appeared next to them holding several small paper cones filled with hard candy. "I thought you might enjoy some candy," he said with his friendly smile, gently patting Blanca Estela on the head, while ruffling Mario's hair.

The four of them, Mario and Mimi, Evita and Blanca Estela, sucked on the candy in silence while the room filled with people. Finally, the lights went out and the black and white movie began, the images dancing a little on the screen and the music sounding a little scratchy, but no one seemed to mind. Blanca Estela noticed that her three companions seemed to know all about the actors in the movie and were familiar with the characters and the plot of the film, as if they had seen it before. She whispered to Mimi, asking her if this was the case. Mimi nodded, but did not elaborate until Mario intervened, explaining, "This is the second time that the movie comes to Revilla, and it was very popular the first time."

Blanca Estela was not able to follow all the dialogue, because the actors spoke with a different accent from the people in Revilla and used some words that she had not heard before. But she understood most of the story, which was about a group of people who were very poor and lived in the same neighborhood. The title of the movie was precisely that, "We, the Poor." When a young woman with a pretty face and a sweet expression appeared on the screen, Evita leaned forward and said, "That's your namesake, Blanca Estela."

She did not know how to respond. After a moment, Evita continued, "Didn't you know? I am sure that you were named after her. My mother says that she was your mother's favorite movie star. And don't they make such a good looking couple?" This question was in reference to the handsome man with the mustache who now appeared on the screen with the girl.

Blanca Estela still did not reply. She felt a little resentful, thinking that Evita seemed to know things about herself that she had not even guessed. She had wondered sometimes why she had not been named after her mother. If she had, she would probably have been called "Lili" for short, which was pretty. Instead, she had been encumbered with the awkward double name, which, especially in the United States, had caused no end of confusion. If she had been named for her mother's favorite actress, and if the handsome actor, who was now singing, looked a bit like that photograph of her father, then perhaps her mother, herself, had wished that she had been named Blanca Estela. Since that was not possible, she had done the next best thing: she had given her daughter her favorite name. Blanca Estela sighed with contentment feeling that, little by little, here in Revilla she was beginning to know her mother and her own origins.

Evita leaned forward again, whispering, "I have an extra movie card of Blanca Estela. Would you like it?"

Blanca Estela nodded, smiling, and said, "Yes, thank you. I would love to have it."

A few days later, during the morning grocery shopping, Blanca Estela ran into her four friends at Chabela's. Mario and Mimi were buying the usual rice and beans (and bubble gum for Mario). Evita wanted coffee and candy, the latter for herself, and Pedro had brought some squash from the ranch to sell to Chabela. Blanca Estela, still distracted and impatient, was trying to remember Mamá Anita's instructions while wondering if Manuel's car would bring Lilia that day. She barely understood Evita's suggestion when she said, "Why don't we put on a show, a musical program?"

"I can play my harmonica," Mario said quickly. "I just learned to play 'Adelita' on the harmonica."

Even Mimi and Pedro seemed to know what Evita was talking about, but Blanca Estela remained in the dark until Evita, noticing her confusion, explained, "We sing and dance and recite poems, and my mother lets me borrow necklaces and earrings and even clothes for costumes, and she allows me to put on lipstick."

"You mean, on the stage, in the theater where they show the movies?" Blanca Estela asked, still puzzled.

"Oh no, the theater is only used for big occasions, like the celebration of national holidays or Mother's Day. We put on our shows in the patio or in one of the rooms of a house. Let's ask your grandmother if she will let us do it in your house," Evita suggested.

"I don't know," Blanca Estela answered doubtfully. "Who comes to watch the show?"

"Friends, or some of the grown-ups, sometimes nobody, but it is still fun to get dressed up in costumes and sing and dance. We can be quite good because we rehearse properly until we get it right. You know what would be very nice? If we could put on a show to welcome your mother home," Evita concluded in a cajoling tone.

Blanca Estela immediately agreed to ask her grandmother for permission to use the house for the show. Mamá Anita was hesitant at first to let them turn the house into a theater, but she finally allowed them to rehearse and perform in the entryway where, she even pointed out, there were already hooks on the walls from which they could hang the sheet or bedspread or whatever they would use for a stage curtain. She did lay down one condition though, that they were not to rehearse when she was taking her afternoon nap or get underfoot when she was doing her housework. Blanca Estela promised to keep to those limits faithfully and to report to her friends what her grandmother had said.

They met that same afternoon, after Mamá Anita's nap, and began by discussing the difficulties of dancing on the uneven floor of the entryway. They agreed that it would have been better to dance in the parlor, where the floor was level *chipichil* stone, but, since that was out of the question, they would have to make do with what they had, because other houses were even less suitable. The largest room in Evita's house, for example, was used as the sewing workshop and, therefore, could not be used for anything else. As for Mario and Mimi's house, Blanca Estela had not gone beyond the front room, and this was small and dark because it had been partitioned off to separate it from the other half, where Nereida had set up a barber's chair for her haircutting business. The rest of the rooms in the Balboa house, like everywhere else, were used for sleeping, cooking or eating and were, therefore, out of bounds for games.

The entryway of Mamá Anita's house it was to be, then, and here they began to rehearse a dance number. It was *"El Jarabe Tapatío,"* and it was to be performed by the two couples of Mimi and Pedro, and Mario and Evita. Mimi generously offered to drop out of the number and let Blanca Estela take her place, but Blanca Estela declined since she had no idea of how the dance was performed. It had been nice to be included, though, and now she did not feel left out, even if she did not take part in that number. During rehearsal of "*El Jarabe Tapatío*," Mario played the tune on his harmonica, and Evita sang along "tra-la-la-la" since there appeared to be no words that went with the music. The dance steps, however, were quite complex, and Blanca Estela was surprised that the four knew them so well. They explained to her that "*El Jarabe Tapatío*" was a folk dance, probably the best known in Mexico, and that all the children learned it in school. She commented that it was a shame that they did not have a record with the music for it. Mario replied that they would have one for the performance, that they would borrow it from one of the teachers. There was no point, however, in borrowing the record early and running the risk of getting it scratched, and besides, Tino still had to work on the phonograph to rig it up to a battery in case there was no electricity when they put on the show.

They also began rehearsing to sing "*Cielito Lindo*" a cappella, since Mario could not both play the harmonica for accompaniment and sing at the same time. Blanca Estela had just memorized the lyrics of "*Cielito Lindo*" when Evita remarked that, since the program was in honor of Lilia's return, Blanca Estela should perform something on her own. Blanca Estela was horrified. Sing or dance all by herself? Never. She could recite a poem, Evita suggested. She did not know any poems and had difficulty memorizing anything, Blanca Estela argued. Nonsense, Evita countered firmly, adding, "I can find a poem that your mother will like, and you can at least memorize a couple of stanzas." There was no way to refute Evita, especially since the recitation was to be in honor of Lilia.

The following day, Evita came to rehearsal with two stanzas marked out of a poem, which she had copied from a book. The poem was about a very rich and powerful king who had a mischievous daughter who had taken a fancy to a star, which she wanted to wear as a brooch. One day the princess had left the palace without permission from her father and had gone to explore the gardens of the Lord in the heavens. There she had plucked her favorite star and pinned it to her dress, where it shone with brilliant light, surrounding her in a halo. The poem went on to relate the outcome of the princess' celestial excursion, but mercifully, Evita had not found it necessary for Blanca Estela to memorize the rest of the lines. She merely showed her the text and encouraged her to read it all.

Blanca Estela read the poem haltingly, for she had never formally learned to read Spanish. Evita then showed her how it should be recited, and Blanca Estela found herself carried away by the cadence of the sounds and the rhythms that conjured palaces, jewels, light and mystery:

*Este era un rey que tenía*
*un palacio de diamantes,*
*una tienda hecha del día*
*y un rebaño de elefantes...*

She later asked her grandmother if she knew the poem, and Mamá Anita said yes, that it was a poem written by a famous poet named Rubén Darío for a little girl named Marguerite. Did Lilia also know the poem, Blanca Estela also wanted to know. Of course, replied Mamá Anita. Most children learned that poem in school, or even before, and Lilia had liked it very much when she was little. Blanca Estela was now inspired to learn at least the fragment assigned to her by Evita, so that she could welcome her mother home with her favorite poem, and perhaps later, when she started school in Revilla, she would learn it in its entirety.

Friday came, and still they had no word as to when Lilia would arrive, but they knew it would be any day. Blanca Estela had learned her lines, but anxiety about her mother's return was beginning to distract her, so that she began to stumble over the recitation, seeming to regress in the quality of her performance. The others were also impatient to get on with the show. They had added another singing number, and Evita had also decided to present a recitation of another poem, one which she had given earlier, during the school year, for the celebration of the Cinco de Mayo, which commemorated the victory of the Mexican forces over the French troops that had invaded Mexico almost one hundred years before.

To quell the nerves and the stage fright brought on by the delay, Evita called for a dress rehearsal that evening. She explained to them that this meant that they had to wear the costumes and set up the stage as for a real performance. Mamá Anita was forewarned of what was coming, and she accepted it, even getting into the spirit of things by providing them with a heavy velvet coverlet of faded gold color to serve as a stage curtain. Mario brought a small ladder on which he stood while he hung up the curtain over a rope, which stretched from one side of the entryway to the other, anchored by hooks on each wall. After hanging up the curtain, Mario set up a small, portable phonograph connected to a battery on which they would play the record with the music for the dance numbers.

Pedro brought a pair of straw hats and two red bandanas for the boys to wear as part of their dance costume, while Evita provided hers and Mimi's. The girls' costumes consisted of very full skirts of brightly patterned cotton and white, peasant-style blouses. To make the look even more festive, Evita added several ropes of glass beads in amber and red, which they wrapped around their necks. Evita's goal had been to approximate the richly decorated folk costumes usually worn for the "*Jarabe Tapatío*," the *China Poblana* costume of the women and the *Charro* outfit of the men.

Blanca Estela, of course, did not wear a costume because she was not part of the dance number, but she decided to wear her nicest dress, which was her First Communion dress. This Mamá Anita would not allow her to do. She should not risk getting it soiled or torn before Lilia had had a chance to see it, Mamá Anita said firmly, and there was no room for discussion. Blanca Estela then opted for her next best, the pale yellow dress that had been her Easter dress. When she put it on, she was surprised to notice that the dress, which had previously fit her loosely and long, now pulled across the shoulders and exposed her knees.

As the girls prepared to dance, Blanca Estela saw Mimi and Evita swirling their skirts around them, setting in motion the red and orange flowers that were printed on the fabric. She also noticed with amazement the transformation of her friends' faces into vivid masks of painted cheeks and lips. At that moment she stopped being an onlooker and a reluctant participant in the performance and wanted nothing more than to be part of their world of make-believe. She asked Evita to paint her lips and put rouge on her cheeks, too, and knelt down in front of her, lifting up her face to receive from Evita the gift of fantasy that an inspired make-up artist can confer.

The rehearsal went smoothly, with very few corrections or repetitions, and at the end of it Evita pronounced that they were ready to present their performance to the public. The only thing holding up the opening now was Lilia's arrival, and it finally happened the following day.

At noon, Manuel's car rolled to a stop outside Mamá Anita's house, and the driver tooted the horn to announce his presence. Almost immediately, the front doors burst open, and Blanca Estela flew out through them in time to see Lilia getting out of the front seat of the car. She hurled herself at her mother and threw her arms around Lilia's waist. She remained like this, with her face pressed against her mother's body, listening to her mother's heartbeats, her own breath rising and falling in unison with her mother's, until Lilia gently disengaged herself. Lilia gave a shaky little laugh and, taking Blanca Estela's face in her hands, kissed her several times, leaving a moist trace where her tears had brushed against Blanca Estela's cheeks.

Mamá Anita appeared then, and Lilia stepped forward to embrace her. Manuel, without waiting for directions, took the suitcase from the back seat and carried it inside the house, leaving the three still on the sidewalk. Mamá Anita then said, trying to recapture her usual brusqueness, "Let's go inside, children. What are we doing out here, trying to get sunstroke?"

Lilia paid Manuel as he was leaving, and the three walked on to the kitchen where dinner was already cooking.

"I have some cool lemonade, *hija*," Mamá Anita said. "Do you want a glass?"

"Oh, yes please, Mamá," Lilia replied, sinking wearily into a chair. "I have been traveling since four o'clock this morning, with only a short stop for a quick snack. I am so hot and thirsty."

"Four o'clock in the morning!" Blanca Estela exclaimed in amazement, leaning against the table next to her mother's chair. "You must have seen the Morning Star at that hour."

Lilia seemed a little disconcerted for a moment, but then she smiled and said, "Perhaps I would have, if I had been looking for it, darling. In the big cities it is difficult to see the stars. They don't shine as brightly there as they do here in Revilla."

During dinner, Blanca Estela let loose a torrent of words, telling her mother about the things that had gone on during her absence. She described the First Communion ceremony and offered to show her the dress immediately, but Lilia said that she would see it later. Lilia asked her if she had liked the handbag, and Blanca Estela said, "Yes," reverently, and added that she kept the mother-of-pearl prayer book in it. She also told her mother about the show which they planned to stage in her honor and added that, immediately after dinner, she would run to tell Evita to prepare for the performance that evening.

"No, Blanca Estela," Mamá Anita interposed firmly. "Your mother is very tired, and she must rest today and this evening."

Blanca Estela looked closely at her mother and noticed that Lilia's face looked thin and pale, particularly against the hair, black as raven wings, which framed it.

"Yes, you must rest," she told her mother, diffidently. "But, tomorrow, tomorrow you will watch our show?"

Lilia smiled and caressed her head. "Yes, darling, tomorrow I will watch the performance that you and your friends prepared."

While Lilia and Mamá Anita still napped, Blanca Estela stole out of the house, very quietly, to go across the street, to look for Evita. She found her in the workshop, singing "Tú, Solo Tú" along with the seamstresses as she sewed pieces of ribbon on the peasant blouses for the dance number. Blanca Estela told her that their performance would have to wait until the following evening, and Evita nodded, seeming more intent on not losing her place in the song, saying only, "Until tomorrow, then. I'll tell the others."

The following day was Sunday, and Blanca Estela, Lilia and Mamá Anita went to Mass. This time the three of them received Communion, and after Mass they hurried home to breakfast. They stopped only briefly to greet Father Mirabal in the church atrium, but on the street they also encountered Leopoldo. He met them with a timid smile, falling in step with them, saying how happy he was to see Lilia home again. Since neither Lilia nor Mamá Anita seemed much inclined to conversation this morning, Blanca Estela felt that it was left to her to make the suitable responses to their friend. In an attempt to contribute something to the discourse, she told Leopoldo about their performance that evening and invited him to come and watch them. She sensed that Mamá Anita and Lilia had exchanged a quick look and that they were not wholly pleased with her suggestion, but Leopoldo accepted the invitation readily.

He said, as they approached Doctor Marín's house, "I must leave you now, since I have promised to have breakfast with Rosalía and my brother-in-law, but I will see you this evening. Thank you for asking me. I am very fond of musical evenings."

After he left them, Mamá Anita pursed her lips and said, "Well, it can't be helped. I know you don't encourage him, but still, he *is* a very good person. Your brother will be happy for his company."

Blanca Estela was immediately alert. "Is my uncle coming to see us?"

"I hope so, child. God grant us that he has a safe trip here. Now, let's hurry, so we can eat breakfast and then clean house and start preparing dinner for him," Mamá Anita replied.

Raúl arrived shortly before dinner, and they soon sat down to eat. When they had finished their dessert of rice pudding, Raúl and Lilia's favorite, they remained at the table while Raúl told them about the roads that his company was building and about a dam that they were going to build later. Blanca Estela looked around the table and sighed with contentment. It was so good to be all together again, her family, half of whom she had not known until this summer. Coming out of her thoughts she sensed again, like that morning with Leopoldo, a certain tension in Lilia and Mamá Anita. Again, she felt that she should try to dispel it and came up with the same solution. She told her uncle about the performance that evening. Raúl laughed with delight.

"A variety show? A musical evening? What a talented niece I have."

Mamá Anita clicked her tongue and said, "Don't be silly, *hijo*. It was just a way to distract these children. Blanca Estela was so impatient for Lilia to come home... Anyway, I am glad that you will be here this evening. This child invited Leopoldo to attend, and Lord knows who else they have asked to come."

"I haven't told anybody else, Mamá Anita," Blanca Estela protested, "only..."

"Yes, yes, child. Nobody is blaming you. Evita will have told everyone, though. I suppose I should prepare some refreshments to offer the visitors, but first, let's get some rest. Lilia, you still look very tired. It will take you days to recover from your trip. And you, son, you must be fatigued also. Blanca Estela, why don't you go lie down for a little while?"

She slid out of her chair groggily and went to kiss her mother as if she were saying good night and then, shyly, also approached her uncle, kissing him lightly on the cheek and saying, "I'm going to take a nap with Domino." When Raúl looked puzzled, she explained, "The cat that you gave me."

Raúl laughed, "You still have that toy?"

She looked at him reproachfully and said, "Of course," and left the grown-ups still at the table, where they went on with their conversation. She continued to hear the murmur of their voices like the faint humming of a beehive while she recited her poem for that evening under her breath until she drifted off to sleep.

When she woke up, she quickly washed her face and put on her yellow dress. Mario arrived as the sun was going down, ready to set up the stage. Raúl helped him hang up the stage curtain while Pedro carried chairs from the parlor and the kitchen to the patio. In the parlor Evita concentrated on making up her face and then doing the same for Mimi and for Blanca Estela. Nereida arrived soon after to run the phonograph, and shortly afterwards the audience began trickling in. María Eva was there and so was Delia from next door. Doctor Marín, Rosalía, Perla and Leopoldo arrived in the doctor's car, where Leopoldo also carried a case of cold soda pop. Blanca Estela asked Pedro if his mother was coming to see them, but he said that she had to stay home with his little brothers. She felt a little sorry for him because the rest of the cast, especially herself, had their families present, but Pedro, himself, did not seem perturbed about his situation.

When everyone had been seated, they began with the dance number involving Mario, Evita, Mimi and Pedro. It went quite well and received enthusiastic applause. Blanca Estela followed with the recitation of the poem. She was proud that she did not stumble over it at all, even though she had learned an additional stanza at the last minute. The poem must have, indeed, been Lilia's favorite, for when Blanca Estela finished reciting it, she looked in her mother's direction, and saw that Lilia's face was radiant and her eyes were shining. Mario followed with a harmonica solo, and they closed with two songs by the entire cast.

The audience rewarded them by applauding warmly and congratulating them. After the performers had taken a bow, Raúl removed the stage curtain that blocked the flow of the breeze through the open entryway, and refreshments were served: Mamá Anita's lemonade and Leopoldo's cold sodas.

Leopoldo stood close to Lilia, looking as if he would like to talk to her alone, but she directed her comments to all those around her.

"That music is so pretty, and I missed it so much when I was across the river. Of course, I haven't felt like listening to music recently, being in mourning," Lilia was saying to Rosalía, who responded with her usual kindness.

"Mourning customs are changing, and it is a good thing. There is enough sadness already in this life that we shouldn't wrap ourselves in any more gloom that we create," said Rosalía.

"It is my daughter that I have to think of. I cannot allow her childhood to be darkened by sadness. That is why I did not object to the children wanting to sing and dance in the house," Lilia continued. "Do you know what I missed most while I was away? I longed to hear again the children's voices singing the *rondas* in the evening. *Doña Blanca*, for example, and... what was my favorite? Yes, it was

*Naranja Dulce.*" She turned to look for Blanca Estela, who had been standing behind her, listening closely. "Estelita, I know you were learning *rondas* and games when I left. Have you learned *Naranja Dulce* yet?"

Blanca Estela looked to Mario for an answer. He shook his head. "No, I don't think we've played that for a long time. Do you want to learn it?"

If that was her mother's favorite, of course she wanted to learn it. "Let's play that," she said. "Teach me."

"Go outside, children, if you are going to play," Mamá Anita said. "There is not enough room here."

They filed out and gathered in the street in front of Mamá Anita's window.

"Let's form a circle," Mario told them and then, for her benefit, he explained, "We're going to sing '*Naranja dulce, limón partido, dame un abrazo que yo te pido.*' When we say the word *abrazo*, we stop, and you embrace the person next to you. Just listen at first, and you'll catch on right away."

She nodded and did as she was told, although the game was a mystery to her. What was this sweet orange or the sliced lemon? Ana why did you embrace your neighbor, as if you were saying farewell? What were the promises that would be forgotten if they turned out to be false? She sang along with her friends and embraced them all, at one time or another, and finally said goodbye as the music played, singing, "*Toca la marcha, mi pecho llora, adiós, señora, yo ya me voy.*" It was like a soldier taking leave of his beloved to go to war.

The moon rose late and hung suspended in the sky like an old gold coin, bathing them in its light and throwing their shadows against the sand that had now turned into powdered silver. The grown-ups began to leave, calling good night to each other and congratulations to the children, who also soon parted to go home and to bed. Later, Blanca Estela, lying in her cot, looked at the sky through the iron bars of the open window. The moon had climbed to the middle sky, and its light, filtering through the bars, turned them into silver ingots. The moon, she thought as she drifted off to sleep, had always been their playmate, the companion of their games.

Raúl was to leave first thing on Monday morning, and Blanca Estela got up early to have breakfast with him. She felt particularly talkative this morning, as if to make up for the silence that prevailed between Lilia and Raúl.

"Did you like my poem, Mamá? Mamá Anita said that you had learned it in school. Do you still remember it? When I start school in September I will learn it, too, won't I? All of it. Will I be in the same class with Mario and Evita?"

"Estelita, stop," Lilia interrupted. "You won't be going to school in September... not here in Revilla."

She stared at her mother, stunned. "But you said..."

"No, darling, don't you remember, when I went away I told you that I would return to take you back with me?"

She had forgotten. So many things had happened since then.

Lilia continued, "We... your father and I... always expected that you would go to school on the other side. I don't want you to forget your English and the things you learned there. You were born in the

United States, and so was your father. He died for that country, so it is only right that you should be educated there."

"But my friends... Mamá Anita... I will miss them..."

"You will be uprooting the child," Mamá Anita intervened.

Raúl added, "This is your home, Lilia, and your daughter's. Why must you leave it and undergo hardships in a strange place? Here you could work as a school teacher, if you wanted to work, or you could marry a man who loves you. You have no need to work in a factory or in a shop, as you will have to do if you go back to the United States."

"We have already discussed all that, and you know my reasons. There is a better future for my daughter over there, better education, and, if in order to give her that I have to work in a factory, I will do it."

Blanca Estela had never been in the middle of an argument among grown-ups before, and their raised voices frightened her. She ran out of the room and towards the only place where she was sure of being alone, the privy at the back of the patio. She wanted to cry, but she would not let the others see her in tears. Why, oh, why must they leave now? She wanted to be near her grandmother. How funny that she had been afraid of her at first. Mamá Anita was like a little steam engine, always huffing and puffing and never still, but so warm and comforting. And her handsome uncle, would she see him again? This reminded her that she wanted to say goodbye to him before he left, and she came out of the privy, drying her eyes.

He was already at the door, carrying his suitcase. She ran to embrace him. "You will not forget me?" Blanca Estela asked him. He picked her up and held her in front of him, as if to see her better. He looked into her eyes and said, very seriously, "No, I will not forget you. I love you very much." He kissed her on the forehead before putting her down and then embraced first Mamá Anita and then Lilia. He held her tightly and whispered, "God bless you, little sister." Then he was gone.

After breakfast, Mamá Anita took all of Blanca Estela's clothes (except what she had on and the First Communion dress), put them in a washtub and started scrubbing them against the washboard. Lilia protested, "Leave those clothes, Mamá. I should be doing that," but Mamá Anita, looking very grim, just shook her head and went on scrubbing.

"I don't know where I'm going to put all these things," Lilia continued. "Blanca Estela has more clothes now than when we arrived. You are always sewing dresses and nightgowns for her, Mamá."

"I made those things for Blanca Estela because I want my granddaughter to look nice," Mamá Anita replied, still brusque. "There is an empty suitcase somewhere that you can take if you need more space to pack these newer clothes in. Oh, Lilia," she added, dismayed, "I hope you know what you are doing. This poor child has already made friends here, and it's going to be hard on her to pick her up and take her to a new place where everyone will be a stranger to her."

Blanca Estela wandered off into the parlor, sat down in the rocking chair, and forlornly rocked herself while she tried to guess where she and her mother were going. Was it back to where they lived before, where her old friends, June and Linda lived? Blonde, English-speaking Linda and June seemed so long ago now. Perhaps she could teach them to sing *"Naranja dulce"* or *"Doña Blanca."* Somehow she couldn't see them holding hands in a circle under the moonlight, singing, *"Si fueran falsos mis juramentos, en otros tiempos se olvidarán."* Besides, you needed more than three children to play those games, and most of the children she knew, her friends, were here in Revilla.

Perhaps she could stay with her grandmother again while Lilia went back across the river to work. The thought shocked her. She was being disloyal to her mother, even thinking of it. She loved her mother more than she loved anybody else (although her grandmother was a close second). How could she bear to be always separated from her, to not see her lovely face and to not have her hand to hold? No, if her mother wanted to go away, then she must go with her. Anything was preferable to the aching sadness that remained when Lilia went away.

She left the rocking chair and went in search of her mother. She found her in the kitchen, stirring a pot of beans, while Mamá Anita hung the laundry to dry over the clothes line.

"Mamá, she asked, "where are we going... is it where June and Linda live, where we were before?"

"No, darling. Now we are going to live in San Antonio. Before, we were in California, which is very far away. Now we'll be much closer to Revilla. We'll come and visit sometimes. You can come and stay with your grandmother during the long vacation. You'll see, it won't be so bad. You will make new friends in San Antonio, but you can still come and see your friends in Revilla when you visit here."

"Why did we use to live in California?" She was trying to make sense of the things that grown-ups did and that you had to get used to. "Why did we leave California?"

Lilia sat down at the kitchen table and told her. "We lived in California because your father was a soldier, and soldiers have to go where they are told. They sent him to a military post there, and we went there to be with him. You were born in Texas, though. Your father was away when you came, and I was staying with his family, who are also your family. You will get to know them better when we live in Texas. I don't guess you remember them, *Don* José and *Doña* María, your grandparents on your father's side. You were still a baby when we went to join your father in California. Then Roberto, your father, went away. His superiors sent him to a place called Korea. He... he never came back. Soldiers go to war and sometimes... sometimes they die."

Lilia gave a deep sigh and roused herself, as if she were coming back from far away. She stood up and said, "Now, Estelita, I have to finish cooking dinner because your grandmother has been working very hard washing your clothes."

Blanca Estela got up from her chair and said, quietly, "I'll be back in just a little while."

"Where are you going?"

"I'm going to tell my friends that I am going away."

"All right, but don't stay out too long. It's almost time to eat."

Next door, she found Nereida, who told her that
Mimi and Mario were out with their brother in the
truck. "Did you want to see them about something?" Nereida asked her.

She felt shy whenever she was around Nereida,
but this time she needed to tell someone her important news. "My mother and I are going away, to live
across the river," she blurted out.

Nereida was interested. "Are you going back to
California?" she asked, a little wistfully.

She was glad that she could give a definitive
reply. "No, we're going to live in San Antonio."

"Oh, San Antonio is pretty, but I still prefer Los
Angeles."

Blanca Estela remembered that Nereida had
liked the hair styles that people wore in California
and wondered if her mother would ask Nereida to
cut her hair again before they left. Suddenly she,
too, wanted her hair cut. Since she was going to a
new place, with new people, she wanted to do
something that would represent this new life. She
asked Nereida, "Will you cut my hair?"

Nereida was surprised. "What? Cut off your
long braids? Yes... you probably would feel better
with short hair. What does your mother say,
though? You haven't asked her? Go ask her, and if
she gives her permission, come back, and I will cut it
in there." Nereida pointed to the barber's chair that
could be glimpsed in the next room.

Blanca Estela went back to the house just in time
to sit for dinner and told her mother that she wanted to cut her hair.

Mamá Anita was shocked at her announcement. "Your beautiful long hair! It's such a pretty shade of brown, too."

Lilia did not respond for a few moments, and then she said, thoughtfully, "Well, perhaps you're right. It is hot, even if you wear it braided. It would be easier to keep it neat when you're in school, and I am working and don't have much time to look after things."

Mamá Anita said nothing else, and they finished the meal in silence.

"Can I tell Nereida that she can cut my hair?" Blanca Estela insisted after they had cleared the table.

Lilia looked at Mamá Anita, but Mamá Anita only said, "You do as you think is best."

Lilia caressed Blanca Estela's long braids and said, smiling, "I will go with you when you have it cut. Is it Nereida who will cut it, or will you wait until we're in San Antonio?"

"Oh, I want Nereida to do it, just like she cut your hair. Can I have it done this afternoon?"

"Fine," said Lilia, "after three."

Before going back to Nereida, she went to look for Evita and, when she found her, she was hard pressed to decide what to relate first, her approaching departure or her impending haircut. She got both things out in the same sentence. "My mother and I are going back to live across the river, and I'm going to get my hair cut before I leave. Nereida is cutting it this afternoon."

Evita was uncharacteristically silent for a moment before saying simply, "Oh," in a little voice. Then she seemed to collect herself and added, "Good, now you'll be able to wear the hairclips that I gave you. Where are you going to live?"

"In San Antonio."

"My married sister, who lives in Laredo, knows some people in San Antonio, and she goes to visit them sometimes. She says there are many beautiful stores there, very large stores. You will like it, I'm sure," Evita concluded, as if she were trying to reassure her. She then went back to tracing a drawing of a bunch of flowers, which she had earlier explained were orchids, on to a pair of pillowcases for the girls to embroider.

Blanca Estela left, feeling a little deflated, to tell Nereida that she and her mother would be coming later to see her.

When Lilia and Blanca Estela arrived for their appointment, Nereida led them through the front room on tiptoe because Delia was sleeping in the back room, trying to get over one of her bad headaches. They followed her to the far side of the room, which had been partitioned off by means of a canvas and wood frame divider. Here, Nereida had her barber's chair and a small dressing table with an attached mirror. Along the outside walls ran several rows of shelving where Tino and Néstor kept the radios and electric irons that people brought to them for repairs, another occupation in which they engaged.

Nereida had Blanca Estela sit in the chair, which was so big that Blanca Estela felt as if she would surely be swallowed up in it. She felt particularly small in it after Nereida pumped a pedal with her foot and raised the chair until Blanca Estela's legs were left dangling in the air. Nereida then wrapped a white towel, which smelled of sunshine, around Blanca Estela and picked up a comb and a pair of scissors from the dressing table.

Suddenly Lilia took Blanca Estela's braids in her hands, caressing the thick plaits, and said, "Cut them like this, so that we can save the braids."

Blanca Estela closed her eyes as Nereida approached with the scissors and, after a long time, she heard a snipping sound and felt her hair being pulled below the ears. She wanted to cry out and tell Nereida to stop, but it was too late—one braid had already been amputated. She clamped down on her teeth and shut her eyes tighter until the second one was off too, and then, suddenly, she had an unexpected feeling of lightness. It was done. She started to get up from the chair, but Nereida pushed her back, saying, "Wait, I haven't finished. I still have to even it all around and shape it."

Mimi and Mario came in as Nereida was making the last trims. They were struck silent when they saw what had happened. "Why did you do it?" Mario asked, accusingly.

"Oh, it was just very hot and heavy. I wanted my hair short, so it would be easy to keep when I—when we—go back across the river," she answered hurriedly, avoiding his eyes.

"You are leaving? You are going back?" Mario turned the question into a statement in a flat voice. She nodded.

"Why?"

She turned to her mother, wishing that she would answer that question, but Lilia was giving Nereida some money and speaking to her in hushed tones.

"My mother says we must go, that it is very important that I should go to school there... " Her voice trailed off, revealing even to her own ears the deep misery that she still felt at the thought of leaving.

Mario turned his back to her and peered into the insides of a large table radio that sat on a shelf.

Then Mimi asked, "Will you ever come back?"

"Oh yes," she replied fervently. "My mother says that I will come back during the long vacation."

"Well, don't forget us," Mimi said as she drifted out of the room.

"No, I will never forget you, and I am coming back," Blanca Estela repeated, speaking to Mario's back because Mimi had already melted away.

Lilia hurried her out of the Balboa house, saying, "Come, let's go home and show your grandmother your new haircut."

For some reason when Mamá Anita saw Blanca Estela's short hair, she passed a hand over her eyes and remained like that for a moment before saying brightly, "Oh yes, what an attractive haircut. You look very pretty, Blanca Estela, very stylish."

"We saved the braids," she told her grandmother, as if trying to reassure her that the damage was not irreversible. "Look, Mamá, show Mamá Anita my braids."

Lilia opened a white silk scarf and revealed the golden brown plaits, tied at the ends with pink ribbons.

"Would you like to keep them, Mamá Anita? That way you will remember me when you see the braids."

"Oh, my darling, I will remember you every day. I do not need the braids to remind me, but yes, I do want to keep them, as a very precious memento of this summer," Mamá Anita cried out and, to Blanca Estela's surprise, she wrapped her arms around her tightly. "Let's put them away somewhere safe. Here, let's put them in this chest," she added when she had composed herself.

Mamá Anita raised the lid of a cedar-lined chest where she kept delicate things, like Lilia's wedding veil, which was now Blanca Estela's First Communion veil. In there, too, was the beautiful blue doll that had been the cause of such adoration and anguish. Blanca Estela lifted the doll gently and surreptitiously checked the back of the dress. Mamá Anita had done a perfect job of mending it. Of the tear caused by the struggle between her and Aminta, there only remained a faint scar.

"Do you want to take her with you?" Mamá Anita asked her, indicating the doll. "I forget—what is her name?"

Blanca Estela shook her head, still looking at the doll. "No, I think that I want her to stay with you. Keep her for me until I come back. Her name..." She looked at her mother to make sure that she was out of earshot. "I don't remember what her name was, but I am now giving her the name 'Anita.'" And she carefully transferred the doll to her grandmother's hands.

There was a knock at the door, and Lilia went to see who it was. She came back to the parlor, followed by Leopoldo, saying, "Look, Mamá, Estelita, Leopoldo brought some photographs. They're pictures of your First Communion, Estelita. Doctor

Marín took them with his camera and is giving them to us. How kind he is. Estelita, you look so pretty in your white dress. How I wish I had been here."

Mamá Anita took the photographs and examined them, saying, "Come, Estelita, let's go out in the patio, where the light is better."

There were three photographs in all, one of Blanca Estela by herself, holding the mother-of-pearl prayer book in one hand and the Communion candle in the other. The second photo showed Blanca Estela with her godmother, Rosalía, while the third was a group portrait with Mario, Doctor Marín and Rosalía. "Do you want to keep these photographs, Mamá Anita?" Blanca Estela asked, her generosity now in full bloom.

"No, I saw you in person. Your mother did not. She must have them. Well, perhaps I could keep one, the one of you and your godmother. I know that you will want the picture with the four of you, especially because Mario is your friend, and your mother will want the one of you. Let's go and thank Leopoldo for bringing them."

They returned to the parlor in time to see Leopoldo release Lilia's hand as he said, "I will think of that... that you will return, soon, at least next year, and then you can tell me..." He stopped when he saw them, and, stammering, he waved away their thanks and hurried out of the house.

Lilia, too, seemed flustered and began to speak rapidly. "Estelita, we have to start packing your clothes. Some of them I won't even iron because they will only get wrinkled again in the suitcase."

She turned to Mamá Anita and said, "Mamá, I am going to leave Blanca Estela's First Communion dress here. It will be better cared for here, hanging in the big wardrobe, than if I crush it inside a suitcase. Is that all right?"

"Of course, leave it here," Mamá Anita replied and then, turning to Blanca Estela, asked her, "Do you want to look at the dress again before I lock the wardrobe?"

"Oh yes, Mamá Anita," she answered reverently, and a moment later she was touching her fingertips to the airy silk that she doubted she would ever wear again.

She then realized that she wanted to ask her grandmother for something. "Please, Mamá Anita, will you give me one thing?"

"What is it, child?" Mamá Anita was surprised.

"Your box of buttons. Your box with the pictures of the boats on the lid."

"You want that? The buttons, too?"

"Well... some of them."

Mamá Anita laughed merrily. "Take it, child, and take as many buttons as you like."

And thus it was that when they rode again in Manuel's car, which was taking them back across the river, she held in her lap the tin box with the boating illustrations that had been her grandmother's gift to her. Inside it there was a wealth of buttons: make-believe pearls, gold and silver coins, glittering shapes of amber, emerald and ruby. Her treasure chest.

It was still early morning, and they were driving towards the east. As they left the town behind them, she turned back for one last look. Mamá Anita was still standing on the sidewalk, flanked by Mario, Mimi and Evita, and they all continued to wave, even as they grew smaller as the distance between them lengthened.

Evita had given Blanca Estela a picture card of the movie star who was her namesake. Mario and Mimi had no farewell gift, but she did not need one to remember them by. As Manuel was loading the suitcases, Mario had reminded her, "Remember, you are coming back next summer, and we will go picking cotton then. I will have a burlap sack ready for you, and I will show you how to pull the cotton bolls."

"Yes, I will come back," vowed Blanca Estela silently as a veil of dust—or was it tears—blurred the landscape behind her. The sun shone brightly, already striking the white walls of the houses of Revilla, and in the distance the stones glimmered in the light like pillars of gold and silver.

◆ ◆ ◆

# Appendix

These are the songs and games that Blanca Estela learned in Revilla in *Pillars of Gold and Silver*. There are no definitive versions of these songs or chants because they have been part of popular culture for so long that the texts vary according to the individual regions of the Spanish-speaking world. I give the versions that the children of Revilla used to sing, but I also note other sources (when I found them) for the texts.

## Chapter I

*Mambrú se fue a la guerra,*
*que pena, que dolor.*
*Mambrú se fue a la guerra,*
*no se si volverá...*
*que do-re-mi, que fa-sol-la...*

But see also: *Naranja dulce, limón partido: Antología de la lírica infantil mexicana*, compiled and edited by Mercedes Díaz Roig and María Teresa Miaja. México: El Colegio de México, 1984. Another source is John Donald Robb's *Hispanic Folk Music of New Mexico and the Southwest: A Self-Portrait of a People*, University of Oklahoma Press, 1980.

In *Quitiplás: Cancionero infantil* (Dirección de Educación Especial, Organización de los Estados Americanos, 1990) *Mambrú* reads, in part:

*Mambrú se fue a la guerra*
*chiribín, chiribín, chin, chin*

*Mambrú se fue a la guerra*
*y no sé cuándo vendrá*
*ja ja ja, ja ja ja*
*No sé cuando vendrá.*
*¿Vendrá para la Pascua?*
*chiribín, chiribín, chin, chin*
*¿Vendrá para la Pascua*
*o para Navidad?*
*ja ja ja, ja ja ja*
*o para Navidad.*
*La Navidad se pasa*
*chiribín, chiribín, chin, chin*
*La Navidad se pasa*
*Mambrú no vuelve más*
*ja ja ja, ja ja ja*
*Mambrú no vuelve más.*

*Mambrú se ha muerto en guerra*
*chiribín, chiribín, chin, chin*
*Mambrú se ha muerto en guerra,*
*lo llevan a enterrar*
*ja ja ja, ja ja ja*
*lo llevan a enterrar...*

## Chapter II

This game is called "Los Colores" (colors) or "Los Listones" (ribbons), but since it did not include any lyrics, I did not find it in the *cancioneros* or anthologies. The object of the game was for each child to guess what color ribbon or similar item the other child was hiding in his/her hand. If the first child guessed right, the other child forfeited the item and was out of the game. If the first child guessed wrong, he or she was out of the game.

The game opened with a child knocking at a door and another child asking, *"¿Quién es?"* The response was, *"La vieja Inés."* (The name was probably chosen because *Inés* rhymes with *es*.) The answer was a ribbon of a certain color.

## Chapter III

Spelled at times "Matarilerileró" and others as "Matarilerilerón." I am not aware that the name of this game has any meaning but is more in the nature of a tongue twister. The first line appears to consist of nonsensical sounds:

> *Amó, ató... Matarilerilerón*
> *¿Qué quiere, usted, Matarilerilerón?*
>
> *Yo quiero un paje, Matarilerilerón.*
> *Escoja usted, Matarilerilerón.*
> *Escojo a (insert child's name)*
>
> *¿Que oficio le pondremos, Matarilerilerón?*
>
> *Le pondremos (insert unpopular occupation), Matarilerilerón.*
>
> *Ese oficio no nos gusta, Matarilerilerón.*
>
> *Le pondremos (insert acceptable occupation), Matarilerilerón.*
>
> *Ese oficio sí nos gusta, Matarilerilerón.*

See also *Naranja dulce, limón partido.*

## Chapter IV

This is how the children of Revilla sang "Hilitos de oro." The song is in the form of a dialog between a messenger from the king and the father of several daughters in whom the king is interested.

*Hilitos, hilitos de oro,*
  *que se me vienen quebrando,*
  *que manda decir el rey*
  *que cuántas hijas tenéis.*

*Que tenga las que tuviera,*
  *que nada le importa al rey.*

*Ya me voy desconsolado*
  *a darle la queja al rey.*

*Vuelva, vuelva, caballero,*
  *no sea tan descortés,*
  *de las hijas que yo tengo,*
  *escoja la más mujer.*

*No la escojo por bonita,*
  *ni tampoco por mujer,*
  *la que quiero es una rosa*
  *acabada de nacer.*

See also the versions in Robb's, *Hispanic Folk Music of New Mexico and the Southwest.* Also Rafael Jijena Sánchez's, *Hilo de oro, hilo de plata.* Buenos Aires: Ediciones Buenos Aires, 1940.

## Chapter V

The children of Revilla played "A la víbora de la mar," which is similar to "London Bridge Is Falling Down," singing these verses:

*A la víbora, víbora*
  *de la mar, de la mar,*
  *por aquí pueden pasar,*

*los de adelante corren mucho*
*y los de atrás se quedarán.*

*Una mexicana*
*que frutas vendía,*
*ciruela, chabacano,*
*melón o sandía.*

*Campanita de oro,*
*déjame pasar*
*con todos mis hijos,*
*menos el de atrás,*
*trás, trás, trás...*

See also the version in *Naranja dulce, limón partido.*

## Chapter VI

This is the version of "La muñeca" that Blanca Estela learned in Revilla:

*Tengo una muñeca vestida de azul*
*Con zapatos blancos y su manto azul.*
*La llevé a la plaza y se me constipó\**
*La llevé a la casa y la niña murió.*

*Brinca la tablita, yo ya la brinqué.*
*Bríncala otra vez, yo ya me cansé.*

*Dos y dos son cuatro, cuatro y dos son seis,*
*Seis y dos son ocho y ocho dieciséis.*

\* Became sick with chest congestion or chest cold.

For other versions see Isabel Schon, *Doña Blanca and Other Hispanic Nursery Rhymes.* Minneapolis,

MN: T.S. Denison & Co., Inc., 1983. Also *Naranja dulce, limón partido* and *Quitiplás*.

## Chapter VII

The following is the refrain of this *ronda* (a game accompanied by a song in which the children join hands in a circle) as Blanca Estela sang it:

*Doña Blanca está encerrada*
*en pilares de oro y plata.*
*Romperemos un pilar*
*para ver a Doña Blanca.*

Other versions read: "Doña Blanca está *cubierta con* pilares de oro y plata."
See Isabel Schon, *Doña Blanca and Other Hispanic Nursery Rhymes.*

## Chapter VIII

Blanca Estela and her friends sang "Naranja dulce, limón partido," thus:

*Naranja dulce, limón partido,*
*dame un abrazo que yo te pido.*

*Si fueran falsos mis juramentos,*
*en otros tiempos se olvidarán.*

*Toca la marcha, mi pecho llora,*
*adiós, señora, yo ya me voy.*

See also *Naranja dulce, limón partido* and *Doña Blanca and Other Hispanic Nursery Rhymes.*